MORENO VALLEY

AUG 3 0 1999

MORENO VALLEY PUBLIC LIBRARY

0-00-01 2751718 3

P9-CKS-934

MVFOL

# Cat on the Scent

# Rita Mae Brown
## & Sneaky Pie Brown

# Cat on the Scent

**WHEELER**
PUBLISHING, INC.
ROCKLAND, MA

★ AN AMERICAN COMPANY ★

Copyright © 1999 by American Artists,Inc.
All rights reserved.

Published in Large Print by arrangement with Bantam Books, a division of Random House, Inc., in the United States and Canada.

Wheeler Large Print Book Series.

Set in 16 pt Plantin.

*Library of Congress Cataloging-in-Publication Data*

Brown, Rita Mae
   Cat on the scent / Rita Mae Brown & Sneaky Pie Brown.
     p. (large print)  cm.(Wheeler large print book series)
   ISBN 1-56895-749-1 (hardcover)
   1. Haristeen, Harry (Fictitious character)—Fiction. 2. Women postal
service employees—Virginia—Fiction. 3. Murphy, Mrs. (Fictitious character)—Fiction. 5. Historical reenactments—Virginia—Fiction 6. Women
detectives—Virginia—Fiction. 7. Women cat owners—Virginia—Fiction.
8. Cats—Virginia—Fiction. 9. Virginia—Fiction. 10. Detective and mystery stories. gsafd. 11. Large type books. I. Title. II. Series
[PS3552.R698C38   1999]
813'.54—dc21                                                    99-31994
                                              CIP

*To a cat queen,*
*Elizabeth Putnam Sinsel*

# Cast of Characters

*Mary Minor Haristeen (Harry)*, the young post-mistress of Crozet

*Mrs. Murphy*, Harry's gray tiger cat

*Tee Tucker*, Harry's Welsh corgi, Mrs. Murphy's friend and confidante

*Pewter*, Market's shamelessly fat gray cat, who now lives with Harry and family

*Pharamond Haristeen (Fair)*, veterinarian, formerly married to Harry

*Mrs. George Hogendobber (Miranda)*, a widow who works with Harry in the post office

*Market Shiflett*, owner of Shiflett's Market, next to the post office.

*Susan Tucker*, Harry's best friend

*Big Marilyn Sanburn (Mim)*, the undisputed queen of Crozet society

*Tally Urquhart,* older than dirt, she says what she thinks when she thinks it, even to her niece, Mim the Magnificent

*Rick Shaw,* sheriff

*Cynthia Cooper,* police officer

*Herbert C. Jones,* paster of Crozet Lutheran Church

*Blair Bainbridge,* a handsome model who lives on the farm next to Harry's

*Sir H. Vane-Tempest,* a modern Midas who proves there is nothing like the greed of the rich

*Sarah Vane-Tempest,* the must younger, fabulously beautiful wife of the imperious H. Vane

*Archie Ingram,* as a county commissioner he has been a strong advocate of controlling development and preserving the environment. Too bad he couldn't preserve his marriage

*Tommy Van Allen,* tall, dark, and handsome, he's been wild as a rat ever since childhood

*Ridley Kent,* an easygoing man who has inherited enough money to sap all initiative. He means well

# 1

The intoxicating fragrance of lilacs floated across the meadow grass. Mrs. Murphy was night hunting in and around the abandoned dependencies on old Tally Urquhart's farm, Rose Hill. Once a great estate, the farm's main part continued to be kept in pristine condition. A combination of old age plus spiraling taxes, and wages forced Thalia "Tally" Urquhart, as well as others like her, to let outlying buildings go.

A huge stone hay barn with a center aisle big enough to house four hay wagons side by side sat in the middle of small one-and-a-half-story stone houses with slate roofs. The buildings, although pockmarked by broken windows, were so well constructed they would endure despite the birds nesting in their chimneys.

The hay barn, whose supporting beams were constructed from entire tree trunks, would outlast this century and the next one as well.

The paint peeled off the stone buildings, exposing the soft gray underneath with an occasional flash of rose-gray.

The tiger cat sniffed the air; low clouds and fog were moving in fast from the west, sliding down the Blue Ridge Mountains like fudge on a sundae.

Normally Mrs. Murphy would hunt close to her own farm. Often she was accompanied by

Pewter, who despite her bulk was a ferocious mouser. This evening she wanted to hunt alone. It cleared her mind. She liked to wait motionless for mice to scurry in the rotting burlap feed bags, for their tiny claws to tap against the beams in the hayloft.

Since no one paid attention to the Urquhart barns, the mousing was superb. Kernels of grain and dried corn drew the little marauders in, as did the barn itself, a splendid place in which to raise young mice.

A moldy horse collar, left over from the late 1930s, its brass knobs green, hung on the tack-room wall, forgotten by all, the mules who wore it long gone to the Great Mule Sky.

Mrs. Murphy left off her mousing to explore the barn, constructed in the early nineteenth century. How lovely the farm must have once been. Mrs. Murphy prided herself on her knowledge of human history, something the two-legged species often overlooked in its rush to be current. Of course, she reflected, whatever is current today is out of fashion tomorrow.

The tiger cat, like most felines, took the long view.

Her particular human, Mary Minor Haristeen, or Harry, the young, pretty postmistress of Crozet, Virginia, evinced interest in history as well as in animal behavior. She read voraciously and expanded her understanding of animals by visiting Virginia Tech in Blacksburg and the Marion DuPont Scott Equine Research Center in Leesburg, Virginia. Harry even studied the labels on crunchy-food bags to make certain kitty nutrition was adequate. She cared for her two cats, one dog, and three horses with love and knowledge.

The flowers continued to push up around the buildings. The lilac bushes, enormous, burst forth each spring. The sadness of the decaying old place was modified by the health of the plant life.

The cat emerged from the barn and glanced at the deepening night clouds, deciding to hurry back home before the fog got thicker. Two creeks and a medium-sized ridge were the biggest obstacles. She could traverse the four miles in an hour at a trot, faster if she ran. Mrs. Murphy could run four miles with ease. A sound foxhound could run forty miles in a day. Much as she liked running, she was glad she wasn't a foxhound, or any hound, for that matter. Mrs. Murphy liked dogs but considered them a lower species, for the most part, except for the corgi she lived with, Tucker, who was nearly the equal of a cat. Not that she'd tell Tucker that....Never.

She trotted away from the magical spot and loped over the long, flat pasture, once an airstrip for Tally Urquhart in her heyday, when she had shocked the residents of central Virginia by flying airplanes. Her disregard for the formalities of marriage did the rest.

Tally Urquhart was Mim Sanburne's aunt. Mim had ascended to the rank of undisputed social leader of Crozet once her aunt had relinquished the position twenty years ago. Mrs.

Murphy would giggle and say to Mim's face, *"Ah, welcome to the Queen of Quite a Lot."* Since Mim didn't understand cat, the grande dame wasn't insulted.

On the other side of the airfield a rolling expanse of oats just breaking through the earth's surface undulated down to the first creek.

At the creek the cat stopped. The clouds lowered; the moisture was palpable. She thought she heard a rumble. Senses razor sharp, she looked in each direction, including overhead. Owls were deadly in conditions like this.

The rumble grew closer. She climbed a tree—just in case. Out of the clouds overhead two wheels appeared. Mrs. Murphy watched as a single-engine plane touched down, bumped, then rolled toward the barn. It stopped right in front of the massive doors, a quarter of a mile away from Mrs. Murphy.

A lean figure hopped out of the plane to open the barn doors. The pilot stayed at the controls, and as the doors opened, the plane puttered into the barn. The motor was cut off. Mrs. Murphy saw two figures now, one much taller than the other. She couldn't make out their features; the collars of their trench coats were turned up and they were half turned away, dueling gusts of wind. As each human braced behind a door and rolled it shut, the heavens opened in a deluge.

A great fat *splat* of rain plopped right on Mrs. Murphy's head. She hated getting wet, but she waited long enough to see the two humans run

4

down the road past the stone houses. In the far distance she thought she heard a motor turn over.

Irritated that she hadn't gone down the farm road and therefore might have missed something, she climbed down and ran flat out the entire way home. She could have stayed overnight in the Urquhart barn, but Harry would panic if she woke up and realized Mrs. Murphy wasn't asleep on the bed.

By the time she reached her own back porch forty-five minutes later, she was soaked. She pushed through the animal door and shook herself twice in the kitchen, spattering the cabinets, before walking into the bedroom.

Tucker snored on the floor at the foot of the bed. Pewter snuggled next to Harry. The portly gray cat opened one brilliant green eye as Mrs. Murphy leapt onto the bed.

*"Don't sleep next to me. You're all wet."*

*"It was worth it."*

Both eyes opened. *"What'd you get?"*

*"Two field mice and one shrew."*

*"Liar."*

*"Why would I make it up?"*

Pewter closed both eyes and flicked her tail over her nose. *"Because you have to be the best at everything."*

The tiger ignored her, crept to the head of the bed, lifted the comforter, and slid under while staying on top of the blanket. If she'd picked up all the covers and gotten on the sheets, Harry might have rolled over and felt the wet sheets and the wet cat. Mrs. Murphy was better off in the middle; and she would dry faster that way, too.

Pewter said nothing but she heard a muffled *"Hee-hee,"* before falling asleep again.

# 2

The slanting rays of the afternoon sun spilled across the meadows of Harry's farm. The hayloft door, wide open, framed a sleeping Mrs. Murphy, flopped on her back, her creamy beige stomach soaking up the sun's warmth. The cat's tail gently rocked from side to side as though floating in a pool of sunlight.

Simon the possum, curled in a gray ball, slept at the mouth of his nest made from old hay bales. A worn curb chain glittered from the recess of his den. Simon liked to carry off shiny objects, ribbons, gloves, even old pieces of newspaper.

Below, in the barn's center aisle, Tucker snoozed. Each time she exhaled, a tiny knot of no-see-ums swirled up, then settled down again on her shoulders.

May, usually the best month in central Virginia, along with colorful Octobers, remained unusually cool this year, the temperature staying in the fifties and low sixties. One week earlier, the last of April, a snowstorm had roared down the Blue Ridge Mountains, covering the swelling buds and freezing the daffodils and tulips. All that was forgotten as redbuds bloomed and dogwoods began to open, lush white or pink. The grass turned green.

This afternoon the animals couldn't keep their eyes open. Sometimes an abrupt change of season could do that, wreaking havoc with everyone's rhythm. Even Harry, that engine of productivity, dozed in the tack room. She had every intention of stripping and dipping her tack, a monotonous task reserved for the change of seasons. Harry had gotten up that morning in an organizing mood but she had fallen asleep before she had even broken down the bridle.

Alone—if one counts being divorced but having your ex much in evidence as "alone"— Harry ran the small farm bequeathed to her by her deceased parents. Farming, difficult these days because of government regulation, made enough money to cover the taxes on the place. She relied on her job at the Crozet Post Office to feed and clothe herself.

In her thirties, Harry was oblivious to her charms. Her one concession to the rigors of feminine display was a good haircut. She lived in jeans, T-shirts, and cowboy boots. She even wore her cowboy boots to work. Since the Crozet Post Office was such a small, out-of-the-way place, she need not dress for success.

In fact, Harry measured success by laughter, not by money. She was extremely successful. If she wasn't laughing with other humans she was laughing with Mrs. Murphy, wit personified, Tucker, or Pewter, the cat who came to dinner.

Pewter, curled in Harry's lap, dreamed of crème brûlée. Other cats dreamed of mice, moles, birds, the occasional spider. Pewter conjured up images of beef Wellington, mashed potatoes, fresh buttered bread, and her favorite food on earth, crème brûlée. She liked the crust thin and crunchy.

In the distance a low purr caused Mrs. Murphy to flick her ear in that direction. The marvelous sound came nearer. She opened one eye, casting her gaze down the long dirt road dotted with puddles of water from last night's rain. She stretched but didn't rise.

The throaty roar sounded like a big cat staking out territory. She heard the distinctive crushing sound of tires on Number 5 gravel. Curious, she half raised her head, then pushed herself up, stretching fore and aft, blinking in the sunlight.

Pewter lifted her head as well.

Tucker remained dead to the world.

Mrs. Murphy squinted to catch sight of a gleaming black car rounding the far turn.

*"Company's coming."*

No one below paid attention. She leaned forward, sticking her head out the second-story space as Harry's nearest neighbor, Blair Bainbridge, cruised into the driveway behind the wheel of a black wide-body Porsche 911 Turbo.

Tucker barked. Mrs. Murphy laughed to herself—*"Dogs!"*—as she sauntered over to the ladder. She excelled at climbing ladders and at descending them. The latter took longer to learn. The trick was not to look down.

She scampered across the dusty center aisle and out to Blair. Harry woke up with Pewter licking her face. Tucker, sniffling about interrupted sleep, emerged into the sunlight.

"Hello, Mrs. Murphy." Blair grinned.

*"Hello."* She rubbed against his leg.

"Anybody home?" Blair called out.

"Be there in a minute," a foggy Harry replied.

The tiger cat walked around the low-bodied, sleek machine. *"A cat designed this."*

*"Why?"* Tucker viewed the car without much enthusiasm, but Tucker never had much enthusiasm when awakened.

*"Because it's beautiful and powerful."*

*"You don't like yourself much, do you?"*

Harry walked out, then stopped abruptly. "Beautiful!"

"Just delivered." Blair leaned against the sloping front fender. "Makes all the crap I do worthwhile."

"Modeling can't be that bad."

"Can't be that good. It's not..."—he paused—"connected. It's superficial." He waved his hand dismissively. "And sooner or later I'll be considered over-the-hill. It's ruthless that way."

"I don't know. You're too hard on yourself. Anyway, it got you this. I don't think I've ever seen anything so beautiful. Not even the Aston Martin Volante."

"You like Aston Martins?" His dark eyebrows rose.

"Love 'em. Not as much as horses, but I love

9

them. The Volante is a sleek car, but you need the mechanic to go with it. This is more reliable."

"German."

"There is that." She smiled.

"Would you like a ride?"

"I thought you'd never ask." She spoke to the two cats and dog. "Hold down the fort."

"*Yeah, yeah,*" Mrs. Murphy grumbled. "*I think we should all go for a ride.*"

"*No room,*" Tucker sensibly noted.

"*I don't take up much room—unlike you.*"

"*What's that supposed to mean?*"

"*Nothing.*" Mrs. Murphy raised her tail straight up, sashaying toward the house as Blair backed out. Mrs. Murphy thought the baritone perfect, not too deep, yet velvety.

"Only one hundred Turbos made for the U.S. market each year," Blair said as he straightened out the wheel.

Pewter waddled toward the house. She gave the $110,000 internal-combustion machine barely a look. "*Don't go so fast,*" she chided her cohort.

To torment her, the tiger cat bounded gracefully onto the screened-in porch, pawing open the unlatched screen door.

"*I hate her,*" Pewter muttered.

"*Me, too.*" Tucker walked alongside the gray cat. "*The biggest show-off since P.T. Barnum.*"

"*I heard that.*"

"*We don't care,*" Tucker replied.

"*You're bored.*" Mrs. Murphy ducked through the doggie door in the kitchen.

10

*"Did she say I was boring?"*

*"No, Pewter, she said we were bored."*

*"Nothing ever happens in May."*

Mrs. Murphy stuck her head out the magnetic-flap door. *"Blair Bainbridge bought a Porsche Turbo. I count that as an important event."*

Pewter and Tucker, walking more briskly, reached the screen door. The corgi sat while the cat opened it.

*"That doesn't count."* Pewter flung open the door.

Mrs. Murphy ducked back into the kitchen. Pewter dashed through the animal door first.

*"What would you like to happen?"* Mrs. Murphy inquired.

*"A meat truck turns over in front of the post office."* Tucker wagged her nonexistent tail.

*"Remember the Halloween when the human head turned up in a pumpkin?"* Pewter's pupils widened.

*"Yech!"* Mrs. Murphy recalled the grisly event that happened a few years back.

*"Yech? I found it. You didn't."*

*"I don't like to think about it."* Mrs. Murphy fastidiously licked the sides of her front paws, then swept them over her face.

She noticed the side of the barn facing north, the broad, flat side where the paint was peeling. A painted ad for Coca-Cola, black background underneath, peeled out in parts.

*"Funny."*

*"What?"* Pewter leaned over to groom her friend, whom she loved even though Mrs. Murphy often irritated her.

11

*"How the past is bursting through—all around us. That old Coke sign—bet it was painted on the barn in the 1920s or '30s. The past bursts through the present."*

*"Dead and gone,"* Tucker laconically said.

*"The past is never dead."*

*"Well, maybe not for you. You have nine lives."*

*"Ha-ha."* Mrs. Murphy turned her nose up.

*"I bet the past wasn't as boring as today,"* Pewter moaned.

*"Things will pick up,"* Tucker advised.

Truer words were never spoken.

# 3

Blair glided down Route 250 toward Greenwood at 60 miles an hour. He was only in second gear and the tachometer wasn't even close to the red zone.

Harry couldn't believe the surge of power or the handling. They hit 0 to 60 mph in 4.4 seconds. The balance of the car astounded her. The old farm Misfit blurred by, then Mirador (Misfit's big sister), then Blair downshifted, turned right, and headed back toward the Greenwood school, the road snaking and the car sweeping around each sharp curve without a shudder, a roll, or a skid.

"Don't you love it?" Blair laughed out loud.

She sighed. "Deep love."

A short stretch of flat land beckoned. He

smoothly shifted. The speedometer glided past 100, then Blair expertly downshifted as a curve rolled off to the right.

Unfortunately, Sheriff Rick Shaw was rolling, too, right out of Sir H. Vane-Tempest's driveway. He hit the siren and snapped on the whirling lights.

"Damn," Blair whispered.

"What's he doing out here in the boonies? He ought to be on Route 29." Harry glanced in the rearview mirror.

"Is it Rick or Cynthia?" Blair squinted at the distant object, which was fast approaching.

"Rick. Cynthia doesn't wear her hat in the squad car."

"That makes sense. Turn your head and the brim hits the window."

"Rick's balding, remember."

"There is that." Blair half smiled as he pulled over. The Porsche stopped as smooth as silk. He lowered the window and reached in the side pocket of the door for the relevant papers as Rick lumbered up.

"As I live and breathe, Blair Bainbridge." Rick bent over. "And our esteemed post-mistress. License, please," he sang out.

"Oh." Blair fished around in his hip pocket, pulled out his crocodile wallet, and handed the license to Rick.

"Blair, do you have any idea how fast you were moving?"

"Uh—yes, I do."

"Uh-huh. You know, of course, that the speed limit in the great state of Virginia is fifty-five miles per hour. Now I don't think that's the smartest law on the books, but I have to enforce it."

"Yes, sir."

"When did you get this vehicle?"

"This morning."

"Uh-huh. Why don't you get out of the car a minute."

In a show of sympathy, Harry unfastened her seat belt and got out, too.

"Lemme see the engine."

Rick popped up the back, revealing a giant turbo covering the engine.

"That's a pain in the ass," the sheriff grumbled.

"It's the turbo, chief, it forces air back in here,"—Blair pointed to the inlet side—"which boosts the horsepower to four hundred. Here's the delivery side."

"Four hundred horsepower?" Rick whispered reverently.

Blair smiled, knowing the sheriff was hooked. "The intake, or flow, is split toward the left and right exhaust turbochargers. The air gets reunited, flows past the throttle, and goes into the cylinder heads in virtually direct sequence." He paused, realizing he was getting too technical. "The pollution level falls below government requirements, which is a good thing. Drive a turbo and be environmentally responsible."

"Uh-huh." Rick ran his hand over the rear fender, which slightly resembled a horse's hindquarters, then ducked his head inside the driver's side. "Not much room in the back."

"Big enough for Mrs. Murphy, Tucker, and Pewter." Harry finally said something.

"I'm surprised they aren't with you." Rick pushed his hat back on his head. "Now in order to be fair here, I need to know a little more about this car. Can we all fit in?"

"Sure," Blair said.

"Tell you what, guys, I'll stay with the squad car. You two roll on," Harry said.

Rick furtively looked around. "Well—"

"No one will know a thing. If anyone stops, I'll say you're investigating a rustling call and I came along for the ride. You're out in the pasture."

"Well—all right," Rick agreed. "If H. Vane-Tempest happens to come by, don't say a word."

"Got his nose out of joint again?" Harry casually asked.

Rick grunted. "He's a little different."

"Different!" Harry giggled. "He's got more money than God and he acts like he *is* God."

"He and Archie Ingram pester me with more calls than anyone else in the county, and this is a county full of nutcases."

Archie Ingram, one of the county commissioners, a handsome man, courtly to women, was so violently opposed to most development schemes that he had attracted radical detractors and equally radical supporters.

"H. Vane is a big noise in the environmental group. I guess he and Archie have to work closely together."

15

"Ideas are one thing. Temperament's another." Rick hooked his thumb in his gun belt. "I predict those two can't stay on the same team for long."

"Sheriff, would you like to drive?" Blair asked.

"Well—"

"Go on."

Rick slipped behind the wheel.

Blair winked at Harry, then folded his six-foot-four-inch frame into the passenger side. "That button will push the seat back or forward. There you go. And you can raise or lower the seat, too."

"Isn't that something?" Rick's seduction would be complete once he touched the accelerator. He reached to the right for the key.

"On the left."

"That's weird."

"A leftover from the great racing days when drivers had to sprint to their cars. If the ignition was on the left it gave them a split-second advantage. The driver could start the car and shift into gear simultaneously."

"I'll be damned." Rick turned the key. The pistons awakened like Sleeping Beauty.

Rick stalled out.

"Takes a while to get used to the clutch. Everything is much more sensitive than you or I are accustomed to—it's not so much about technology, it's about feel."

"Yeah." Rick engaged the clutch and touched the gas, then shot down the road.

Harry folded her arms across her chest,

watching the car lurch into second. It would take Rick a few more tries.

She walked back to the squad car, sat down, and clicked on the two-way radio.

Milden Hall, the estate of Sir H. Vane-Tempest, was immediately behind her. The overlarge sign, emblazoned with a gold griffin on a blood-red field, swung slightly in the breeze.

Harry turned off the radio, swung her legs out, and closed the door. The day was too pleasant for sitting in the car. She walked back toward the sign. A car cruised around the corner, having turned off 250.

Harry waved and Susan Tucker pulled her Audi to the side of the road.

"What are you doing out here?"

Harry walked over to her best friend. "Joyriding. Blair bought a Porsche Turbo and as luck would have it, Rick Shaw came out of H. Vane's driveway just as we slowed down to eighty-something."

"Where's Blair now? In jail?"

"No. He's letting Rick drive the Turbo."

Susan laughed. "That's a good one."

"What are you doing out here?"

"On my way to drop off books for Chris Middleton. I want to persuade him to give a talk at the high school for career day."

Chris was a small-animals veterinarian, one of the best.

"Good idea."

"And then I have to meet Mim, Her Royal Pain in the Ass, at the club. She's fussed up

17

about this board meeting over the water supply. The county's been fighting about the reservoir so long I don't know why she still lets it get to her."

"We've got to do something with the development in the northwest corner of the county. They need water."

"Exactly, but the reservoir plan is already outdated and it hasn't been built yet." Susan pouted for a minute. "Archie Ingram, as usual, wants to turn the clock back to 1890."

"Make it 1840. Then he could own slaves." Harry approved of conservation but Archie Ingram took it too far.

"Good one, Harry." Susan smiled. "Oh, that reminds me, the battle reenactment at Oak Ridge—you have to be there."

"No I don't."

"Yes you do, because Ned needs camp followers."

Ned was Susan's husband, a lawyer by trade and a re-enactor in Civil War battles on weekends. The latter was becoming a passion.

"Susan, I hate that war stuff."

"Living history."

"I'll think about it."

"Harry..." Susan lowered her voice.

"Susan..."

"You do it."

"Takes two women to keep your husband happy these days."

"That's right, girlfriend. And I even have your costume."

"Susan, you're both nuts."

"You'll look fetching in a bonnet."

"I'm not wearing period clothes—period!"

Harry heard the distant, distinctive sound of the Porsche. "Push on, because Rick will be embarrassed if he gets back and finds you here. We don't want Blair to get a ticket."

"Tell Blair that Ned expects him in the First Virginia." That was the name of Ned's unit. The re-enactors were fanatical about detail, down to the last button.

"I will." Harry kissed her on the cheek. Susan kissed air in return, then drove away.

By the time the Porsche drove into view, Harry was back leaning against the squad car. A beaming Rick Shaw stayed behind the wheel.

"You deserve a car like that, Sheriff."

"I never drove anything like that in my life," Rick said, his voice full of wonder. He wouldn't get out of the car. He was like a child at Christmas, sitting under the tree, fondling his favorite present.

"I just had to have it." Blair smiled. "Boys with toys, as Harry would say."

"Hate to leave this baby." Rick finally slid out from under the wheel. He walked alongside the front of the car, running his top finger over the curving, graceful lines. "Kind of like an egg on its side."

"Yes."

Rick opened the creaking door of the squad car. "Blair, stay inside the speed limit."

"Yes, sir."

"Harry, mum's the word."

"Okay." She smiled at Rick, whom she liked even though he chided her about being an amateur detective. His word was *busy-body*.

He flicked on the radio.

"Car 1. Car 1."

"Car 1," Rick answered.

"Where you been, boss?" Deputy Cynthia Cooper's voice crackled.

"Sir H. Vane-Tempest's. His wife says Archie Ingram threatened her husband with bodily harm. H. pooh-poohs it. Said they simply had a disagreement over sensitive environmental issues."

"Oh la!" Coop sang out.

"See you in ten. Over and out." Rick started the motor and Harry backed away from his window. Rick winked at her, then pulled out, made a U-turn, and cruised back to 250.

Blair folded his arms across his muscled chest. "Man fell in love before my very eyes."

"Doesn't everyone?" Harry enjoyed her double entendre, for Blair was stunning to the point of leaving women breathless—and a few men, too, for that matter.

"How about you, then?" He held open the driver's-side door, ushering her into the cockpit.

Harry sat still, inhaling the rich leather smell as she reached for the key on her left. Blair closed the passenger door behind him.

"Ready, Eddy?" She turned over the key.

"Shoot the goose, Bruce."

"I never heard that."

"Maybe it's shoot the juice." Blair laughed.

She did and they roared into Greenwood, around the little town, and back to Crozet by every back mountain road she could remember.

When they finally pulled into her driveway, Tee Tucker burst through the animal door of the house, then pushed open the screen door, happy to see her mother.

Mrs. Murphy turned to Pewter, both of them reposing on the kitchen table, forbidden to them and therefore more appealing. *"That dog will never learn."*

Pewter tapped her skull with one extended claw. *"Dog brains."*

Mrs. Murphy jumped over to the window over the kitchen sink. *"They're coming inside. Off the table."*

Pewter waited until she heard the screen door slam before leaving the table.

"Hi, kids," Harry greeted her cats, who ignored her.

*"Make her suffer for leaving us here."* Mrs. Murphy stalked into the living room.

Pewter, knowing some manner of food would be placed on the table, decided to be mildly friendly.

Harry spied the cat hair on the table and wiped it off with a wet dishrag. "You were on the table."

*"Was not,"* Mrs. Murphy called from the living room.

*"Was too,"* Tucker tattled.

*"Shut up, you little brownnose,"* Mrs. Murphy yelled at the dog.

"Blair, thank you again for letting me drive a dream." She opened the refrigerator door, removing corn bread and butter. Not that she had made the corn bread; Miranda had given her a big pan of it Friday after they left work.

"Any time."

"Oh, I forgot to tell you. Susan drove by while I was waiting for you and the sheriff. She said Ned expects you in the First Virginia for reenactment at Oak Ridge."

"I'll call him."

"I didn't know you were into that battle stuff."

"I'm not. They're short of bodies."

"Isn't it expensive to get the gear?"

"Yeah, but I can't complain if I've just bought a Turbo, can I?" He laughed. "Some of these guys are a little extreme, but I'm looking forward to it."

*"Extreme?"* Mrs. Murphy sardonically replied as she walked back to the kitchen, pointedly not paying attention to Harry. *"They're a quart low."*

*"I think it's fascinating."* Tucker sat down on Blair's foot.

*"You think anything's fascinating that has dead bodies in it."*

*"Well, dogs eat carrion. That's what they're for, I guess."* Pewter pressed against the refrigerator door. *"Nature's garbage collectors."*

*"People hang out deer for a few days,"* Tucker rejoined.

*"Better gut them the minute you kill them or*

*you'll have some terrible-tasting deer.*" Mrs. Murphy wasn't fond of venison, but she could eat it if prepared in buttermilk.

Pewter moved back to the table. "*There aren't going to be any dead bodies at the reenactment, just people pretending to be dead.*"

"*The way things have been going, the commission meeting coming up might have a few dead bodies.*" Tucker giggled.

Pewter turned her full attention on Harry, who had set out some thinly sliced roast beef.

"Stay on the floor." Harry read her mind, not difficult under the circumstances.

"*One teensy piece,*" Pewter begged.

"*Me, too.*" Tucker had been transformed into Miss Adorable.

"No," Harry said, but without much oomph.

"*She'll weaken if you sit by the chair.*" Pewter hurried to get on Harry's right side.

"*You say that every time.*" The tiger cat laughed but she hurried to Blair's side, figuring he'd weaken before Harry.

"I had no idea that Sir H. Vane-Tempest pestered Sheriff Shaw so often."

"Tempest in a teapot is what Miranda calls him." Harry stuck her knife into a pot of creamy homemade mustard. "But Archie's picking fights with everyone. Even though he and H. Vane seem to be in a phase of political agreement. He's even fighting Mim."

"Not a smart move."

"Getting on the wrong side of Sir H. isn't smart either. His net worth is more than the gross national product of Chile."

*"Mrs. Murphy, what do you know about H. Vane?"* Tucker never took her eyes off Harry's hands.

*"He doesn't have cats or dogs, which bespeaks an empty life."*

Blair dropped her a sliver of roast beef, which she daintily ate.

"Are you going to the commission meeting?" Harry asked her guest.

"You bet. It's going to be the best show this spring."

# 4

Archie Ingram, a handsome man in his early forties, smiled at the assemblage. The only hint that he was nervous was the tension in his cheek muscles. The classroom at Crozet High School spilled over with people, many standing in the hall. A topographical map of the county was on a bulletin board behind the front table.

"I told you we should have used the auditorium," Archie complained to Jim Sanburne, the mayor of Crozet, as well as Mim's husband. As mayor he chaired the county meeting in his town.

"Archie, these meetings usually number three people, each of whom wants a zoning variance for a trailer, a business, or a nursing home. The only reason all these people are here is that you've stirred up a hornet's nest."

"Bullshit," he growled at the large, genial man.

Jim ignored him, waving a greeting to the Reverend Herbert Jones.

"Jim, I brought my dowser." Herb held up the wooden divining rod, which worked well despite naysayers.

"Spare me," Archie muttered under his breath, his eyes scanning the room, resting a second on the beautiful Sarah Vane-Tempest before darting away.

"What?" Jim asked

"Where's Tommy Van Allen?" Archie demanded. "I'm not delaying this meeting one more time for him."

"I don't know. I called and he wasn't at work."

"Typical." Archie tapped his pencil on the tabletop. "The only reason he ever wanted this thankless job was to find out when and where we'd be making road improvements and granting commercial zoning permits. Gives him more time to put together a good bid."

"Come on, Arch, you don't believe that."

"The hell I don't." Archie snapped his mouth shut like a turtle.

Harry, Mrs. Murphy, Tucker, and Pewter sat in the middle next to Harry's colleague in the post office, Miranda Hogendobber. Also there were Susan and Ned Tucker; Harry's ex-husband, Fair Haristeen; and Boom Boom Craycroft. The widow Craycroft was not Harry's favorite person.

Blair accompanied Mim's daughter, Marilyn.

Little Mim, as she was known, stood up in

front with her mother, who was already poring over the large map of the county.

Sir Henry Vane-Tempest—called H. or H. Vane by everyone—sat off to the side, his horn-rimmed spectacles sliding down his long nose. He had taken the precaution of bugging each county commissioner's office. Once a week the transcript was discreetly brought to him at his farm by Tareq Said, head of Said and Trumbo Investigations. Vane-Tempest made certain that his wife knew nothing of this. No one knew and H. would keep it that way. Next to him was Ridley Kent, a rich ne'er-do-well whose primary occupation was staring at women's bodices. He happened to be sitting beside a good one. Sarah Vane-Tempest was H. Vane's trophy wife, an elegant blonde whose cool beauty owed little to the expensive clothes she wore.

"The gang's all here," Susan said to Harry.

"Frightening, isn't it?" Harry sarcastically replied.

"Holding negative feelings will eat you up and destroy your good health," Boom Boom crooned.

"Shut up, Boom."

"That's exactly what I'm talking about." Boom Boom cast her violet eyes at Harry.

Archie noticed Mrs. Murphy sauntering up to the map. "Get that cat out of here."

"*I beg your pardon.*" Mrs. Murphy stared at him.

"Mary Minor Haristeen, those animals have no place here." Archie pointed to Pewter, on her lap, and Tucker, seated at Fair's cowboy-booted feet.

*"Hey, Murphy, jump on the table and blow a tuna fart right in his face,"* Pewter called out.

*"How rude."* Mrs. Murphy giggled but she did jump on the desk to stare Archie directly in the eye.

"Murphy—" Harry called to her.

*"You are a sorry excuse for a mammal."* Mrs. Murphy insulted Archie, who blinked as she spoke.

"She's saying that she's a resident of Albemarle County, too, and the water supply affects her." Mim's upper-class voice hushed the room.

"That's right, honeybun," Jim, not upper-class, said.

Everyone laughed.

"Then at least keep this feline with you," Archie told Harry.

Mrs. Murphy, the full attention of the room on her, flopped on her side, cocking her head at the audience.

"Isn't she adorable. She knows we're talking about her," one of the older ladies said.

*"Gag me,"* Pewter sniped.

"Mrs. Murphy, come back here," Harry said firmly. She was put out at Mrs. Murphy's showing off, but secretly she was also enjoying Archie Ingram's discomfiture. He could be so pompous.

Naturally, Mrs. Murphy flopped on the other side, again gazing at her fans. She emitted a honey-coated meow.

27

"Precious," another voice cooed.

Even Tucker looked queasy.

Harry handed Pewter to Fair, stood up, and stepped along a row of desks to the center aisle. "Madam, you get off that desk."

*"One for the money, two for the show, three to get ready and four to go,"* the tiger cat sang out, sat up, grabbed Archie's pencil in her teeth, and leapt off the front table.

"Hey!" Archie boomed as everyone in the classroom laughed at him. "Hey, I want that back."

Mrs. Murphy pranced over to Sarah Vane-Tempest, dropping the pencil at her expensively shod feet.

*"I can't believe you did that,"* Pewter hollered at her.

*"Watch me."* She skidded out of the hallway, dodging legs, and finally sat down under the water fountain. By the time Harry caught up with her, she was intently grooming the tip of her tail.

"Monster."

*"Broccoli eater."*

"If you even move your eyebrows I'm taking you out to the truck."

*"Take me to Blair's Porsche. I don't want to sit in the truck."*

"Don't you mouth off at me," Harry warned her.

*"Who else am I going to mouth off to?"*

Harry paused, wondering whether to take her back into the meeting or go directly to the truck. Well aware of Murphy's lethal temper, she thought the cat would be safer in sight than out of sight. She scooped up the silky-coated creature, holding her bottom while Murphy leaned on her shoulder, winking at passersby.

By the time Harry reached the classroom door her seat had been taken. Pewter stood on Fair's lap, paws on his shoulders, looking for her buddy. Upon seeing Mrs. Murphy, she jumped down and walked to the back of the room.

Meanwhile Archie was explaining to the assembled why the reservoir plan was outdated. He couldn't resist reminding them that he had always been an opponent of unchecked growth. However, the population had grown, the water supply had not, and as a public servant he had to find a solution. Before he could finish his presentation, the county commissioner next to him dropped his tablet. It hit the floor with a loud clatter.

Archie glared as Donald Jackson bent over to pick it up, tipped off balance, and fell over, still in the chair.

Jim Sanburne quickly hopped out of his seat to assist Don, which made Archie look like a jerk, since he was standing above the fallen man.

Irritated, Archie continued reading off his figures.

"Archie, we know all that." Don tried to divert him.

"Everyone in this room knows the cost of building a new reservoir?" He slapped his hand on the table, the papers in his other hand shaking.

"Yes. It's on the handout sheet. You don't need to read that. In case anyone missed a handout sheet, a new reservoir in the northwest quadrant will cost us thirty-two million dollars."

"What's wrong with rehabilitating Sugar Hollow?" a voice from the middle piped up.

Sugar Hollow was the site of an old reservoir.

"After what Hurricane Fran did?" Archie imperiously dismissed the question.

"Not so fast, Archie." Ned Tucker spoke up. "Given the importance of the issue, a feasibility study on reviving Sugar Hollow isn't a frivolous suggestion."

"Maybe we need them both," Sir H. Vane-Tempest suggested in his soothing voice.

"And where would the money come from?" Little Mim asked a sensible question yet received a frown from her mother.

Big Mim preferred to speak before her offspring did, at which time she expected Little Mim to rubber-stamp whatever she had said. Aunt Tally, leaning on her silver-handled cane, cast a sharp eye at her family. The handle itself was carved in the shape of a hound's head. It had become Tally's signature accessory.

"From my pocketbook," Miranda good-naturedly called out.

A few people laughed. Others nodded.

"The county's population has tipped over 112,000." Jim, deep voice rumbling, folded his hands. "The original plan for the reservoir between Free Union and Earlysville was drawn up in 1962, when the population was half of what it is today and projections were not even close to our current rate of growth."

"That's the problem. Unrestrained growth," Archie again said.

"We can't throw people out." Jim sighed, tacitly acknowledging the problem.

"No, but we can certainly put the lid on development."

"You've done a good job of that all by yourself," Sir H. Vane-Tempest jocularly interjected.

"With little support from my colleagues." Archie's eyebrows twitched upward as he stared at the Englishman. "You've been opposed to growth, H. Vane, and I appreciate your vision."

"Un*planned* growth. A master plan for this county would go a long way to solving these woes." Sir H. Vane-Tempest appeared to shift politically ever so slightly.

"We don't have a master plan!" Archie's eyes narrowed. What was Vane-Tempest up to?

"This reservoir plan is not worth the paper it's printed on." Don Jackson shook his head. "Earlier commissions did not foresee this population boom nor the encroachment of Richmond and even Washington, on weekends, anyway. Our infrastructure is woefully inadequate and that includes our water supply."

"Wouldn't it make sense to identify all of our water resources?" Fair Haristeen stood up. "We have the runoff from the Blue Ridge Mountains, which I believe figured into the original reservoir plan. We have the remains of the reservoir at Sugar Hollow. We have the Rivanna, Mechum, and James Rivers, which may yet prove useful."

"He's right." Boom Boom smiled, which made the men smile back.

"Yuk," Harry whispered to Mrs. Murphy and Pewter.

"And if we try to dam up the rivers, do we know what the state will do to us? Ha!" Archie threw up his hands. "To say nothing of the catastrophic environmental damage."

"We can't be the only county trying to absorb new people." Sir H. Vane-Tempest now stood up. In his early seventies, exuding vitality, he was well turned out, although the ascot seemed pretentious for the occasion. "The concept of a major reservoir serving ourselves and even the lower counties, such as Buckingham, isn't a frivolous idea."

"Well, what about the water table?" Dr. Larry Johnson joined in. "Whatever we do, we have to examine the underground effect. This isn't just about building a reservoir."

Archie sat down, folding his arms across his chest.

Don leaned forward. "Precisely the reason for these local meetings. Our commission has to present your ideas to the state. There's no way Albemarle County can fund a reservoir. Even if you double taxes, we can't pay for it."

"So we have to go to Richmond no matter what?" Jim Sanburne half asked, half informed the audience.

"Too much government! Richmond will only make it worse. Look at the bypass." Aunt Tally referred to a bottled-up traffic mess that the state couldn't resolve, each plan being worse than the former.

People nodded their heads in agreement.

"There's got to be enough water under the ground. Got to be." Ridley Kent shook his head.

"Ridley, if you had a brain you'd be dangerous." Vane-Tempest guffawed at his own joke.

Ridley, not one to take offense, laughed back. "I mean it. There're underground rivers as well as overground rivers."

"Exactly. Identify the water sources." Fair spoke again.

"I agree, but aren't these feasibility studies also expensive?" Blair finally spoke. As a relative newcomer to Crozet he had learned to wait his turn. Of course, you couldn't wait your turn until you knew your place on the totem pole, which he was finally figuring out. Given his income and his stunning good looks, he hovered in the middle, much higher than had he been shorn of his attributes. Not being southern, there were moments when the elaborate, unspoken rules overwhelmed him. Harry usually translated for him.

"Hideously expensive." Archie leaned forward again.

"We know there's plenty of water, plenty." Herb Jones's gravelly voice filled the room. "But no matter how much we have, no matter where it is, we can't dam it up or pull it up without goring somebody's scared cow."

"I resent that!" Archie jumped up.

"Sit down, Arch," Jim calmly commanded.

Archie didn't listen. "You're implying that because my farm is in the path of the reservoir I stand to gain. I think I stand to lose!"

"Oh, hell, Archie, I implied nothing, but you proved my point." The room erupted in laughter, then quieted as the elderly minister, beloved of all, continued. "There's no way a project like this can go forward without enriching some and harming others. Once the state comes in and appraises your land or exercises eminent domain and claims land for the so-called greater good, whatever they do is going to be a real shell game."

"You got that right." Susan's husband, Ned, chimed in.

"And what about the bids for the jobs? Who would build the reservoir? You don't think that's political?" Vane-Tempest stood up again.

"Well, H. Vane, I'm not in the construction business." Archie glared at his former colleague, since he mistakenly assumed the criticism was directed at him.

"No, but Tommy Van Allen is." Vane-Tempest appeared triumphant.

"He's hardly my best friend." Archie cleared his throat. "What are you implying?"

"Gentlemen, Van Allen's books are open. I have known him all my life." Jim Sanburne wanted to get this meeting over with.

"Means you've known Archie all his life, too. You have my sympathy," Vane-Tempest catcalled, tired of Archie's oversensitivity. A few people laughed. Sarah elbowed her husband to stop.

"You know, if I weren't an elected official, I'd smash your face in." Archie clenched his fists, surprising people. He had a temper but he was taking offense where only leavening humor was intended.

"That's quite enough." Mim rose, facing the gathering. "We need more information. If we ask the state for another study it will be at their convenience and our expense. We are perfectly capable of identifying water sources ourselves. Once we have done that we can formulate our own plan and then present that plan to the state—a preemptive strike, if you will. Archie and Donald, you take the Keswick-Cismont area."

"Wait a minute. We have to vote on this." Archie's face changed from red to pale white.

"Call to question," Miranda said.

"There's no motion on the floor," Jim said.

"I move that the county commissioners identify all possible water sources in Albemarle County before our next meeting." Boom Boom succinctly put forth the motion.

"I second the motion," Vane-Tempest said.

"Call to question," Miranda repeated.

"All those in favor say aye." Jim cast his gaze over the room.

"Aye," came the resounding reply.

"Opposed."

"Me," Archie said. "I've got enough work to do."

"If you want to be reelected to the county commission you'd better change your attitude," Mim warned. Coming from her it was no idle threat.

As the meeting broke up, Boom Boom pushed her way to the back. "Harry, don't forget you're going to Lifeline with me Thursday night."

"I know." Harry showed no enthusiasm.

"Eight at the church."

"Eight."

"*Ha-ha,*" Mrs. Murphy giggled. *"Boom Boom's got her."*

*"She promised. Poor Mom. She got caught on that one."* Tucker thought it was funny, too, for Lifeline was a group that looked inward, a spiritual awakening larded with lots of psychobabble. Harry was going to hate every minute, but she'd been hornswoggled into it in front of her friends last fall and now that a new cycle of Lifeline was starting, she had to make good on her promise.

Miranda bustled out, surrounded by her church friends. They sang in the choir at the Church of the Holy Light. "See you tomorrow, Harry."

"Bright and early." Harry smiled.

Fair caught up to her and leaned down. "Do you think someone has paid Archie off to be so obstructionist? It doesn't make sense. He's so touchy."

"He's opposed to anything that will allow more people to move into the area. A reservoir would do that. At least, I think that's what's

36

going on. He's saying one thing but doing another."

Fair smiled at his ex-wife's shrewd observation, but wondered what had happened to Archie Ingram, never the most likable man but always a principled one.

Boom Boom, her back to Harry, was talking to Blair about his Porsche.

Sir H. Vane-Tempest and Sarah hurried by, glancing over their shoulders. Archie was in slow pursuit. They escaped out the front door as Ridley Kent bagged Archie, demanding to know when the next meeting would be.

"I don't know." Archie shoved him aside.

Don Jackson, together with Jim Sanburne, caught up with Archie. "Jesus, Arch, what's the matter with you?"

"Nothing. These studies will take forever. I'll be an old man before we come to any conclusion, and the state will do whatever they want, which would be the rape of Albemarle County, her natural resources, her extraordinary beauty, and her historical value."

"Can't be that bad." Jim frowned, worried for Arch, who had a promising political future if he could learn to control his temper.

"It will take forever. Christ, some of us will be pushing up daisies." Then he stormed out the door.

*"He's scared,"* Mrs. Murphy said to her friends. They could smell the fear, too.

# 5

Harry shot mail into the brass mailboxes as Mrs. Murphy sat on the ledge underneath the top section of boxes. The bottom section contained the big boxes, big enough for Murphy to sit in. Harry hummed to herself as Miranda played with the computer at the right side of the open counter.

As much as Miranda hated computers, the tiny post office had finally received one and Miranda had applied herself to the instructions that came with it. Being a bright woman, she had figured the machine out but she didn't like it. The green letters on the screen, a touch fuzzy, hurt her eyes.

Also, every time the power fritzed out, which happened often in the country, down went the computer. She could figure much faster with her trusty scale. No matter what the computer said she still double-checked with the scale.

Both women, early risers, came to work at seven. Usually, by the time residents opened the front door of the post office much of the mail was sorted—except during holidays. In late spring a few love letters filtered in, a few postcards from those taking early vacations, and the bills never stopped. Harry's secret ambition was to burn everyone's bills, announce she'd done it, and see what happened. The night of April 15, when lines curled across the railroad tracks as people hastened to dump their

IRS forms in the mail, her ambition flamed beyond disposing of bills—she wanted to tear down every IRS building in America. She figured every other postal worker felt the same.

Low clouds and a light drizzle didn't dampen her mood. The warmth of spring brought out the best in Harry.

A squawk from the computer elicited "I know I did it right, why is it talking to me?" from Miranda.

"Zero out and try it again."

"I don't feel like it." Miranda, chin up, strode away from the offending machine.

A knock on the back door awakened Tee Tucker. Before she could bark, Susan Tucker, her breeder, jumped inside. She held her umbrella out the door, shook it vigorously, then closed the door, propping the umbrella to the right of it.

"Gloomy day, girls."

"Good for my irises," Mrs. Hogendobber, a passionate gardener, replied.

"Miranda, did you make orange buns again?" Susan sniffed the beguiling scent.

"Indeed, I did, you help yourself."

Susan gobbled one before Miranda finished her sentence.

"Pig." Harry laughed at her best friend.

"It's true." Susan sighed as she licked her lips. "I might as well live up to my billing." She ate another one.

*"She'll ask for a rowing machine next Christmas,"* Mrs. Murphy remarked.

*"Won't use it. No one ever uses those things,"* Tucker said.

*"Boom Boom uses hers."* Pewter opened one eye. She'd been snoozing on the chair at the small table in the rear.

*"She would."* Mrs. Murphy stuck her paw in an open mailbox. *"Don't you love the way the clear window on bills crinkles when you touch it?"*

*"Bite it."* Pewter egged her on.

*"Better not. Mom's still mad at you for your shameless display at the meeting last night."* Tucker, ever obedient, chided her.

*"Hee-hee."* Mrs. Murphy's whiskers twitched forward.

Susan walked over to scratch her ear. "You were the best part of the water-commission meeting."

"Say, wasn't Archie a pip?" Mrs. Hogendobber, beyond sixty, although she'd never admit her exact age, used slang from her generation's youth.

"Pip? He was a flaming asshole." Harry laughed.

"Don't be vulgar, Harry. That's the trouble with you young people. Cursing betrays a paucity of imagination."

"You're right." Harry smiled. "How about my saying that Archie was fraught with froth."

"A firth of froth or a froth of firth?" Susan kissed Murphy's head.

*"I like that,"* Murphy purred.

"What's a firth?" Mrs. Hogendobber asked.

"I don't know. It sounded right." Susan laughed at herself.

"To the dictionary, girls." Miranda pointed to the old Webster's, its blue-cloth case rubbed shiny, the cardboard sticking out at the corners.

"Is there really such a word?" Harry wondered.

Miranda silently pointed to the Webster's again.

Susan sat down at the table, thumbing through. The orange buns screamed under her nose. She snatched another. "*Firth,* old Scandinavian word meaning an 'arm of the sea.' "

"The English language is a lifelong study," Miranda pronounced.

The Reverend Herbert Jones strode up to the big counter, the ladies on the other side. "I smell orange."

"Come on in," Harry lifted the divider.

He helped himself to an orange bun. Pewter ate one when no one was looking. It made the cat so full she couldn't move. The humans were surprised that Pewter wasn't begging until Miranda counted the orange buns.

"Susan, did you eat four?"

"Three."

"Uh-huh." Miranda sternly reproached the cat with a look.

It had no effect whatsoever.

"This whole water business worries me." Herb licked his fingers, then found a napkin. "I don't know why Archie is behaving the way he is. He's known about the old study for years." His voice shot upward. "The various conservation groups in the county are on top of this one. Anyway, there are more-pressing political issues."

"Like what?"

"Like a new grade school in Greenwood."

"Yeah, that is pretty important," Harry agreed.

"That fop Sir H. Vane-Tempest—and if he's a knight or a lord or whatever, I'm John the Baptist—" Herb arched an eyebrow, "called me up and chewed me out for having too much brass on my foraging cap."

"What?" The three women stared at him.

"Like a fool I agreed to be in this reenactment. Now look, girls,"—he always called them girls, and there was no point in mentioning that might not be desirable—"I'm no fanatic. I agreed to fill out the ranks. He wants me to be one hundred percent accurate, though. He says that no real soldier would have all that brass on his cap because it's just one more thing to keep clean."

"Exactly what is on your cap?" Miranda asked.

"VA 1st—and then he said I had to wear something called a havelock—it's a piece of white canvas that buttons over the cap. He said it might be hot and a real soldier would want to keep the sun off. I told him I'd spent enough money and if I wasn't one hundred percent accurate that was too bad. He huffed and puffed. Finally I told him he wasn't an American, and far more important, he wasn't a Virginian and he shouldn't tell one born and bred how to dress. My great-granddaddy was

42

*in* the war. His was living high on the hog in England. He sputtered some more and said nationality had nothing to do with it. This was living history." He shook his head. "Obviously, the man has nothing better to do with his life."

"What about Ned?" Harry turned to Susan. "Is he getting obsessive?"

"He started out like the Rev." She smiled at Herb when she said that. "Now he's really into it. Why do you think I'm getting involved?"

*"That settles it. I'm going."* Mrs. Murphy spoke from the depths of the mail cart.

*"Fat chance,"* Tucker replied.

*"I am too going and I'll tell you why, midget fatso."*

*"I'm not fat."*

*"You're so low to the ground, how can I tell?"* The tiger cackled. *"I'm going because there were Confederate cats. They were vital to the war effort. We kept mice out of the grain supplies."*

*"What about Union cats?"* Pewter, a glorious Confederate gray, said.

*"We don't mention them."*

"What are you all talking about?" Susan, sensitive to animals, asked them.

*"The reenactment,"* came the reply.

"You know Blair Bainbridge bought everything authentic, not reproductions but real stuff. Must have cost him a fortune," Herb mused.

"I'd kill for his Porsche." Harry's eyes clouded over.

"You'd have to." Susan poked at her. "You can't even afford a new truck."

"Ain't it awful?" Harry hung her head in mock despair.

"Your ex is going as a cavalry officer. No one can find a jacket large enough for him, so he's wearing a period muslin shirt and gray pants."

"I hope he's considered the small fact that most of our horses aren't accustomed to continuous gunfire and cannon fire."

"He mentioned that." Herb folded his arms across his chest so he wouldn't reach out and grab another orange bun. He was on yet another diet and he'd cheated already.

"I have mixed emotions about Civil War reenactments. I think we're glorifying violence," Harry said. "I can't help it, I think there's a nasty reactionary undertow to all this."

"Never thought about it." Susan wrinkled her brow. "I figured it was what they said, living history. Besides, Ned gets dragged to so many things with me, I have to go along with this."

"Well, if it's living history, then why aren't we reliving inventing the reaper or the cotton gin? Why are we instead reliving the most horrible thing that's ever happened to this country? Sixty percent of the War Between the States was fought on Virginia soil. You'd think we, of all the people, would have the sense not to glorify it."

"Maybe it's not over." Herb stared at the ceiling.

*"He hit the nail on the head."* Mrs. Murphy played with her tail.

# 6

Later that afternoon the clouds grew darker still.

Deputy Cooper walked through the back door. "Hey."

"Hey," Harry answered.

"Where's Miranda?"

"Ran home for a minute." Harry pointed to a chair. "Sit down."

"Have you seen Tommy Van Allen?"

"No."

The two cats, dozing in the canvas mail cart, woke up, sticking their heads over the top.

"He's been missing for two days—two days that we know of—and his plane is missing, too."

Mrs. Murphy put her paws on the edge of the cart, with rapt attention.

"Cynthia, how could his plane be missing for two days and the airport not realize it?"

"They thought the plane was in Hangar C, the last hangar for repairs. Apparently Tommy had scheduled a maintenance check for Monday morning."

"How could the plane take off and not return without anyone noticing?"

"I wondered about that myself. The airport closes at midnight. He could have gone off then, and he *is* in the habit of staying a night or two at his destination. Still, it's odd."

*"I know where the plane is!"* Mrs. Murphy shouted.

"Quiet." Harry shook her finger.

The cat jumped out of the cart and bounded into Cynthia's lap. *"I don't know where Tommy is but I know where the plane is."*

"She's affectionate." Cynthia scratched her ears.

*"Don't waste your breath,"* Pewter advised Mrs. Murphy.

*"Do you really know where the plane is?"* Tucker asked.

*"Tally Urquhart's old barn. I'll take you there."*

Rain rattled on the windowpane.

Pewter settled back down in the mail cart. *"Wait for a sunny day."*

Mrs. Murphy jumped off Cynthia's lap back into the mail cart, where she rolled over Pewter. *"You don't believe me."*

*"I don't care."*

*"Sunday night when I came to bed wet—that's when I saw the plane."* She swatted the inattentive Pewter.

"Temper tantrum." Harry rose and separated them.

"Has anyone picked up Tommy's mail?" Cooper asked.

"His secretary." Harry held Mrs. Murphy on her shoulder.

Miranda came through the back door. Cynthia asked her about Tommy.

"He'll show up. It's hard to hide a six-foot-five-inch man," Miranda advised. "He's done this before."

"He stopped drinking," Harry reminded her.

"Maybe he slipped off the wagon." Miranda frowned.

"*I know where the plane is!*" the cat bellowed.

"God, Murphy, you'll split my eardrum." Harry placed her on the floor.

# 7

The longer days helped Harry finish her chores when she returned home from work. She pulled Johnny Pop, her 1958 John Deere tractor—as good as the day it was built—into the shed.

When she cut the choke the exhaust always popped—one loud crack—which made her laugh. She cleaned stalls, throwing the muck into the manure spreader. Since it was raining she'd have to wait until the ground dried before spreading anything on it.

Harry always put her equipment back in the shed. Her dad had told her that was the only way to do it. Stuff would last for decades if well built and well cared for.

She missed her father and mother. They were lively, hardworking people. As she grew up she realized what good people they really were. They'd had a German shepherd, King, when she was in her teens. King lived to an advanced age and when her mother died, King followed. Harry told herself that one day she'd get another German shepherd but she hadn't gotten around to it, maybe because a shepherd would remind her of her mother and make the loss even more apparent.

Tucker had been given to her as a six-week-old puppy by Susan, one of the best corgi breeders in Virginia. Harry didn't like small dogs but she learned to love the bouncing, tough corgi. Then she decided if she brought in a shepherd puppy it would upset Tucker—another reason to procrastinate.

Actually, the shepherd would upset the cats more. Tucker, outnumbered, might have been happy for another canine on the place.

She dashed back to the barn, rain sliding down the collar of her ancient Barbour. "I've got to rewax this thing." Water was seeping through the back of the coat.

The phone rang in the tack room. "Hello."

"Harry, Ridley Kent here. I've agreed to help Archie canvass landowners. I'm looking at a topo map and a flat map. You've got a creek in your western boundary."

"Yep."

"Strong creek?"

"In spring, but even in summer it never dries out completely. The water comes down from Little Yellow Mountain."

"What about springs?"

"There's one at the eastern corner."

"North or south?"

"Northeastern."

"Have you ever had your well run dry in a drought?"

"No. Neither did Mom and Dad, and they moved to this farm in the forties."

"Thanks."

"Sure." She hung up the phone.

*"Mother, there's an underground spring in the depression in the cornfield,"* Tucker told her. *"I can hear it."*

Harry rubbed the dog's soft fur. "I don't have any treaties on me."

The horses, munching hay in their stalls, lifted their heads when Mrs. Murphy jumped on the stall divider from the hayloft. Pewter, on the tack trunk, her favorite spot, watched her nimble friend. She could jump like that if she wanted to but she never wanted to; it jarred her bones.

*"Simon's found a quarter,"* Murphy announced.

*"Don't tell,"* a tiny voice complained.

*"I don't want your quarter,"* Tucker called up as the possum's beady little eyes peered over the hayloft ledge.

Harry looked up at him. "Evening, Simon."

He blinked, then scurried back to his nest. Simon wouldn't show himself at first but over time he'd learned to trust Harry. That didn't mean he was going to talk to her. You had to be careful about humans.

The rain pounded down.

Harry checked the barometer in the tack room. The needle swung over to stormy. She walked up and down the aisle. She'd filled each water bucket, put out hay, put new salt cubes in the bottoms of their feed buckets. But Harry liked to double-check everything. Then she unplugged the coffeemaker in the tack room, folding up the cord and slipping it in the top drawer of the tall, narrow chest of drawers. She kept bits in those drawers as well as hoof-picks, small flat things. She'd learned her lesson when the mice ruined her first coffeepot by chewing through the cord. They had electrocuted themselves but they could have started a fire in the barn. Since then she ran light cords through a narrow PVC tube that she attached to the wall. This was the only exposed cord.

Harry also kept fire extinguishers at both ends of the barn plus one in the hayloft. Right now she was in less danger of fire than of being blown off the surface of the earth.

She paused at the open doorway. "You know, I'd better close the barn doors." She walked to the other end and pulled the doors closed. Then she returned to the end of the barn facing the house. "Kids, you with me?"

Three little heads looked up at her. "*Yep.*"

She pulled the barn doors at that end closed, with a sliver of room for her to squeeze out. Then she ran like mad for the screened porch door. The two cats and the dog jetted ahead of her.

"*I hate to get wet,*" Pewter yowled.

"*Slowpoke.*" Mrs. Murphy pulled open the door.

"You guys are smart." Harry admired her brood.

The animals shook on the screened porch. Harry removed her coat and shook it, too. "I swear—when it dries I will rewax it."

She lifted a thick-piled towel off a peg, kneeling down to dry off the animals.

Apart from the rain drumming on the tin roof it was a quiet night. She made herself a fried-egg-and-pickle sandwich, fed the animals, then sat down to read *The Life of Cézanne* but couldn't keep her eyes open. Low-pressure systems made her sleepy.

Mrs. Murphy listened to the rain. *"As soon as it dries we're going over to the old barn."*

# 8

An open one-pound can of gunpowder sat on the butcher-block kitchen table. Paper cartridges, laid out in rows like tiny trapezoidal tents, covered one edge of the table. Ridley Kent bent his handsome head over the litter. Determined to out-authenticate everyone, he was rolling his own cartridges. It wasn't as easy to roll sixty grains of 2F black powder as he had anticipated.

Rolling with both hands, he then fumbled with the tie-off. Outside the rain beat down the kitchen window. It was a filthy night.

"Damn it to hell!" he exploded when the paper opened, spilling gunpowder over the table. Now he'd have to count out grains again.

It occurred to him to line up sixty grains behind every piece of paper. That served the purpose, too, of calming him down so he wouldn't botch his next tie-off job.

Archie Ingram came through the door, sending the carefully cut paper sailing around the room.

"I could kill you, Archie."

Archie hung his raincoat on the doorknob to drip. He surveyed the white papers, then knelt down, picking them up. "Get a grip."

"Do you know how long I've been sitting here with these cursed things?"

"Half the day?"

"Two hours. It took one hour just to cut the paper."

"Right weight. You've done your home-work. After all, you could have cheated and bought ready-mades."

"Not me. Plenty of others do."

"Here, let me show you how to do this." Archie sat down, took a flat knife, and scraped the sixty grains into the paper, rolling it so a tiny piece, the longest piece, stuck over the final edge. He tied off the end. "Where'd you get the dowel?"

"Made it." Ridley referred to the wooden dowel, about half an inch with a head cut like a bullet head or minnie ball. Rolling the paper on this wooden dowel made the task more congenial but Ridley's fingers, none too steady at any time of day, still couldn't tie off the cartridge.

"And I suppose you'll go as an officer?"

"Since I'm one of the few who can afford the gear, yes," came Ridley's testy reply.

"Don't even think about giving an order. You give enough in real life."

"What did officers do?" Ridley questioned, half laughing.

"Die by the truckload."

"I've no intention of doing that. Anyway, the Union men fire over our heads and we fire over theirs. Aren't the rules never to point a firearm directly at your opponent, and not to ram a real ball down your rifle?"

"Yes. But don't give orders. You're new to this and even though you're a—"

"Colonel."

"How perfect," Archie slyly said. "You don't give orders. You walk by the side of your men, on the front corner."

"I'll ride."

"Ridley, you can't ride a hair of a horse. Walk or be an artillery officer."

"All I have to do is walk along. I think I can manage that."

"Listen, bonehead, Fair Haristeen's worried about riding and he can *ride*. None of the horses are accustomed to gunfire. You'll walk."

"But I've got yellow trim on my uniform and a golden sash for my sword," Ridley protested.

"Light blue. Infantry. Don't make an ass of yourself. Take this back to Mrs. Woo and have her sew on blue facings. Her shop is that little building behind Rio Road Shopping Center. Just do what I tell you. I know what I'm talking about and I don't want to see you make a fool of yourself."

Ridley wanted to say, "You're making a fool out of your own self. Why worry about me?"

Archie droned on. "We're going to shut up H. Vane. The man thinks he can run the world. Pompous limey! He's upset because we're filling the rank with men who aren't true re-enactors. I said we had to do it. The public will be in attendance and we need this battle to warm up for the Wilderness reenactment."

"Still bodies in that Wilderness." Ridley shuddered.

"There's so many bodies in the ground in Virginia, you can't plow without hitting one, especially around Richmond."

"Maybe that's why our crops grow so well."

Archie narrowed his greenish eyes. "You're not taking this seriously."

"Seriously enough to spend good money."

"Hell, Ridley, if you aren't throwing your money away on women..."

"You've got room to talk?" A thick auburn eyebrow jutted upward.

Crimson washed over Archie's face. He blushed easily. "A gentleman doesn't discuss those matters."

"Who said we were gentlemen?" Ridley laughed.

"We were raised gentlemen even if we can't always be gentlemen." A guilty conscience haunted the county commissioner.

"Archie, one of these days you're going to get caught, and if your wife doesn't kill you somebody else will." A half-smile gave Ridley a rakish air. "You're a Casanova in disguise."

"What's the disguise?" Archie liked the description more than he cared to admit.

"Pug ugly." Ridley laughed.

Archie breathed in, thought a second, then laughed himself. He rolled another cartridge. "Charles Bronson wasn't classically handsome."

"Charles Bronson's ass would make your Sunday face," Ridley teased, for Arch was good-looking.

"Ridley, you really know how to hurt a guy." Archie's gloom lifted a bit.

Ridley could make anyone laugh. His infectious spirit, too often fueled by booze, made him a boon companion. Women adored him. The compliment was returned.

Ridley got up, returning with a three-banded Enfield rifle. "Four hundred and eighty dollars. Was I robbed?"

"No, that's the going price."

He polished the brass on the musket.

"If you're behind a line of infantry, you hold your rifle so that the first and second bands of your weapon are over the ear of one of your men." He pointed to the part of the barrel. "That way no one will get a singed ear."

They worked quietly, then Ridley, voice low, said, "Arch, if you don't mend some fences you're going to lose your commission seat. Mim's in a rage."

Archie flared his nostrils. "She is?"

"What did you expect? You acted like a jerk at the commission meeting." He smiled to soften his words. "You didn't seem like yourself."

Archie shrugged. "I'm sick of being the

55

bad guy in the county-commission meetings."

"You're only the bad guy to the developers. Plenty of people think you're doing a fine job. No one understands why you're so emotional about the reservoir, though. I'm on your side, Arch, that's why I'm telling you what others won't tell you. You need to mend fences," he repeated.

"H. Vane is behind this."

"He may be behind it but I'm telling you Mim's in front of it." Ridley put his cartridges in stacks of ten. "And why did you deny Vane-Tempest's request for a zoning variance last winter? Establishing a quarry on the north side of his land is a good idea. No one will see it and it will create jobs."

"He needed better plans."

"Come on, Arch, his plan included a responsible solution to reclaim the pits. It was environmentally progressive." Ridley lowered his voice. "Are you on the take?" Archie's jaw fell slack. Ridley pressed. "That's what some people are saying. I'll never tell but I'd sure like to know because you're acting like you're a nickel short of a dime these days. People think hard-line environmental groups are slipping you money. Crazy. But they're talking like that."

Archie got up, heading for the door. Ridley ran after him. "Arch! Come on, Arch. I'm trying to help."

"Help? You accuse me of betraying the public's confidence!"

"I don't want you to lose what you've worked so hard to get. Come on, sit down."

Archie rejoined him. "I am not on the take."

"Okay." Ridley paused. "Hey, did you hear that Tommy Van Allen is missing?"

"He's not missing. He's probably in Santa Fe or Buenos Aires, for God's sake. That is the most self-indulgent man I've ever met."

"Rick Shaw called me. They're treating it as a missing-persons case. His plane is missing, too."

"I'm glad we never pitched in and bought that twin engine. I don't know how I could have fallen for that."

"It was fun...our flying club, but I don't get the power charge from flying that you guys do."

"At least you could afford it." Archie absent-mindedly polished the brass bands on the rifle.

"Tommy and I already knew how to fly, of course, courtesy of the U.S. Air Force. And H. Vane learned in the RAF. Maybe being up in the air again reminded me too much of my service days or maybe I really am up in the air. It was too close for comfort."

"Blair sure learned quickly. I thought a pretty guy like that would chicken out. I'd rather he had dropped out instead of you."

"I can't warm to that guy." Ridley offered Archie a beer. He passed. "He's not cold-blooded but he's not hot-blooded either. Like last fall, when he had that affairette with Sarah Vane-Tempest—"

Arch interrupted, "He did not."

"The hell he didn't. They were discreet about it, that's all."

"I can't believe she'd go to bed with Blair Bainbridge," Archie said with disgust.

"Didn't last long. Maybe he got bored with her or she got bored with him. Then, too, I wouldn't want H. Vane breathing down my neck."

"What's H. Vane expect, marrying a woman half his age?"

Ridley walked to the fridge. "Drink a beer, buddy, you look peaked."

"Huh? Okay." Archie took the cold beer, peeling back the pop-top. "I know I've been irritable. Too much work, Ridley. Just too much. My wife complains that she never sees me and since she only complains when she does see me, I don't want to go home." He drank a long, slow swallow. "Being a county commissioner can sometimes, well, let me put it this way—if there's a buffoon, an asshole, or a certifiable psycho, not only will I meet them campaigning they'll show up in my office. And this reservoir stuff brings them all out of the woodwork."

"Forget about it for a night. I'll make popcorn. We can tell lies about the women we've conquered."

"Sounds good to me." Archie drained the beer can, got up, and fetched another.

# 9

The rain stopped Wednesday morning. That evening after supper, Mrs. Murphy gathered Pewter and Tucker on the screened-in porch.

*"Four miles is too far in the muck. Let's wait a few more days,"* Pewter whined.

*"For all we know, the plane will be gone by then."* Mrs. Murphy sniffed the wind, a light breeze out of the west. *"I'm heading out."*

*"I'll go with you."* Tucker's big ears moved forward.

*"I'm staying home."* Pewter sat down.

*"Chicken,"* the dog teased her.

*"I'm not chicken. I don't feel like getting dirty, especially since I've just given myself a bath."*

*"Well, let's go."* Murphy opened the screen door, Tucker immediately behind her. The door flapped twice. Pewter watched them bound over the meadow by the barn. She felt a pang of missing out but not enough to follow. She walked back inside, deciding to curl up on the 1930s chair with the mohair throw. She liked to snuggle in the mohair but wished Harry were wealthy enough to afford cashmere. Pewter craved luxury.

Reaching the first creek dividing Harry's property from Blair Bainbridge's, the cat and dog were stopped by high water.

*"Ugly."* Tucker paced the bank.

*"Let's go up to the beaver dam."*

*"If it's standing."*

59

*"Hasn't been that much water. Come on."*

*"I hate those beavers."* Tucker did, too.

*"We'll be across before they know it."*

A quarter of a mile upstream the log-and-sapling lodge dominated the creek along with the sturdy dam the beavers had constructed.

Carefully, Mrs. Murphy put one paw on the dam. She tested its sturdiness, then sped across, small splashes of water in her wake.

Tucker whined but followed. Her progress wasn't as graceful but she made it. They were halfway across Blair's easternmost meadow before the beavers emerged from their lodge to inspect their dam.

Lights at Blair's place caught their attention. A white Land Rover was parked in the driveway.

*"Wonder what Archie's doing at Blair's?"*

Mrs. Murphy kept moving. *"Trying to borrow the Porsche."*

They laughed until they reached the ridge, about seven hundred feet above sea level. They paused at the top, which bristled with rock outcroppings. Although only four miles across, the terrain was rugged in parts.

After catching her breath, Mrs. Murphy nudged Tucker. *"Ready?"*

*"Yeah."*

They swept down the ridge, skirting the thorn creepers and the underbrush, where they startled rabbits and one lurking fox. Mrs. Murphy hoped the bobcat was hunting somewhere else tonight.

The last creek had an upturned tree fallen over it. Mrs. Murphy danced across it. Tucker chose to swim the creek.

60

The abandoned buildings of the Urquhart farm shone silver in the moonlight, the slate roofs sparkling as though obsidian.

The doors to the barn were shut.

The two animals circled the barn, searching for burrows, preferably uninhabited. Mrs. Murphy looked up.

The Dutch door of a stall was partially open, flapping in the gentle breeze.

*"I'll try it."* Mrs. Murphy squatted down, paused a second, then sprang upward, reaching the slight opening before the top door banged back again. She dropped to the old hay on the stall floor.

Walking over to the big doors, she pulled with her paw just enough to create a crack. Tucker wedged her nose in and both cat and dog pushed. The big door creaked back on its overhead track just enough for the powerful dog to push herself inside.

Tucker stopped. Tommy Van Allen's plane was still parked in the middle of the vast center aisle. *"I'll be."*

*"You sniff around the plane,"* Mrs. Murphy ordered. *"I'll get in the cockpit."*

The tiger unleashed her claws, vaulting at a stall post. She shimmied up, reaching a massive cross beam, and walked along the top of it until the white plane was directly underneath, ten feet below.

*"That's a big drop, Murphy."*

*"I know."* Murphy stared down at the wing, backed up a bit, then jumped off the beam. She hit the wing with a thud, sliding a little in the

61

process, leaving red clay marks to disturb the pristine whiteness.

*"You okay?"* the dog called.

*"Yes, but it's slick."* The cat tiptoed to the edge of the cockpit. She easily opened the door, as the handle was large and turned down, and the door was slightly ajar. Then she hopped inside, leaving the door hanging wide open. The odor of old leather filled her nostrils.

*"See anything?"* Tucker called up.

*"Lots of dials and a throttle."*

*"Blood?"*

*"No, squeaky-clean."*

Tucker, somewhat disappointed, returned to the task of sniffing around the plane. The odor of gas killed other scents.

Mrs. Murphy poked at knobs, put one eye close to the throttle to see if anything had fallen into the slidpath. She hopped around, unwittingly leaving muddy paw prints as a signature.

Finding nothing, she readied to jump back down on the wing. Then, on the pilot's-side door, she noticed a leather pocket like a map pocket on an old car door. She reached over but couldn't quite get to it. She reached again and caught the very inside of the pocket, slowly moving the door toward her. She didn't want to shut the door since the inside handle might not open easily.

With one paw, claws out, she pulled open the pocket while with the other paw she held the door from closing. She fished in the pocket, pulling out the only thing in there, a folded-over map, used so many times, the creases were worn to nothingness. She grabbed it between her teeth, hopping onto the wing. She skidded on the flap side of the wing and launched herself to the soft center-aisle turf below.

The two friends walked to the door, squeezed through, and opened the map in the moonlight. Mrs. Murphy carefully sat on the edge of the map so it wouldn't blow away; she loved the smooth feel of paper under her bottom.

"*What is it?*" Tucker strained to make sense of the colors and lines.

"*Your face is too close. Step back.*"

"*Oh.*" She did as instructed. "*It's the U.S. Geological Survey map for the county. Pretty colors.*"

"*Can you carry this back home? I'll hide it in Simon's house.*"

"*Why not leave it here?*"

"*Because I think someone will come back for it.*"

"*Tommy?*"

"*No. Tommy's dead.*"

"*How do you know that?*"

"*I don't. Cat intuition. I saw two people leave this plane. One had to be Tommy, a very tall person, but it was raining, fog was swirling down, and I couldn't get a good look. Plus I was already at the creek and had climbed up in the oak tree. The other person was short.*"

"*Anyone would be short compared to Tommy Van Allen.*"

"*Tucker, put your paw on both corners. If I can*"

look down at this map maybe I can see better. ”
The cat drew herself to her full height, glancing
down. *“Hmm. Pieces are outlined. ”*

*“Maybe an old flight path. ”*

*“These are more like squares and a big outline
outside that. ”*

*“Was there a flight plan up there?”*

*“No. ”*

*“Why would two people take off, not tell
anyone, and land here? And one of them is now
missing. ”*

*“I haven’t a single idea. But they planned to
put the plane in the barn. I really think they did. ”*

*“You don’t think the fog and bad weather
drove them down?”*

*“There are better places to land than Tally’s
old airstrip. There are lots of airstrips in Albemarle
County. To come down here you have to shoot
between Little Yellow Mountain and that ridge
we crossed. It’s not threading a needle but you have
to be pretty darned good, especially with the
downdraft and winds that swirl around mountains.
Whoever landed here in the fog was a hell of a pilot. ”*

*“Tommy was good. ”*

*“But it wasn’t Tommy. I saw him hop out
and open the doors. At least, I think that was
Tommy. ”*

*“How will we ever get Harry over here?”*
Tucker wondered.

*“Only if she visits Tally or if she rides over. She
hardly ever comes this way, because the second
creek crossing changes every time there’s a storm.
Who knows how long it will take the humans to
find this plane?”*

*"If Rick Shaw is logical he'll eventually search each private airstrip."*

*"That's true. I wonder when he'll get to that?"* The cat noticed Mars, pulsating red in the sky. *"I do believe whoever flew that plane will be back for this map."*

*"There have to be thousands of survey maps of the county. This one isn't valuable."*

*"If it has fingerprints on it, it is."* Mrs. Murphy studied the map again, paying attention to the hand-drawn lines. *"That's it."*

*"What?"*

*"The big outline—it's the watershed. I remember from the map posted on the bulletin board at the commission meeting. I was up on the desk. I could see it clearly."*

# 10

"Do I have to do this?" Harry leaned against the truck door.

"Yes." Miranda offered no hope of escape. "I'll take Mrs. Murphy, Pewter, and Tucker home with me. No one will miss supper. If you take them home, you'll be late."

"All right." Harry climbed up into the old Superman-blue 1978 Ford half-ton.

*"Good luck, Mom,"* Mrs. Murphy saucily called out.

She needed more than luck. She needed the patience of Job. Lifeline, held in the basement of the Lutheran church, provided support and direction for many seekers.

65

Harry thought she had direction enough, and as for support, she was raised not to broadcast her troubles.

The adherents of this self-discovery process really surprised her, though. Ridley Kent; Cynthia Cooper—of all people; Dr. Hayden McIntire, Larry Johnson's much-younger partner; and several other people she'd known for years were among the crowd that filled the church basement.

Boom Boom stuck next to her.

The leader of the group, Bill Oster, worked at the University of Virginia library. It had taken years of training for him to become a group leader.

"Each of us carries negative programming, negative information. The purpose of Lifeline is to clear that away so you can more fully experience the people around you and so you can more fully experience yourself. It's strange, isn't it? We are raised to practice good manners, we're taught how to treat other people, but we're not taught how to treat ourselves. The first task, therefore, is to establish a proper relationship with yourself."

Boom Boom beamed with each word, casting significant glances at Harry. By the end of the evening Harry couldn't say she'd heard anything silly but she couldn't say the program was for her either. By nature a self-contained person, she found the idea of exploring emotions or even cleansing herself of negativity in front of others to be anathema. Still, she had to admit the ideas were worth considering.

"I hope you'll return," Bill Oster warmly said.

"You are a motivating leader." Harry, manners to the fore, complimented him.

"And that means you won't return." He believed in constant honesty, which at times had a touch of ruthlessness to it.

"No." Harry hated to be direct in this fashion. It violated everything she'd been taught all her life. "It's not for me but I think it's a good process."

He clasped both her hands in his. "If you change your mind you know where to find us. We start new groups every six weeks."

Boom Boom, disappointed in Harry, said, "Would you go if I weren't part of the group? I'm training to lead a group but I can put it off for another six weeks."

"It has nothing to do with you, Boom."

"Eventually you overcome your discomfort level."

"You have to want to and I don't. Whatever my deepest inner flaws are, I've learned to live with them."

"That's not the point." Boom Boom felt rejected because Lifeline was rejected.

Cynthia joined them. "Boom, Harry is the stubbornest woman I've ever met. Neither of us can talk her into anything. Besides, she kept her promise."

"That's true." Boom Boom offered her hand to Harry, who graciously shook it.

"Thanks, Boom."

"Will we ever be friends?"

"I—I don't know, but our relationship has

improved." Harry was truthful. Ever since Boom Boom's fling with Fair, the very sight of her set Harry's teeth on edge, but she was able to have a civil conversation with her now.

A somewhat mollified Boom Boom Craycroft bid them good-night.

"You're the last person I'd think to find in a group like this," Harry confided to Coop. "Well, Ridley Kent is a big surprise, too."

"I was getting jaded," Cynthia softly replied. "I see liars, drunks, irresponsible shits day in and day out. The drug dealers are a real treat, too. I was losing my faith in the goodness of people."

"Guess you would."

"I thought, this can't hurt me and I might even learn something."

"Good for you. No wonder I haven't seen you around much lately."

"Actually, this is my first night. I've been on overload because the spring flu is moving through the force. In the last month we've had two or three people out each week. I'm pulling a lot of overtime, anyway."

"When things even out, come on over. We'll have a Chinese-and-video night."

"Great. I'll bring the Chinese."

Harry walked Coop to her car, then hopped into her truck.

As she walked through Miranda's door she smelled freshly fried liver, not her favorite.

Miranda sat at the table, the animals eating from places set for them. Sheepishly Harry's hostess said, "They're the only creatures I can get to eat fried liver with me."

"I'll eat fried liver."

"You don't really like it."

"I wouldn't buy it in a restaurant but everything you make tastes good."

"I happen to have a piece left, smothered in my special sauce with caramelized onions. And I know you love brussels sprouts, a hint of molasses and lemon with them, but only a hint."

As Harry ate this unexpected feast, Miranda peppered her with questions to satisfy herself that Lifeline wasn't leading people away from the Scriptures.

"Didn't mention the Bible. It's about personal growth, not religion."

"The two are connected."

"Now, Miranda, I am not capable of a theological discussion. You take that up with Herbie. After all, the meetings are held in his church."

"People need the Good Book."

"Lifeline and Christianity are not mutually exclusive." A brussels sprout melted in her mouth.

"The essence of Christianity is forgiveness."

"I think in Lifeline they teach you to forgive yourself."

This thought hit Miranda like a Ping-Pong ball: It bounced off but left a small impression. She would have to ponder it. "Seems you got more out of Lifeline than you realize."

# 11

Pewter, wild-eyed and puffed up, charged through the animal flap at the back of the post office. *"Come quick!"*

Without arguing, Mrs. Murphy rushed outside, closely followed by Tucker. Pewter's short, furry tail disappeared around the corner to the front of Market Shiflett's grocery store. She leapt onto the fruit display outside the front door.

Mrs. Murphy followed, finding herself amid the banana display. *"Ever see a banana spider?"* she hissed.

She soon forgot about the furry spiders hiding among the yellow bunches because inside, Sir H. Vane-Tempest and Archie Ingram were shouting at the top of their lungs. A small crowd was gathered, including Market Shiflett, who stood beside the screened front door of his store. It was still too cool for air-conditioning.

"You've forgotten—" Vane-Tempest sputtered.

"I've forgotten nothing."

"You've forgotten who your friends are." Vane-Tempest stepped closer to Archie, who suddenly hit him on the left cheek. He lashed out so quickly that Archie surprised both himself and the Englishman.

Reeling backward, Vane-Tempest lifted a soft hand to cover the red mark.

Still in a fury, Archie taunted the old man.

"You're the one who forgets, Vane-Tempest, and it will catch up with you!"

Before the Englishman could lunge forward, a rattled Archie had backed out of the store, parting the gaggle of people.

Harry stuck her head out of the post office, since the shouts had penetrated even there. She stuck it back in. The altercation was none of her business. Besides, people were soon pouring into the post office, all telling their versions of the tale.

Mrs. Murphy moved over to sit on the apples. *"Friendship is like a love affair. When it sours, pfff-t!"*

*"Ours won't."* Pewter rubbed her cheek against the slender tiger.

*"We're cats. We're smarter than people,"* Murphy purred. She liked attention and she especially liked being groomed.

*"Don't you wonder what's happened?"*

*"It's the rock quarry,"* Pewter said.

*"That was ages ago,"* Mrs. Murphy remembered.

*"Some people are on slow fuses,"* Pewter remarked.

Tucker stepped away from the fruit stand to better see the cats. *"Bet there's a woman involved."*

*"Maybe,"* Mrs. Murphy noted.

*"Who would go out with H. Vane-Tempest apart from his very expensive wife? A puff adder, that man!"* Pewter likened people to animals.

*"Who said it was H. Vane?"* Tucker winked.

*"Gross,"* came the tiger's tart comment.

They walked over to the post office, going in by the front door as yet another resident opened it. Sir H. Vane-Tempest was loudly explaining his side of the story.

"He's become irrational. He thinks everyone is against him. Even Aileen has noticed it. I spoke to her last week about Archie's personality disintegration."

Aileen was Archie's wife.

"It's difficult being on the county commission when opinion in the county is so divided," Miranda offered.

"He asked for the job," Big Mim tartly observed.

"Won't have it for long," Little Mim said, which made her mother smile slightly.

"Ever since the storms this winter when Sugar Hollow washed—the terrible flooding—he's not been the same," Vane-Tempest said.

"It can't be that," Miranda shrewdly noticed. "You don't think so either."

Vane-Tempest eyed her. "Well—well, whatever has come over him has been intensifying since that time. I was the man's friend...when no one else wanted to hear about preserving the environment."

Tucker interrupted. *"He's sure tooting his own horn."*

"Quiet," Harry reprimanded her.

Vane-Tempest continued. "He's argued with everyone. Aileen says he hardly speaks to her when he comes home at night. He goes into his den and pores over papers and maps. And yes, I am angry that he lobbied the commission to deny permission for me to establish a rock quarry. But I'll get over it."

"Will *he*?" Mim sharply said.

"I didn't act that badly," Vane-Tempest defended himself. "He did."

"He certainly did today." Little Mim played with the soft leather weave of her Bottega Veneta bag.

"You should have offered him a share of the business when his term expired." Mim surprised everyone with her comment, then added, "Really, people, how do you think anything gets done here?"

"That's a bribe," Miranda said firmly.

"No. You don't ask him to vote your way, you simply offer him a job when his term expires. It's done in Washington on an hourly basis and the pity of it is, it isn't done well. We'd have better government if it were."

"Cynic." Vane-Tempest smiled.

"Realist." Mim tapped her foot on the polished wooden floors, polished with use. "People in government can't make money while they're in government. So you must use your position to develop contacts for when your term expires."

No one said a word for a minute. Mim had a way of boring straight to the heart of a problem. The truth was that Archie, a small printer by trade, didn't make much money. The county-commission post carried no stipend and the time it sucked up diverted his attention from a business that could have been more lucrative.

"He'd never give up his business." Vane-Tempest betrayed his own thoughts, which was exactly what Mim had hoped to achieve by being forthright. Being an Englishman, he couldn't have known she was baiting him. The Virginians knew exactly what she was doing, which was why they fell silent after she spoke.

"Aileen could run it." Little Mim worked well with her mother despite her irritation with her overbearing parent. "She runs it anyway."

"Archie lacks the common touch and a good printer has to be able to deal with people who have little idea of how long it takes to print anything or what it costs. You're right. He ought to turn the whole business over to Aileen. As for why he wanted to be a county commissioner, well, he has his pet concerns, but truthfully, he wanted the power." Vane-Tempest cracked a knuckle, revealing his rare nervousness.

*"Human meetings waste time,"* Pewter blandly noted. *"Everyone has to express an opinion. Then everyone else has to rebut it or add to it. I say shut up and get the job done."*

*"They can't,"* Mrs. Murphy shrewdly observed. *"Most cats are roughly equal, if you think about it. I mean, we can all jump about the same height, run about the same speed. They're very different from one another. Their talents are wildly different. The only way they can survive is to talk to one another and reach a consensus. All herd animals are like that. We're not herd animals."*

*"Neither am I,"* Tucker protested.

*"You're a pack animal. Same difference."*

*"I am an individual."*

*"I never said you weren't an individual, Tucker. But dogs tend to run in packs and kill in packs."*

*"I herd cows, sheep, anything. I'm not a hunting dog."*

*"You're an argumentative one."* Mrs. Murphy flicked her tail.

*"Tucker is the exception that proves the rule."* Pewter didn't feel like a fight. Hearing Archie and H. Vane was enough for her.

Vane-Tempest threw back his shoulders. "I can't talk to Arch, obviously, but I do think some of you can. Maybe you can cast oil upon the waters."

" 'Yet man is born into trouble, as the sparks fly upward.' " Miranda quoted Job, Chapter 5, Verse 7.

"What's that supposed to mean?" the Englishman mildly inquired.

"I don't know. Just popped into my head." Mrs. H. laughed at herself.

Just then the Reverend Herbert Jones pushed open the door. Everyone stopped to stare at him.

"What do you think?" Herb asked.

He stood there, shoulders back, head erect, wearing his Confederate sergeant major's uniform with the red facings of the artillery.

Then everyone started talking at once.

*"Odd,"* Tucker said.

*"Why?"* the cats asked.

*"Like the dead coming to life, isn't it?"*

# 12

The Reverend Herbert Jones, accustomed as he was to the confessions of his flock, still managed to be surprised by them.

He ushered Archie Ingram into his cozy library, where Herb's two magnificent cats, Lucy Fur and Elocution, snoozed on a bearskin rug before the fire. Herb had shot the bear as a boy. Lost in the woods, he had riled the normally passive animal although he didn't know how he had done it. All he knew was that a black bear was charging him. Luckily he had his .22 rifle, but it was too light to bring down the animal. He stood his ground, waited, and then fired, hitting the beast in the eye and killing it instantly. And then he started to shake all over. His daddy, thanks to the gunfire, found him.

Archie Ingram took a seat near the fire.

"I'll be brief, Herb. I'm having an affair. My wife suspects. Sooner or later this will blow up in my face. Even though we've drifted apart, I know I have a good wife but...I can't seem to help myself. And the strange thing is, I don't feel guilty."

Herb poured a small glass of port, Dow's 1972, for Archie and for himself. Port and a fine cigar were the perfect finish to an evening. He'd sworn off cigars, missing them terribly, but he still enjoyed his evening glass of port. Stashed away in his small wine cellar he had a bottle of Cockburn's from 1937. He was saving it for a special occasion but he could never figure out what would be that special.

He held the glass in his hand, admiring the ruby color, which came to life as the firelight flickered through it. "Archie, we've known each other a long time."

"Yes, we have."

"How old are you now?"

"Forty-three."

Herb sipped, leaned back in his chair, and thought awhile. "Ever think how wine is made?"

"Peasants step on grapes."

Herb laughed. "I guess we could say the grapes are bruised and tortured, but out of this suffering, combined with time, comes a liquid of refinement and comfort. I enjoy port, you know. I've got bottles ranging from the recent—say ten years ago—all the way back to 1937. Port improves with age. Men do, too. You're being bruised now."

"Except I'm the one committing the sin."

"You hurt yourself more by sinning than you hurt anyone else. Some people never realize that. You're at a vulnerable age."

"Yeah, youth is checking out..."

"And leaving no forwarding address." Herb laughed. "It's a a hard time for both men and women. Takes us differently, though. So many marriages break up."

"I don't want to lose my wife."

"Then you'd better lose the other woman."

Sweat poured down Archie's face. "I know that. Each time I see her I tell myself, this is it...break it off and then..."

"Younger?"

"A little," Archie admitted.

A rueful smile covered the minister's expansive face. "You've heard that feminist joke, 'When God made man she was practicing.' I don't think of myself as a feminist but I agree with that one." He paused. "Arch, there's not a man alive who hasn't been torn between two women at one time in his life. And I expect there isn't a woman alive who hasn't been torn between two men at one time in her life. Pray for guidance. Consider what has drawn you to the other woman and what has drawn her to you. There may be answers there that surprise you."

"Should I tell Aileen?"

"I can't answer that." He shook his head. "I don't know."

Archie drained his glass. "Crazy time."

"You've ruffled a lot of feathers lately. I always say it's easy to be an angel if no one ruffles your feathers."

Archie carefully placed his glass on the coaster. "Everybody wants something, don't they?"

"Most times, yes. Quid pro quo makes sense in the business world but it has no meaning in the spiritual world. God's love is unconditional."

Archie smiled weakly. He wanted to believe that but he didn't. No matter, talking to Herb had helped him. He now felt he could sort this out somehow, over time.

As Herb opened the door for Archie and

waved good-bye he noticed how cool it was. May could be tricky.

# 13

Mrs. Murphy loped along fields swallowed in darkness, skirting the creek dividing Harry's land from Blair Bainbridge's picturesque farm. She wanted to visit the 911 Turbo. The humans hadn't given her enough time to thoroughly inspect the car.

A movement out of the corner of her eye caught her attention, about fifty yards away, a swaying in the bushes along the upper creek.

She stopped. In a split second she whirled around, blasting for home as fast as she could run. She heard the quick swish of the spring grasses behind her. Longer strides than hers were gaining on her.

With a surge of her own turbo, Mrs. Murphy ran flat out, her belly skimming the earth, her tail horizontal, her whiskers and ears swept back.

She charged into the paddock on the west side of the barn where Poptart, Gin Fizz, and Tomahawk were munching.

*"Help me!"* She streaked past Harry's horses.

The three horses spread out as the forty-pound bobcat tore over the earth. They pawed, snorted, and ran around, forcing the big cat to weave. It gave Mrs. Murphy just enough time to dodge into the barn and climb into the hayloft. She ran to the open hayloft door.

*"Tucker, help me!"*

The horses continued to chase the bobcat, who easily evaded them.

The powerful animal slid out of the paddock to sit outside in front of the hayloft, where she eyed her quarry above.

The owl, on a trip back to her nest with a mouse, swooped low over the bobcat but the animal wasn't afraid.

Simon, in the feed room, gobbling up sweet feed that had fallen on the floor, froze stiff. He was all ready to flop over and play dead if necessary.

Gin Fizz, old and wise, ordered the others, *"Make a lot of noise. We've got to wake Harry."*

Pewter, asleep on the kitchen table, woke up at the din of neighing and dashed to the window. Seeing in an instant what was going on, she hurried into the bedroom, leaping on Harry with all her weight.

"Uh." Harry opened one eye.

*"Tucker, wake up!"* Pewter shouted at the dog, sleeping on her side. *"Bobcat!"*

"Huh?"

*"The bobcat's sitting under the hayloft and she'll get Murphy."*

"Where's Murphy?"

*"In the hayloft, stupid!"*

Tucker shook her head. Why did cats hunt at night? Nonetheless the corgi scrambled to her feet and barreled through the animal door in the kitchen door.

*"Wake up! Wake up!"* Pewter jumped up and down on Harry.

The neighing and snorting finally filtered into Harry's ears.

"Dammit!" She shot out of bed, switched on a light, and grabbed her shotgun from the closet. She slipped four shells into the pocket of her robe, which was half on, half off, as she ran in her bare feet for the kitchen door.

Tucker squared off against the bobcat, who was spoiling for a fight.

*"Don't risk it."* Mrs. Murphy leaned so far over the hayloft opening, she nearly fell out.

The bobcat coolly waited until Harry switched on the outside lights. Then she turned, calling over her shoulder, *"Beware, little cousin, the hunter can become the hunted."*

With one mighty bound the bobcat cleared the paddock fence and ran out the northern side, Gin Fizz giving chase.

By the time Harry reached the fence line she saw the bobcat cruising along, maybe one hundred yards out. She put down the shotgun to climb over the fence.

"You guys all right?" In the moonlight she carefully checked the horses for scratches or injuries. Dawn was a half hour away. Then she hurried back to the barn, looking up at her friend. "Are you all right? Come down here so I can see you."

She walked into the barn and clicked on the lights. As Mrs. Murphy was backing down the ladder, Harry ducked her head in the feed room to see if any mice were in evidence.

"Simon."

Simon was playing possum. He'd been so traumatized by the bobcat that when he heard Harry's voice he couldn't move forward or backward, so he dropped over.

One eye opened when Harry cut off the light.

Mrs. Murphy landed on the tack trunk. "Let me look at you. If I have to make a screaming run over to Chris Middleton's at this hour I won't stay friends with our vet for long. You'd better be okay."

*"I am."* Mrs. Murphy's fur was still puffed.

Tucker, who'd run around the other side of the barn in case the bobcat pulled a fast one, trotted down the center aisle from the back.

"Brave dog." Harry patted the broad head.

*"I'm a corgi."* Tucker shrugged.

*"Thanks, Tucker. I owe you one."* Mrs. Murphy jumped down to rub along Tucker's side.

The three walked back to the house, Harry stepping lively since her bare feet were cold.

Pewter greeted them at the door. *"I told you not to hunt far from the barn!"*

*"You stayed inside, chicken."*

*"I'd have come out and fought if I had to,"* she growled.

And in truth, Pewter could be a lion when needs be.

Mrs. Murphy laughed now that the danger was over. *"Close call."*

Harry, wide awake, made a pot of coffee as she fed the animals. She'd grown up in the country. She understood the ways of predators. She knew that life could change in the blink of an eye. One false step and you were a bigger animal's breakfast—or a smaller animal's, if it was smart and strong enough.

# 14

Oak Ridge rises out of the land south of Lovingston, Virginia. Built in 1802 by a Revolutionary War veteran, one of the Rives family of Albemarle, the estate was buffeted from the scalding rises and freezing plunges of unregulated capitalism. The originator of Oak Ridge rode the economy like the tides. His progeny fared less well and over the nineteenth century the place changed hands, sometimes for the better, sometimes for the worse.

Finally Thomas Fortune Ryan, a local boy born in 1851, made good in the New York stock market and bought the place he remembered from his impoverished childhood. By that time, 1904, Ryan was the third-richest man in America—true riches, for there was no Internal Revenue Service.

He set about creating a great country estate, not on the scale of Blenheim but on a Virginia scale, which meant he kept a sense of proportion. The mansion was twenty-three thousand square feet, and eighty other smaller houses, barns, and water towers completed the plan. A hothouse, built as a smaller version of London's famed Crystal Palace, sat below the mansion.

The place bore the mark of a single, overriding, rapacious mind. An alley of oak trees guided the visitor to the main house from the road—the northern, back side of the house. The grander entrance was on the other, southern side facing the railroad tracks because that was how Mr. Ryan rode to his country estate from New York, in his sumptuous private car. The buggies, phaetons, gigs, and the occasional coach-and-four drove up the back way.

Given that the glory days of rail travel were over, the approach now was from Route 653, the paved highway to Shipman, the back road.

The re-enactors camped on the miles of front lawn and former golf course, their Sibley tents resembling teepees, common tents and larger officers' tents dotting the verdant expanse like overlarge tissues.

The re-enactors would have to tramp a half mile to the oak tree, reckoned to be 380 years old. The Yankees would rise up out of the eastern woods surrounding Trinity Episcopal Church, while the Southerners would be marching due north from the edge of Mrs. Wright's hayfields.

The view was better for the public from the oak tree and it reduced the possibility of a raid on the main house.

Having that many people on her front lawn caused the petite and pretty Rhonda Holland some inconvenience, but she bore it with good grace. John, her dynamic husband, delighted in strolling along the neatly laid out avenues of tents to chat with the fellows cleaning rifles, fiddling, and singing. A convivial man wearing a floppy straw hat, he had plans for Oak Ridge as magnificent as Thomas Fortune Ryan's.

John worked more slowly than Ryan, thanks to the proliferation of government agencies choking him with regulations, but he never gave up.

The entire Holland family was on hand to view the reenactment, as were thirty thousand other people, a far larger crowd than anyone had anticipated.

Add in the five thousand re-enactors, including camp followers, and there were a mess of people.

Harry sat on a camp stool. Tucker sat next to her, and Mrs. Murphy and Pewter lounged on a camp table spread with maps. The cats weren't supposed to come but they'd hidden under the seat of the truck, then raced to freedom when the door was opened.

Pewter nibbled on a square of hardtack. *"How could they eat this stuff?"*

*"With difficulty,"* the tiger said, watching Fair Haristeen struggle with his gold sword sash.

"Here." Harry wound it around his middle, the two tasseled ends of the sash tempting Mrs. Murphy, but not enough to leave her perch, just enough for her to swat at the tassels when he walked by.

Fair, a twinkle in his eye, said, "I love it when you fuss over me."

"Stand still." Harry commanded but she smiled when she said it.

"You know I never looked so good as when you bought my clothes."

"Fair, stand still. You're a vet. Coveralls aren't that glamorous. You look the same now as when we were married."

"Meant my Sunday clothes." He playfully pinched her buttock. "I liked it best when you undressed me."

"Pulease." Harry drew out the word. Pretending to ignore the banter, she secretly enjoyed it. "There. A proper Confederate officer."

"I'd rather be improper."

"What's with you? Maybe the prospect of battle is an aphrodisiac." She laughed.

"No, *you're* the aphrodisiac. I'm only doing this for Ned Tucker." He kissed her on the cheek.

A shout outside the tent sent them onto the grass avenue.

Archie Ingram and Sir H. Vane-Tempest fought in Sir H.'s tent, next to Fair and Ned's tent. Archie, lean and quicker than the Englishman, cracked him hard on the jaw.

The larger man, about forty pounds overweight, sagged for an instant against the corner tent pole. The tent wobbled dangerously. Then Vane-Tempest collected himself, lunging for Archie, grabbing him by the waist and bulling him out onto the grassy avenue.

Sarah, in a pale melon gown complete with hoop skirt, rushed out. Smart enough not to get between them, she hissed, "Stop it!"

The men paid no mind.

Vane-Tempest clumsily ducked Archie's blows but enough landed that red marks swelled on his cheeks. Archie danced around him. One solid blow from Vane-Tempest would have picked the smaller man off his feet, then sent him crashing to the ground.

Fair watched for a moment, then grabbed Archie's upraised hand. Archie whirled around and caught Fair on the side of his head.

Ned Tucker, running from the other end of the avenue, seized the Englishman before he could land a telling blow on Archie. Although thirty years older than Archie, Sir H. wanted to fight.

Vane-Tempest shook Ned off more easily than Ned thought he could. The two antagonists pounded each other again.

Herb Jones, dressed in his artillery sergeant major's outfit, hurried out from the headquarters tent. Larry Johnson, Hayden McIntire, and a host of other Crozet men followed.

Two men from Rappahannock County dashed over, canteens banging against their hips.

The four of them finally separated Vane-Tempest, who was sputtering "bloody this" and "bloody that," from Archie, who grimly said nothing.

Sarah rushed to her husband's aid. He needed ice held to his cheek. He grandly pushed her aside with one arm and advanced on Archie once more. Fair and Bobby Forester, from Rappahannock, lunged for him again.

"Leave me alone!" the florid peer of the realm commanded.

Herb Jones strode into the middle of everyone. "Gentlemen, save it for the Yankees."

This made everyone laugh except for Archie and his opponent. Even Vane-Tempest evinced a small smile.

Tucker, Mrs. Murphy, and Pewter sat quietly at their campsite, watching the exchange.

"*They can't abide each other.*" Tucker scratched her ear.

"*H. Vane gave beaucoup money to Archie's campaign last year.*" Mrs. Murphy swatted at a fly. "*You'd have thought they were two peas in a pod then.*"

"*Guess Archie didn't keep his promises.*"

"I'll settle with you later." Archie's jaw jutted out, his facial muscles tense.

"You'll settle with me? That's a laugh." Vane-Tempest smoothed his hair with his right hand. "And you had no business invading my tent in the first place!"

"Archie, come with me." Herb put his hand under Archie's elbow. "Fair, you keep an eye on H. Vane until we draw up in formation."

"Yes, sir." Fair saluted.

The gray line parted as Herb propelled the county commissioner toward the HQ tent.

Men listened to Herb. He'd attended VMI and then fought in Korea, where he experienced a revelation about his calling on earth. When he returned home he entered the seminary, which provoked no end of amusement among

88

his contemporaries. They'd known him as a hell-raiser at military school.

"Now, Arch, what is the matter with you? You're becoming..."

"A liability," Archie snapped, his knuckles bleeding.

"I was going to say 'an embarrassment.' " Herb didn't mince words. "You're an elected official."

"We're in Nelson County now, not Albemarle." Archie hung his head, half mumbling.

"You know this will get into the papers."

Archie glumly said nothing as Herb continued to guide him toward the large HQ tent.

As the crowd dispersed, Sarah allowed herself a flash of temperament. "H., you're a perfect ass."

"And you're a perfect bitch," he evenly replied.

"That does it. You can play soldier by yourself. I always thought this was silly to begin with, grown men dressing up and waving swords about. At least your father was a real soldier."

"That's below the belt, Sarah." His mouth clamped shut like a vice. "But then that's your favorite geography, isn't it? You forget I served in the RAF. I just didn't have the good fortune of being born in time for the big war."

Fair, face reddening because he didn't want to hear this exchange, stepped away from the sparring couple. "You won't run after Arch?"

"No." Vane-Tempest turned on his booted heel and disappeared into his tent.

Mrs. Murphy and Pewter ran over and peeped under the tent flaps. Sarah, cooling down, walked inside after her husband.

"Why do you let him get under your skin?"

Vane-Tempest sagged heavily on a big trunk. "A man who's been bought ought to stay bought."

"Oh, Henry,"—she called him by his Christian name—"you didn't contribute that much."

"Five thousand dollars at the county-commissioner level seems rather large to me. We aren't talking about the Senate, my dear, and I didn't leave the money in a brown paper bag either. I'm not that crude." He motioned for her to stop speaking as Ned Tucker entered the tent.

"Think you can go out today?"

"Why not?" Vane-Tempest answered the soft-spoken lawyer, Susan's husband.

"You took a couple of good pops to the face."

"He can't hit that hard."

Not exactly true, since Archie had rocked him with the blow to the jaw, but his punches were light otherwise.

"Can you put this aside? I mean, you two are marching in the same company."

Vane-Tempest shrugged, the shrug of superiority. "He won't bother me. I apologize for losing my temper in the first place. I don't like his attentions to my wife."

"Henry!"

He laughed. "He does look at you all the time."

"That's not why you were fighting. Leave me out of this."

"It's none of my business." Ned took a step back to leave. "But please keep a lid on it out there."

The two kitties ducked their heads, scampering back to Fair and Harry.

*"What'd you make of that?"* Mrs. Murphy felt something was unexpressed, something beyond anger.

*"Unevolved."* Pewter scooted in under the tent bottom, nearly emerging between Harry's feet. *"Humans are unevolved."*

"Where have you two been?" Harry pointed a finger.

*"Eavesdropping."*

"I'm taking you to the truck. I'll leave the windows cracked, but you all aren't going to get into that crowd. I can't believe you snuck under the seat of the truck to begin with, little devils."

That fast and without consulting each other, the cats tore out of there.

"Mrs. Murphy! Pewter!" Harry ran after them and Fair started after her but the bugle called him to formation.

*"Should we stay just in view or dump her?"* Pewter asked.

*"Let's just stay in sight and run her to exhaustion."* Mrs. Murphy laughed, turning to see Harry, mad as a wet hen, tearing after them, Tucker right at the human's heels.

# 15

Sarah Vane-Tempest rustled with each step, her long pastel skirts swaying. H. Vane and company had departed to join their regiment, already marching toward the old racetrack on the west side of the oak tree. From there they would wheel out of sight, marching southeast until the land flattened out. They'd be at the edge of beautiful hayfields.

Her parasol provided some relief from the warming sun. She twirled it in irritation.

Mrs. Murphy and Pewter raced by her. She barely noticed them but she did notice Blair Bainbridge, long legs eating up territory as he hurried to fall in with his regiment. He waved as he dashed by.

Harry, panting, slowed down by Sarah. The cats slowed, too, walking the rest of the way but keeping well ahead of Harry.

Miranda Hogendobber joined Harry and Sarah. She'd been in the hunter barn, which was on the way to the oak tree from the main house. She'd brought Fair some hotcakes, a recipe from her grandmother, who remembered the time of Virginia's sorrows. Since Mrs. Hogendobber's great-grandfather had ridden with the cavalry, she gravitated toward the barn.

"The more I think about those two the madder I get." Sarah's parasol whirled savagely.

"Making me dizzy," Mrs. Hogendobber remarked. She meant the twirling parasol.

"What I should have done is crown them with

it." Sarah stopped twirling. "They're like two little boys fighting over a fire truck."

"Exactly which fire truck?" Harry got to the point.

"The zoning variance." Sarah closed her parasol. "H. Vane is still livid over Archie squashing his request for a variance to open the quarry. His revenge is to push for the reservoir."

"But Archie appears to support the reservoir, although, God knows, he has obstructed everything. I told Fair after that commission meeting that Archie is saying one thing but doing another. Who knows what he's really going to do about the reservoir when the chips are down?" Harry hated politics, especially in her own backyard.

" 'Appears' is the operative word. Behind the scenes he's doing everything he can to retard progress. My husband knows all of this, of course." She sighed. "Henry adores political intrigue."

"So what side *is* Sir H. on?" Harry bluntly asked.

"His own." Sarah laughed, spirits a bit restored.

"Well—" Miranda fanned herself with a program advertising whalebone corsets and hoop skirts as well as bayonets and haversacks. "I hope they mend their fences."

"Ego! Neither one will make a peace offering." Sarah tapped her foot with the closed parasol. "How did women wear these things?" She pushed her crinolines forward, and the entire bell of the skirt flowed with them. "The heat doesn't help." A warm front had moved in and the weather was sticky.

*"If you were dropped out of a plane you'd be safe."* Tucker snickered.

Sarah glanced down at the dog, a frown on her pretty mouth; it was as if she knew what the corgi was saying to her. "Damn! I forgot H.'s extra canteen. He'll be furious."

"What's in the canteen?"

"Glenlivet." She raised an eyebrow. "He's cheating. I really do think this authenticity thing has gone too far. Do you know they even have rules about how to die?"

"You're kidding!" Harry laughed.

"If you're shot you have to fall down with your head to the side so you can breathe, with your firearm in your hand a bit away from your body. There are other rules but that's the only one I remember. And they decide who will be injured, who will die, and who will survive. That's if it's a general reenactment. If it's a *true* battle reenactment, like Sharpsburg, the men take on the identities of real soldiers. They have to fall in the exact spots where the real soldiers were hit."

"Strange," Miranda muttered.

"Rules for dying?" Harry stooped over to pick up Pewter, who had slowed.

"The obsession with violence. The obsession with *that* war, especially. No good ever came of it." Miranda shook her head.

Harry disagreed with her. "The slaves were freed."

"Yes," Miranda said, "free to starve. The Yankees were hypocrites. Still are."

Sarah, raised in Connecticut, smiled tightly. "I'm going back to get my lord and master's canteen. I'll see you at the battle." She turned and ran as fast as pantaloons, a hoop skirt, and yards of material would allow. Her bonnet, tied under her neck, flapped behind her.

Harry and Miranda reached the beautiful oak tree. Fair had given them tickets for seats on a small reviewing stand. They took their places.

*"Follow me!"* Mrs. Murphy joyfully commanded as she scampered to the base of the tree, sank her razor-sharp claws in the yielding bark, and climbed high.

Pewter, a good climber, was on her tail.

Tucker, irritated, watched the two giggling felines. She couldn't see anything because everywhere she turned there were humans.

Harry shaded her eyes, glancing up at the cats, who sat on a high, wide branch, their tails swishing to and fro in excitement. She nudged Miranda.

"Best seats in the house." Miranda laughed.

Tucker returned to Harry, sitting in front of her. *"I can't see a thing,"* the peeved dog complained.

"Hush, honey." Harry patted Tucker's silky head.

A low drumroll hushed everyone. A line of Union cannons ran parallel to Route 653. The Confederate cannons, fourteen-pounders, sat at a right angle to the Union artillery.

The backs of the artillerymen were visible to the crowd. As both sides began firing, a wealth of smoke belched from the mouths of the guns.

In the far distance Harry heard another drum. Goose bumps covered her arms.

Miranda, too, became silent.

*"Do you think if Jefferson Davis had challenged Abe Lincoln to hand-to-hand combat they could have avoided this?"* Pewter wondered.

*"No."*

Pewter didn't pursue her line of questioning; she was too focused on all she could see from her high perch. The tight squares of opposing regiments fast-stepped into place. On the left the officer in charge of his square raised his saber.

Ahead of the squares both sides sent out skirmishers. For this particular reenactment, the organizers had choreographed hand-to-hand combat among the skirmishers. As they grappled, fought, and threw one another on the ground the cannons fired now with more precision, the harmless shot soaring high over everyone's heads.

Harry coughed. "Stuff scratches."

Miranda, hanky to her nose, nodded.

As the drumbeats grew louder the crowd strained forward.

They could hear officers calling out orders. The Union regiment at the forefront stopped as the Confederates, still at a distance, moved forward.

"Load," called out the captain.

The soldiers placed their muskets, barrels out, between their feet. As the officer called out further loading orders, they poured gunpowder down the barrels and rammed the charges home.

"*Ha!*" Pewter was watching Fair, struggling with his frightened horse.

Mrs. Murphy, knowing Fair was a fine rider, didn't find it quite as funny as Pewter did. *"I don't think anyone knows how to get the horses used to this noise and the sulphur smell."*

Fair's big bay shied, dancing sideways. At the next volley of cannon fire the horse reared up, came down on his two forelegs, and bucked straight out with his hind legs, a jolting, snapping, hell of a buck. Fair sat the first one but the succeeding ones, spiced up with a side-to-side twisting action, sent him into the sweet grass with a thud. The horse, no fool, spun around, flying back toward the hunter stables. Fair, disgusted, picked himself up, then looked around, realized he was in a battle, and ran over to join his unit.

Sir H. Vane-Tempest, on the front corner of the first regiment, grimly stared into the billowing smoke. Archie Ingram was farther back in the square, as was Blair Bainbridge. Ridley Kent marched in the second unit behind them.

Mrs. Murphy strained to see through the smoke, which would clear, then close up again with new fire. Reverend Herb Jones, red sash wrapped around his tunic, sat on an upturned wagon to the rear of the battle. The heat had exhausted him.

Dr. Larry Johnson and Ned Tucker were in the third line of the regiment, faces flushed. Everywhere the two cats looked they saw familiar faces in unfamiliar clothes. The smoke thinning over the men's faces like a soft silver veil made them look even more eerie.

The first volley of rifle fire from the Yankees rolled over the turf with a crackle: Small slits of flame leapt from muzzles. Mrs. Murphy hoped they would be smart enough to keep their hands away from the barrel nozzles when ramming home the next charge. A man could lose fingers or part of a hand that way if a spark smoldered deep down in the gun.

By now all but one of the mounted officers had bought some real estate. The only animal moving forward was a huge Belgian draft horse, the horse calm as if on parade.

A few "corpses" dotted the field. Then a shroud of smoke enveloped the field as all guns fired at once. *Pop, pop, pop,* rifles and handguns reported between the rhythmic firing of the elegant cannons.

*"Poor suckers died blind."* Mrs. Murphy's whiskers twitched.

*"Ugh."* Pewter shuddered. *"Only a human would die for an idea."*

*"That's the truth."* The tiger blinked when a bit of smoke floated over the branches. *"You know, they can't accept reality. Reality is that everything is happening at once to everybody. There's no special sense to it. So humans invent*

*systems. If one human's system collides with another human's system, they fight."*

*"The only reality is nature."* Pewter, not a philosophical cat like Mrs. Murphy, was nonetheless a smart one.

*"True enough."* The cat squinted as the smoke cleared. She saw Sir H. Vane-Tempest break from the ranks, never to be outdone, and sprint toward the enemy.

A loud *crack,* another volley of cannon fire and he went down, a hero to the cause.

The battle grew more intense. Tucker, since she couldn't see, lay on the reviewing stand between Harry's feet. She hated the noise, and the sulphur fumes offended her delicate nose.

After fifteen more minutes of the hardest-fought section of the reenactment, the Yankees broke and ran. That, too, was choreographed. It would never do for the Union troops to wallop Southerners on Southern turf unless it was a precise reenactment of an actual battle won by the Yankees. Not only was this a sop to Southern vanity, but it was also pretty accurate. The North hadn't begun to routinely chalk up victories until the latter part of the war, when victories in the west ensured victories in the east, and tens of thousands died.

The drummers kept drumming as the last smoke wafted over the flat expanse of hayfield, formerly an old airfield. The routed Yankees ran toward Route 653, collected themselves, and turned left, heading for the racetrack.

The wounded, in the name of authenticity,

were being carried off on stretchers. A few of the dead had gel packs, which squashed when they fell. The fake blood gave them a realistic appearance.

As the last of the wounded were carried to the hospital tent the dead began to stir. The cats sat in the tree and laughed. Tucker watched with curiosity. She'd moved to the front of the reviewing stand.

One corpse didn't move.

A Confederate, resurrected, walked by without paying attention.

Archie Ingram, formerly deceased, also walked by. He stopped, nudging the body with his boot. Nothing happened.

Many people in the crowd were walking back to the main house, unaware of the unfolding drama.

That fast the two cats backed down the tree, streaking across the field.

*"Tucker!"* Mrs. Murphy hollered.

The dog left Harry, just now noticing the curious sight, to join the cats.

Archie, down on his hands and knees, turned over the body. It was Sir H. Vane-Tempest.

Mrs. Murphy reached Vane-Tempest before Pewter or Tucker.

As the breathless gray cat caught up, the tiger sniffed the body. *"Powder,"* was all she said.

The corgi, famous for her scenting abilities, gawked for an instant. *"He looks like a piece of swiss cheese."*

# 16

People slowly began to return to the field. At first the sight of Archie kneeling over Vane-Tempest looked like acting. Distraught, he loosened the older man's collar.

Harry, a sprinter, had been the first person out from the sidelines. She grasped Vane-Tempest's wrist to take his pulse. Irregular. His breathing was shallow.

Miranda, slower but hurrying, motioned for Dr. Larry Johnson to join her. The gray-haired Confederate dumped his weapon and ran. Reverend Jones solicited a four-wheel drive to take him to the victim.

Vane-Tempest, in shock, stared upward with glassy eyes. His lips moved.

Larry tore open his tunic. The bullet holes, neat, could have been drawn on his chest except that blood oozed out of them.

Susan Tucker jumped into a farm truck parked on the side out of view of the battle. She pressed hard on the horn, making her way through the crowd, looking for Sarah. Sarah, returning with her husband's canteen, was slowed by the distance, the heat, and now the retreating crowd. Susan caught sight of her at the hunter barn, standing at the open door, shielding her eyes against the sun.

Finally reaching Sarah, she shouted, "Get in."

"Oh, God, he's really mad at me, isn't he?

I had to catch my breath for a minute. It's sweltering in this dress."

Susan didn't answer Sarah. She was trying to return to the battlefield as fast as she could, given the crowd, which slowly got out of her way as she laid on the horn.

She pulled up close to where Larry was working on Vane-Tempest. Sarah, at first, didn't realize it was her husband lying on the ground, the focus of grim activity. Susan nudged her out of the farm truck.

Sarah stood by the truck door for a second, then ran for the prostrate figure. She tore away her hoop skirt to run faster.

"Harry, keep people away," Larry ordered, then barked at Miranda, "See to Sarah."

Sarah, mute, fought Miranda. Boom Boom ran up to help the older woman. Together they pulled Sarah a short distance from her husband so Larry could work unmolested.

"Hold his head still. You might have to clear his mouth out." Larry spoke low, and calmly.

Harry, on her knees, placed a hand on either side of Vane-Tempest's florid face as Larry crossed one hand over the other and pumped on the wounded man's chest with all his weight.

The two cats watched, as did Tucker. She put her nose to the ground but knew it was hopeless; too many feet had trod the earth, too many guns had been fired.

*"Shot in the back for sure,"* Mrs. Murphy softly said.

*"What a terrible accident."* Tucker hung her head.

*"No accident,"* Mrs. Murphy crisply remarked. *"Three bullets in the back is no accident."*

Pewter stared at the tiger.

Archie knelt on the other side of the gasping man. "I'm sorry. I'm so sorry."

Vane-Tempest blinked. His eyes cleared for a moment and he seemed to recognize everyone. But his left lung was filling with blood.

In the distance an ambulance squealed.

Harry watched Larry work. She'd known him all her life as a family doctor but this was the first time she had seen him dealing with an emergency. She admired his cool proficiency and his physical strength. In his middle seventies, Larry acted like a man in his fifties.

The ambulance rolled out onto the field. Within seconds the crew, headed by Diana Robb, had Vane-Tempest on a stretcher and inside the vehicle. Larry hopped in behind, and the door slammed.

"Waynesboro," Diana called to Harry and Miranda. "It's the closest hospital."

Miranda and Boom Boom guided Sarah back to the farm truck. They squeezed in, heading to Waynesboro, a good twenty-five miles away and up over treacherous Afton Gap.

As the humans continued to mill around in disbelief, Mrs. Murphy suggested, *"Fan five feet apart, and move toward the tree."*

*"What are we looking for?"* Tucker inquired.

103

*"Spent bullets. The holes in his chest were made by clean exits."*

Archie, shaking, walked toward the main house, a vacant look on his face. Harry caught up to him.

She called over her shoulder, "Come on, kids."

*"In a minute,"* Tucker barked.

*"Hurry. It won't take long for one of these fools to grind the bullets into the earth,"* the tiger urged.

*"Found one."* Pewter stopped.

The other two ran over. Sure enough it was a lead bullet, fattish, with three concentric rings on the bottom and a squashed nose lying in the grass.

*"Can't call her back."* The tiger thought out loud. *"Tucker, carry it in your mouth."*

The corgi happily pinched the bullet between her teeth.

*"Don't swallow,"* Pewter teased.

They trotted after Harry, who eased Archie toward the hunter barn.

"I need to get back to my tent."

"Arch, there will be questions. You're better off here."

"I didn't shoot him." Archie was beginning to comprehend the full impact of this dolorous event.

"Of course you didn't. However, why subject yourself to strangers or even friends asking questions you may not be emotionally prepared to answer? Come on in here. I'll find Cynthia Cooper. I know she's around."

"This is Sheriff Hill's territory," Archie vaguely protested.

"I know that but it can't hurt to have an Albemarle deputy with you. Archie, trust me."

His emotions crystallized into anger. "Trust you! For Christ's sake, you're the goddamned postmistress. You don't know what you're doing."

He pushed right by her, plunging into the crowd.

Harry said nothing. She walked into the barn. Fair was brushing down his horse. He looked up.

"Hi."

"H. Vane's been shot."

"What?" Fair stopped, brush held midair.

"Shot through the back."

"Really shot?" It was sinking in.

"Really shot."

"Some fool was back there actually firing bullets? Of all the stupid—"

"Maybe it wasn't stupid."

"Don't let your imagination run away with you, Harry. Who would shoot H. Vane on purpose? He's not worth the lead." That popped out of his mouth before he realized it.

"A lot of men marched behind him, including Archie Ingram. You know how people think."

"It's absurd." He paused. "Is he going to make it?"

"I don't know. Larry Johnson worked on him. He's on his way to Waynesboro Hospital."

"Well, they've dealt with gunshot wounds before."

Tucker walked up to Harry and opened her mouth, dropping the bullet smack onto Harry's foot.

*"Good job."* Pewter praised the dog.

Mrs. Murphy studied her human's face. Harry bent over to pick up the fired bullet.

"Good Lord," she said, then stared at Tucker, who smiled back.

# 17

Miranda's house, centrally located behind the post office, provided a gathering place for old friends. Her cooking drew them in as well. Few things delighted Miranda Hogendobber as much as feeding those she loved and even those she didn't love. Holy Scripture bade her to love all mankind but many times she found the theory easier than the practice.

Harry helped serve apple cider and Tom Collinses. Boom Boom had remained at the hospital, but then Boom Boom flourished amid tragedy, especially if the tragedy was visited upon someone other than herself. However, since she and Sarah were friends, her staying on might serve some good purpose.

Cynthia Cooper sat next to Fair. They were both such light blonds they could have been twins, although they were not related, not even distantly, which is always a disappointment to a true Virginian.

"I can understand someone taking a shot at Archie but not Sir H. Vane-Tempest." Cynthia sipped the most delicious apple cider she had ever tasted. In conjunction with Miranda's piping hot scones it was perfection.

"You don't know that it was on purpose." Harry passed around the silver tray filled with jellies, preserves, and unsalted butter. She thought the shots were intentional but she wanted to see what others would say.

"Actually, I should be the one to say that." Cynthia dumped mounds of persimmon jelly on her scone.

"You're off duty." Harry smiled at her.

"Tell me again about the bullet." Cynthia split open the scone, releasing a thin waft of moist, fragrant air.

"Tucker dropped it at my feet and I gave it to Sheriff Hill."

The dog, greedily gobbling the raw hamburger mixed with raw egg that Miranda had made for her, didn't even glance up when her name was spoken. Nor did Mrs. Murphy or Pewter, faces deep in cooked, diced chicken.

"I wonder why she picked it up?" Miranda thought out loud.

"Maybe it had blood on it," Harry replied, then noticed that everyone stopped eating for a moment. "Sorry."

A light rap on the back door followed by a "Yoo-hoo" diverted them from the unpleasant thought.

"Come in," Miranda called from the kitchen.

Herb Jones eased through the door, a blade of cooling night air following him. "Any word?"

"No."

He sat down. Harry offered the minister his choice of beverage. He requested coffee since Miranda always had a pot on the stove. Miranda bustled in with a tray of fresh scones. She set them on the tea trolley.

"Sit down, Miranda, you work too hard," Herb told her.

"I will in a minute." She walked back to the kitchen, returning in moments with a cup of hot coffee.

"People are already saying that Archie shot him." Herb dabbed his lips with a cocktail napkin. "That's all they're talking about. Even Mim, who's usually circumspect, says it bears all the marks of Archie's scheming."

"Scheming? In front of everyone?" Harry said.

The taciturn Fair spoke up. "That's her point. No one will ever be able to prove that Archie fired at H. People can talk all they want. They can't prove it. Archie's devious by nature."

"Fair, I'm surprised to hear you say that." Miranda's voice shot upward.

"He's played both ends against the middle all his life. That doesn't mean he's bad, just devious."

"Can't they test weapons?" Miranda directed the question to Cynthia.

"Yes." She swallowed, then continued, "And I'm sure Sheriff Hill will do just that. But everyone was loading and firing so all the barrels will be filled with powder. And no one was supposed to have real bullets. This could prove very interesting."

"You know, H. Vane has spent a lifetime abusing his body. I wonder if he can pull through this." Harry watched Mrs. Murphy and Pewter change dishes. "Why do they each think the other one got something better?"

"*We don't.*" Mrs. Murphy brushed a bit of chicken off her chin.

"*It's our food dance,*" said Pewter, nose in the bowl.

"*It is not.*" Tucker giggled.

"*It is too,*" Murphy called to the tailless dog. "*I can smell what she has in her dish and she can smell what I have in mine. We like to do it, that's all. You stick your face in your food and inhale it. We cats have more delicacy of manner.*"

"*And more taste buds,*" Pewter said.

"*You do not.*"

"*Yes we do. We even have better taste buds than they do.*" Pewter indicated the humans.

"*That's not saying much.*" The dog sat down. She was too full to stand.

"You all are getting awfully chatty over there," Harry reprimanded her pets as the decibel level of their conversation increased.

Three pairs of eyes glared at her but the animals did pipe down.

"Where's Susan?" Herb asked.

"I don't know, but before Archie left the campground he asked Ned to represent him."

"Harry, why didn't you say something?" Cynthia was surprised.

"It doesn't mean he did it. The only reason I know is I passed Susan on my way out of the hunter barn." She paused. "I can't stand

Archie Ingram. I really don't give a damn what happens to him and I might even lower myself to enjoy his discomfort."

Everyone stared at her, including the animals.

"Harry, your mother didn't raise you to be like that," Miranda chided her.

"No, but my mother didn't have to deal with Archie after he became a county commissioner either. He got the big head. Anyway, I can't always be a proper Virginia lady. I'm too young to be that proper." A raffish grin crossed her face.

"Lifeline." Cynthia half smiled.

"I'd sooner bleed from the throat. How do you stand it?"

Since no one there had realized that Cynthia attended the self-help group, they smiled nervously, waiting for her rejoinder.

Cynthia smiled reflexively. "I've seen people bleed from the throat."

"I'm sorry," Harry apologized, genuinely upset with herself.

"Does it work?" Fair innocently asked.

"I've only been once but I think it will teach me techniques to handle situations better. It's not really therapy or anything, more of a learning session."

Miranda was dying to ask more questions but decided she'd do it in private.

The phone rang.

"Hello." Miranda didn't cover the mouthpiece. "Mim." She listened. "He's what!" She listened some more. "Thanks." Miranda hung up the phone and ran over to the television.

She clicked on Channel 29's news. An interview with Archie Ingram was in progress. Archie, dressed in a three-piece suit and a turquoise tie, was answering a reporter's questions. He stood outside the county offices.

"—unfortunate incident. I realize many will point the finger at me because of my recent strained relationship with Sir H. Vane-Tempest but our friendship is deeper than this recent disagreement."

"What is the nature of the disagreement, Mr. Ingram?"

"We have different visions of how best to serve Albemarle County—political differences."

The reporter interrupted before Archie could cite his record. "It's about water, isn't it?"

"I'm sick of talking about the damn reservoir!" Archie's face purpled. "Yes, we disagree but I wouldn't shoot him over it."

"But at the meeting at Crozet High School last week—"

"The hell with you, lady." Archie walked off camera.

The cameraman swung around and followed him. Archie loomed into the lens of the camera, and the camera bobbled. The sound of it hitting the sidewalk could be heard, then the picture went black for a second. The image switched back to the studio.

"Is he stone stupid or what?" Harry blurted out.

"You know, the funny thing is, it would make

sense if someone had shot Archie. Doesn't make sense that H. got it." Herb shook his head.

"Maybe Archie was the target and H. Vane got in the way," Harry said. "There's a lot of H. Vane and not much of Archie."

*"Archie's protesting too much,"* Mrs. Murphy announced to no one in particular and everyone in general. *"He's covering something up."*

*"Yeah, he's covering up that he shot H. Vane in broad daylight before thirty thousand people."* Tucker stood up again, felt the effort too great, and sat back down.

*"Something else."* The tiger blinked, then swayed in that way that cats do, a light forward and backward motion.

# 18

Sarah Vane-Tempest slept at the hospital for two nights. When her husband was moved out of intensive care and onto the critical list, she allowed Miranda to take her home.

Exhausted, raccoon-eyed, Sarah invited Miranda in for tea.

"Honey, I brought some quiche. I'll warm it up for you while you take a shower. By the time you're finished the food will be ready."

"If the hospital calls, come get me even if I'm in the shower."

"I will, and don't worry. You've worried enough for three women." Miranda smiled. "Anyway, Blair Bainbridge is taking a turn with your husband. I had no idea they'd gotten that close."

"Outsiders. They both feel like outsiders since their families aren't from Virginia. Oh, well, it is like the Cotswolds, so H. mostly loves it here." Vane-Tempest had been born in a particularly lovely part of England.

"Go on now." Miranda pushed her in the direction of her bedroom.

She warmed the oven and unwrapped her homemade breads, the dishcloths slightly damp to prevent them from drying out. She hummed a hymn as she set the table.

Miranda held that the way a woman organizes her kitchen tells you everything you need to know about her—that and her shoes.

Sarah's kitchen, the latest in high-tech gadgetry, boasted an enormous brass espresso maker from Italy. It rested on the marble countertop.

Velvet-lined drawers contained Tiffany silver for everyday use. The evening silver was locked in the pantry. Miranda couldn't imagine using Tiffany silver for breakfast and lunch.

The refrigerator, dishwasher, microwave, and double oven had black, shiny surfaces. At the top of the wall, six inches from the ceiling, a green neon line acted as molding. It was all very playful and hideously expensive, but at least it was extremely well organized.

While the quiche warmed, Miranda opened the closet. Two Confederate uniforms hung there, each of them clean. Both sported the blue facings of the infantry.

Sarah walked back into the kitchen, her slippers scuffling.

Miranda turned around. "Two uniforms?"

"You know how H. gets when he suffers these—deliriums."

"Mmm." Miranda did know.

Like many wealthy people, H. Vane-Tempest rarely glided into an activity. He jumped in with both feet, spent oo-scoobs of money for equipment, only to abandon the passion a year or two later. Since he had nothing to work for anymore, he needed constant new challenges to occupy his mind. He had bought every possible book on the War Between the States, going so far as to pester the government of England to let him see any correspondence Queen Victoria might have penned on the matter.

Sarah sat down, eyes half closed as the moist aroma of fresh bread curled into her nostrils. "Rye?"

"And cornbread." Miranda opened the oven, removing the warming breads. Hotpads at the ready, she pulled out the quiche.

They ate in silence, Sarah haggard from the crisis. Anyone who knew Miranda Hogendobber longer than a half hour would figure out that the good woman made a lot of room for both your personality and your situation.

"Herb says port is fortifying. Might it pick you up?"

"Put me down. I'm so worn-out I don't

trust my system," Sarah replied. "Do you think he'll be all right, Miranda?"

"I don't know. He's in God's hands."

"God's hands are full."

Miranda smiled. " 'Beloved, do not be surprised at the fiery ordeal which comes upon you to prove you, as though something strange were happening to you. But rejoice insofar as you share Christ's sufferings, that you may also rejoice and be glad when his glory is revealed.' " She drew a breath. "First Peter. I forget the chapter."

"How do you remember all that?"

Miranda shrugged. "Just do. When I was a little girl my sister and I would have memorizing contests. You've never met my sister, have you?"

Sarah shook her head.

"Lives in Greenville, South Carolina. Loves it." She cut another piece of quiche for Sarah.

"I'm full."

"Just a nibble. You need your strength."

Sarah poked at the bacon-and-cheese quiche. "You draw such comfort from the Bible."

"Were you raised in the church?"

"Yes. Episcopalian. *Very* high church."

"I see." Miranda sipped sparkling water. "You might enjoy a more, mmm...personal church."

"Perhaps," came the noncommittal reply.

Miranda marveled at how beautiful Sarah was, even exhausted. Impeccably groomed, hair the perfect shade of blond, eyes startlingly blue, strong chin, full and sensuous lips—Miranda noted these visual enticements. She herself felt no pull toward female beauty. It was rather like watching a sleek cat. She felt men paid dearly for such wives.

"A cup of coffee?"

"No. I've imbibed enough caffeine in the last two days to qualify me for a Valium prescription."

"Well then, I'll just clean up and be on my way. Would you like me to call someone to stay with you tonight? I'd hate for you to wake up and be frightened."

"Boom Boom will come over, after one of her interminable Lifeline meetings. I don't know why. She keeps meeting the same men over and over again."

"Yes." Miranda wanted to say that was probably the point. "Will you be all right until then?"

"Of course I will. You were a dear to tend to me."

"I wasn't tending to you. I was enjoying your company."

# 19

*"Bite her leg,"* Mrs. Murphy ordered Tucker.

*"I will not. That will get me in trouble. You get away with everything."*

*"No, I don't."*

*"You bite her, then."*

*"Cats scratch. Dogs bite."*

*"Bull."*

116

Pewter piped up. *"Nothing's going to work. Forget it."*

They looked out the truck window forlornly as Harry passed Rose Hill, Tally Urquhart's place.

*"Bite her!"*

*"We'll go off the road."* Tucker bared her fangs at Mrs. Murphy.

*"My, what big teeth you have, Grandma."* Mrs. Murphy burst out laughing, joined by Pewter.

*"I hate you."* Tucker laid her ears against her pretty face.

"What's going on here?" Harry, eyes on the road, grumbled. "If you all can't behave I'm not taking you out again."

*"She told me to bite you."* Tucker indicated Mrs. Murphy by inclining her head.

A lightning-fast paw struck the dog on the nose. A bead of blood appeared.

*"Oo-oo-oo,"* the little dog cried.

"Dammit, Murphy." Harry pulled off the road onto the old farm service road of Rose Hill. She stopped, checked the dog, opened the glove compartment for a tissue and held it to the long nose. "You play too rough."

*"Tough."* The tiger thought the rhyme funny. Pewter had to laugh, too.

*"Bunch of mean cats,"* Tucker whined.

*"Play it for all it's worth, bubblebutt."* Mrs. Murphy stepped on Tucker's back, then stepped on Harry's lap.

The driver's-side window, halfway open, was her goal. She soared through it off Harry's lap.

"Mrs. Murphy!" Harry shouted.

The cat sat outside by the driver's door, her lustrous green eyes cast up at her mother's livid visage. *"I've got something to show you."*

*"Good idea."* Pewter stepped on the dog, then on Harry's lap, and then she, too, jumped out of the truck, although not as gracefully as Mrs. Murphy.

*"You don't know where I'm going."*

*"Yes I do."* Pewter loped down the grassy lane.

*"Don't go without me. Oh, don't you dare go without me,"* the dog howled.

"Jesus." Harry opened the door, struggling out with the dog in her arms. The corgi was heavy.

Before Harry's feet hit the ground Tucker wiggled free, landed, and rolled. She hopped to her feet, shook her head, and tore after the cats.

"Tucker, you come back here!" Harry called. "I don't believe them."

She ran after them. Little good that did, as all three barreled on, out of reach but clearly in sight. The cats didn't deviate or dash off the lane as usual. Harry watched, cursed, then hopped into her truck and followed them at fifteen miles an hour.

In ten minutes Tally Urquhart's stone cottages and the huge stone hay barn came into view.

Harry pulled into the middle of the buildings, cut the motor, and got out just as the cats pushed open the barn door a crack and flattened themselves to get inside. She beheld two paws—one tiger, one gray—sticking through

118

the slight gap in the door. It was as though they were waving at her to follow.

Tucker put her sore nose in the door and pushed. She, too, squeezed inside.

"They're trying to drive me crazy," Harry said out loud. "Really, this is an orchestrated plan to send me round the bend."

She walked to the door, rolled it back with a heave, and blinked.

"Holy shit."

*"You got that right,"* Mrs. Murphy cat-called.

# 20

Warm spring light flooded the barn, illuminating Rick Shaw's face as he stood under the wing of the Cessna. Behind him a young woman dusted for fingerprints.

Not a drop of blood marred the shiny surface of the airplane or the cockpit, although there were muddy paw prints on the wings and the cockpit. No dings, dents, or smears of oil hinted at foul play.

The wheels of the small plane were blocked. In fact, everything was in order. The gas tank was almost full. They could have crawled up into the Cessna to cruise through creamy clouds on this, a gorgeous day.

Cynthia spoke to Tally Urquhart. Miss Tally's sight remained keen, her hearing sharp, but her powers of locomotion had diminished. After fervid wrangling sprinkled with the utterance of unladylike epithets, she had agreed to stop driving. No longer able to ride astride, she allowed herself the pleasures of driving a matched pair of hackney ponies, to the terror of the neighbors. Her major-domo, Kyle Washburn, had the honor of transporting her to her many clubs and good deeds. It was also his duty to hang on when she took the reins. There were many in Albemarle County who thought no amount of money was too much to pay Kyle.

"I told you that," Tally snapped.

"I know it's irritating, ma'am, but my job is to check and double-check."

She tossed her white curls, hair still luxuriously thick. "Tommy Van Allen put his plane in my big hay barn and walked away, never to return. And I heard nothing."

"At no time did you hear a plane buzz the house?" Cynthia braced herself for the blast.

"Are you deaf? No."

Kyle stepped in. "Miss Tally is in town a lot, Deputy. Anyone who knows her and her busy schedule would have no trouble landing here when she was out of the house."

"You hear anything?" Cynthia smiled at him.

"No."

"Mr. Washburn." She leaned toward his weathered, freckled face. "How could this plane sit here and you not know it?"

"Winter hay barn," Tally snapped as though that simple description would be enough for any intelligent person.

"Miss Tally fills this barn up with hay in the fall. Usually I open it wide in May. Air it out. I'm behind this year—a little."

"So you two think whoever parked the plane here—do you park a plane?—well, whoever did this knows Miss Tally's schedule?"

"Yes," Kyle answered while Tally glared. This was damned inconvenient and she knew the situation would bring her bossy niece over to once again interfere.

Using her cane with vigor, hand clutched over the silver hound's head, Tally stalked Harry.

"I don't know any more than you do." Harry shrugged.

"You know a good deal less." Tally pointed her cane at Harry. "You say you chased these varmints here?"

"*I'm no varmint,*" Tucker yipped.

"They led me right to the barn."

Tally studied the animals at Harry's feet.

"Sometimes animals know things. Your mother had a marvelous sense of animals. She could talk to them and I swear they talked back," Tally said, her smile momentarily tinged with melancholy. Then, steeling herself, she again eyed Harry. "You get used to it. By the time you're my age everyone's dead. Dead. Dead. Dead. No use crying over spilt milk." She took a little breath. "And if you ask me, Tommy Van Allen is dead, too."

Rick, respectfully silent until now, asked, "Why do you say that, ma'am?"

"Tommy Van Allen is wild as a rat. He'd be here if he were alive."

"Some people think he was selling drugs, made a big haul and disappeared," Rick suggested.

"Piffle."

"Ma'am?"

"He might use them. He wouldn't sell them. That boy was a lot of things but stupid wasn't one of them. He wouldn't sell drugs." She pointed her cane at Rick's chest. "Every time something happens around here everyone yells 'Drugs.' Too much TV." She turned to Harry. "You're a nosy kid. Always were. In the blood. Your great-grandfather was nosy."

"Which one?"

"Biddy Minor. Handsomest man I ever saw. Had to know everything, though. Killed him, of course."

Rick, a student of local crime, said gently, since it wouldn't do to correct her, "It was never proven."

She raised an eyebrow, barely deigning to refute his prattle. "Proving and knowing are two different things, Sheriff. Just like I know Tommy Van Allen is dead. I know it. You have to prove it, I suppose."

"Ma'am, we can't convict anyone without proof."

"Convict them?" Her thin voice rose. "Convict them—they're out on the streets in six months."

Rick blushed. "Miss Tally, I feel exactly the same way but I have a job to do. I'm elected to this position."

She softened. "And so you are. Well—what else do you want to know?"

122

"Can you think of any reason why someone would want to kill Tommy Van Allen?"

She paused thoughtfully. "No more than anyone else. By that I mean he had his share of angry ex-girlfriends, his share of people who plain didn't like him."

"Can you think of any reason why someone would shoot Sir H. Vane-Tempest?"

"Pompous, silly ass." She shrugged her bony shoulders. "You're going to canvass my neighbors, aren't you? Surely one of them heard this airplane."

"We'll speak to everyone," Rick assured her.

A crunch of tires on gravel turned all heads in the direction of the Bentley Turbo R pulling into the open barn.

Tucker barked as the motor was cut off and one elegant leg swung out the driver's side. "*Mim!*" The little dog rushed forward to greet the haughty Mim, who nonetheless loved dogs. She bent over to pat Tucker's head, and the dog happily tagged at her heels.

"Don't you start telling me what to do." Tally's lower lip jutted out.

"I'm not. I'm here to help." Mim stopped to study the plane. "Extraordinary," she said quietly.

"If you all don't need me any longer I'll go." Harry began to move toward the open door.

"Go on." Sheriff Shaw nodded.

Cynthia called out, "I'll catch you later."

Miss Tally placed her left hand on Harry's arm. Her thin ring gleamed. "Mary Minor, you never believed the story about my brother shooting your great-granddaddy because Biddy walked up on his still, did you?"

"No."

She nodded, satisfied. "Good girl."

Harry herded Mrs. Murphy, Pewter, and Tucker into the truck, hearing Mim say, "Now, Aunt Tally, why would anyone put a plane in your barn?"

"To give me excitement in my declining years."

# 21

That evening Harry walked out to the creek dividing her land from Blair Bainbridge's. A soft *squish* accompanied each step. Pewter picked her paws up, periodically shaking them.

*"It was much worse the other night,"* Mrs. Murphy nonchalantly remarked.

*"I'll have to spend half the night washing my feet."*

*"Stick 'em under the faucet,"* the dog joked.

*"Never."* Pewter shook her paws again.

Harry stopped at the creek. The sun was setting, crowning the mountains in pink clouds suffused with gold.

Tucker sat down.

*"I'm not sitting down in this,"* Pewter complained.

*"You're cranky. Bet you've got a tapeworm."*

*"I do not!"* The cat slapped at the dog, who laughed.

*"You should talk."* Mrs. Murphy hated those monthly worm pills but they worked. She knew Tucker sometimes cheated and spit hers out. Then she'd feel bad, Harry would discover evidence of roundworms, and Tucker would really get a dose of medicine.

Harry drank in the sunset and the sound of peepers. She studied her animals; uncanny, as though they knew where the plane was stashed.

It occurred to Harry that whoever deposited Tommy Van Allen's airplane would not be happy to know that she had discovered it. But someone would have eventually done so. She didn't think she'd be in the line of fire.

But Sir H. Vane-Tempest was.

"Just doesn't compute," she said out loud.

*"It's not our problem."* Pewter felt that suppertime started with sunset. She turned to face the distant house, hoping Harry would take the hint.

Instead Harry climbed the massive walnut tree. Mrs. Murphy joined her, as did Pewter.

*"What am I supposed to do?"* the dog whined at the base of the tree.

*"Guard us, Tucker,"* Mrs. Murphy said.

*"I might have to,"* the dog grumbled, *"and lest you forget, egotist of all time, I ran and chased the bobcat."*

*"You did. I really am grateful."*

*"How often do humans climb trees?"* Pewter watched Harry swing her legs as she sat on the low, wide branch.

*"Not very often. As they get older they don't*

*do it at all, I think,"* Mrs. Murphy answered. *"You see so much more from up here. You'd think they'd want to keep doing it."*

*"No claws. Must be hard for them."* Pewter kept her claws dangerously sharp.

*"Everything's hard for them. That's why all their religions are full of fear. You know, hellfire and damnation, that sort of thing."*

*"And being plunged into darkness."* Tucker agreed with the tiger cat.

*"If they could see in the dark as well as we do, their gods would be dark gods."* Mrs. Murphy pitied humans their wide variety of fears.

*"If they were bats their gods would be sounds."* Tucker suffered no religious anxiety. She knew perfectly well that a corgi presided over the universe and she ignored the cats' blasphemous references to a celestial feline.

*"How long do you think Harry will live?"* Pewter rubbed against the cobbled trunk of the tree.

Walnuts, beautiful trees, possessed the exact right type of bark for cats to sharpen their claws on—and it was good to rub against, too.

*"She's strong. Into her eighties, I should say, maybe as long as Tally Urquhart,"* Murphy replied.

*"Then why are humans scared, really? They live much longer than we do."*

*"Nah. Just seems longer."* Tucker giggled.

The cats laughed.

Mrs. Murphy watched Harry hum to herself, swinging her legs as she enjoyed the slow shift of colors from pink to salmon to blood-red shot through with fingers of gray. She truly loved this human and wished Harry could be more like a cat. It would improve her life.

Harry suddenly noticed the animals all observing her.

She burst out laughing. "Hey."

*"Hey back at you,"* they replied.

"Isn't it beautiful?"

*"Yes,"* came the chorus.

*"It's time for supper."*

*"Pewter,"* Mrs. Murphy corrected her.

Pewter fell silent. If she complained she'd probably be stuck out in the walnut tree longer. With luck, Harry's bucolic rapture would pass soon.

*"Do you ever worry about who will take care of Mom when we're dead?"* Tucker soberly asked Murphy.

*"She'll bring in a puppy and a kitten by the time we're old. We'll train them."*

*"I'm not training any kitten,"* Pewter huffed.

*"That's because you have nothing to teach the next generation."*

*"Aren't we clever?"* Pewter boxed Murphy's ears.

Murphy boxed right back, the two felines moving forward and backward on the heavy branch as Harry laughed at them. Pewter whacked Murphy hard and the tiger slipped. She grabbed at the branch with her front paws but her hind legs dangled over the edge.

"Here." Harry reached over and grabbed her

by the scruff of the neck, pulling her up. She put the tiger cat in her lap.

Pewter advanced on Murphy.

"Don't you dare or I'll fall off." Harry shook her finger at Pewter, who grabbed her finger. She sheathed her claws but her pupils were big so she appeared ferocious.

*"Who will open the cans if Harry gets hurt?"* Murphy spit in Pewter's face.

"Now that's enough!" Harry tapped the tiger's head with her index finger.

It didn't hurt but it was irritating.

A sweet purr attracted everyone's attention. A pair of headlights, a mile off, swung into view. Blair pulled into his driveway. He got out of his car, then opened the door for Little Mim.

*"Can she see?"* Pewter asked Murphy.

*"It's clear enough. She can see that far. Interested, too."*

*"Who wouldn't be interested in the Porsche,"* Tucker said.

*"She's curious about him."*

*"Oh."* Tucker watched a twig by the creek. *"What was that about Biddy Minor? Miss Tally said curiosity killed him?"*

*"I don't know. Long before my time. That's way back in our great-grandmothers' time, I guess."*

*"You'd think they'd talk about it."* Pewter backed down the tree. If the others weren't going home, she was. There might be some dried crunchies left in the bowl on the countertop.

*"Maybe they did and we didn't hear it. But I don't think Harry's talked about it."* Mrs.

Murphy hopped out of Harry's lap and backed down the walnut also. She talked as she felt for her footing, the slight piercing sound of her claws sinking in bark audible even to the human. *"Maybe she made a passing reference. It would have happened in the twenties, I think."*

*"That long ago?"*

Murphy reached the bottom as Tucker walked over to her. *"Well, if Biddy was Harry's great-grandfather, you figure he was born in the 1880s, not much later than 1900 for sure."*

*"Let's look it up in the family Bible,"* Tucker suggested, *"when she's asleep."*

*"Okay."* Pewter would have agreed to anything just to get to the house.

Harry "skinned the cat," turning upside down from the branch and dropping to the ground below.

*"Very good,"* Murphy praised her.

As they walked back together Harry asked them, "Did you all know about Tommy Van Allen's plane?"

*"Yes,"* Mrs. Murphy and Tucker replied.

Pewter said nothing because she hadn't seen it before, even though Mrs. Murphy had told her everything.

Harry smiled at them, oblivious to their answers.

"Smart kids."

*"Sometimes,"* Tucker, more modest than the cats, responded.

*"What I don't like about this is it's too close to home."* Murphy emphasized *home.* *"Tally Urquhart's only four miles away."*

*"It doesn't concern Mom no matter how far away or how close it is."* Pewter had taken to calling Harry Mom even though she had been raised by Market Shiflett and she occasionally helped out in the store.

*"This is a small town. Everything concerns everybody and we led Mom to what may become damaging evidence for someone else. We were stupid."* Murphy realized her mistake.

*"I never thought of that."* Tucker pressed closer to Harry.

*"Me neither. I wish I had."*

*"Don't worry until they find a body,"* Pewter said.

*"Whoever landed that plane had guts. The fog that night was thick as Mrs. Hogendobber's gravy. Bold ones like that do things other people don't dream of, they take wild chances. Whoever was with Tommy probably killed him, which means I saw the killer. I couldn't tell you one thing about him, though, except that he was shorter than Van Allen. But whoever killed Tommy can't be but so far away."*

*"You don't know that."* Pewter played devil's advocate.

*"But I do."* Mrs. Murphy dashed ahead a few paces. *"What would someone far away have to gain by removing Tommy Van Allen—"*

*"And removing H. Vane-Tempest,"* Tucker interrupted.

*"He's still hanging on."* Pewter wasn't convinced.

Mrs. Murphy continued her thoughts. *"If Van Allen has some distant relatives who might inherit his construction business, well, it might be someone far away, but I doubt that's the case."*

*"Everyone will know when his will is read."* Pewter shrugged.

*"Since no one knows that he's dead yet the will won't be read. His property will stay intact,"* Murphy said, her tail straight out horizontally.

*"Someone has to run the business."* Tucker began to feel uneasy.

*"Whoever is vice president of his corporation will. But think about it, it doesn't matter who runs the business. What matters is where the profits go. And they won't go into anyone's pocket until he is legally declared dead."*

*"Mrs. Murphy, if the killer stands to profit from Tommy's death then the body must be revealed."* Pewter was hungry and frustrated. This didn't make a bit of sense to her.

*"Exactly."*

*"I don't get it,"* Tucker forthrightly said, her voice high.

*"Be patient."* Mrs. Murphy smiled at them as they caught up to walk beside her. *"Whoever killed Tommy is in no hurry. I don't know what Virginia laws say about when you're legally declared dead, but I guarantee you our killer knows. Someone has a great deal to gain by this."*

*"Could be love gone sour."* Pewter searched for a different tack.

*"Could be."* Murphy inhaled the sharp fragrance of the shed bursting with wood shavings.

Pewter was happy they were home.

Tucker was growing more concerned by the minute. *"You're making me nervous."*

*"Maybe we're looking at this from the wrong angle."* Mrs. Murphy bounced through the screen door when Harry opened it. She liked to let Harry open it. It wouldn't do for Harry to know all her tricks. *"Maybe the question is, what do Tommy Van Allen and H. Vane have in common?"*

*"Nothing,"* Pewter said.

Tucker demurred. *"Plenty."*

The two animals looked at each other as Harry wiped off the kitchen counter and pulled out cans of food.

*"They don't have anything in common."* Pewter defended her position. *"Tommy is young and handsome. H. Vane has got to be in his seventies. The face-lift makes him look a little younger."*

*"He had a face-lift?"* Tucker asked.

*"I can always tell. The eyes. The faces lose some of their expressiveness—even with the good jobs,"* Pewter authoritatively declared. *"But those two don't have anything in common. Tommy is divorced. H. Vane is happily married, or appears to be. Tommy is wild and boisterous, H. Vane has a stick up his ass."*

*"My turn. If you're finished."*

Pewter waited by her food bowl, which said LOYAL FRIEND. *"I'm finished, I think."*

*"Okay, they're both well-off. H. Vane is beyond well-off. He's Midas. But they can do whatever they want. They belong to the same clubs. They go to the same parties. They both like to fly. And Tommy was going to do the reenactment."*

*"Every man in Crozet was going to do that. That's not enough."* Pewter purred when Harry scooped out tuna.

*"Maybe Tommy had an affair with Sarah."* Tucker buried her face in her food.

They tabled the discussion until after they ate.

Harry whistled, tired of her own whistle, and turned on the radio. She liked the classical station and country and western. She tuned to the classical station out of Lynchburg. She heated the griddle, pulled out two slices of bread and two fat slices of American cheese. She loved cheese sandwiches, dressing them up with mayonnaise and hamburger pickles. Sometimes she'd squirt on ketchup, too.

Tucker finished first, as always. *"Hurry up."*

*"You don't savor your food."* Pewter did, of course.

*"It tastes good to me. I don't know why you hover over yours."*

*"Tucker, you're such a dog,"* Pewter haughtily replied.

Mrs. Murphy, a slow eater, paused. *"If Tommy slept with Sarah, the question is, did H. Vane know? He certainly seemed friendly enough to Tommy."*

Pewter pitched in her two cents. *"H. Vane would hardly kill Tommy, then get it in the back himself. This is screwy."*

*"No, it isn't. We haven't found the key yet, that's all."* Murphy was resolute.

*"And now that we've somewhat compromised*

Mom we'd better figure this out." Tucker had lived with Mrs. Murphy a long time. She knew how the cat thought.

"Yes."

Pewter, food bits clinging to her whiskers, jerked her head up from the bowl. "She'd stick her nose in it even if we hadn't taken her to the airplane. Even Miss Tally said it was in the blood."

"You got that right." Mrs. Murphy thought Pewter looked silly. "Remember what she said about Biddy Minor?"

"Curiosity killed him," Tucker whispered.

"I thought curiosity killed the cat." Pewter swallowed some carefully chewed tuna.

"Shut up." Murphy hated that expression. "I prefer 'Cats have nine lives,' myself."

"Well, I only have one. I intend to take good care of it." Tucker snapped her jaws shut with a click.

# 22

The shadows etched an outline of the budding trees onto the impeccably manicured back lawn of the Lutheran church. The Reverend Herbert C. Jones, in clerical garb, fiddled with his fly rod as he stood on the moss-covered brick walkway to the beige clapboard office, window shutters painted Charleston green.

He'd finished his sermon for Sunday and since this was Tuesday he felt on top of the world. True, his desk contained four mountains of neatly ordered paperwork but a man couldn't work around the clock. Even the Good Lord rested on the seventh day. And the afternoon, balmy and warm, enticed him from the grind of paperwork. He got his fishing rod and went outside.

Usually Herb parked the church's 1987 white Chevy truck on the corner to let people know he was at church. Since he received many calls to pick up this and drop off that for a parishioner in need, it was also useful for the truck to sit ready, keys in the ignition. However, at the moment the Chevy had a flat left-front tire, which irritated him no end because he'd endured a flat just last year on the right front and had replaced both front tires. He had parked the Chevy in the brick garage behind the office until he could fix it. Lovely winding brick paths meandered from the church to the garage, formerly the stable, and to his graceful residence, a subdued classic in flemish bond.

The tail of the Chevy poked out from the garage. His Buick Roadmaster was parked next to the old truck.

"I'll stand here and cast at the taillight," he told himself.

Lucy Fur watched her human with detached amusement. Mrs. Murphy and Pewter were visiting from the post office. The animal door that Harry had installed there was a godsend because the animals didn't have to lurk by the front door waiting for a person to open it. All too often the human would close the door fast or step on them, because humans lacked a sharp sense of how much space they took up or how much other creatures needed. They were always bumping into things, stepping on tails, or tripping over their own feet. With the animal door at the rear of the old frame building the creatures could come and go at will. The cats especially enjoyed prowling the neighborhood to visit other cats.

Lucy Fur, a gorgeous young Maine coon cat, had walked into Herb's life one stormy night. He kept her because Elocution was getting on in years and he thought a younger companion would do her good. At first Elocution had hissed and spit. That lasted two weeks. Then she tried the deep freeze. Every time the kitten would walk by she'd turn her back. After a month she accepted Lucy Fur, teaching her the duties of a preacher's cat. The first, for any cat, is to catch mice. However, there were communion wafers to count, vestments to inspect, sermons to read, parishioners to comfort, and a variety of functions to attend.

Both cats excelled as fund-raisers, mingling with the crowd and encouraging generosity with both checkbooks and food.

The three cats sat abreast in the deep window ledge of the house. Sunlight like golden butter drenched their shiny fur. They watched Herb wryly.

Herb put his right foot back as he lifted his right arm. He wiggled a minute, then cast toward a taillight. He'd done better.

"Damn," he muttered under his breath,

reeling his line, a tiny lead weight dangling on the end, his hand-tied fly, white and speckled black, slightly above it.

"*Is this some Christian ritual?*" Pewter asked.

"*Not the way he does it.*" Lucy Fur giggled.

Again, the gentle reverend cocked his wrist, placed his feet in the correct position, and softly flicked his line out. This cast was worse than the first one.

"Hell's bells." His voice rose.

"*Might prayer help?*" Mrs. Murphy dryly noted.

"*As far as I know there is no prayer specific to fishing.*" Lucy Fur's opinion was an informed one. She studied her texts.

"*What about Jesus talking to the men casting their nets?*" Mrs. Murphy suggested.

"*Luke 5, Verses 1 through 11. It's the story where the men fished all night, came up empty, and Jesus told them to go out and throw their nets. They caught so many fish their ships began to sink. And that's when Simon Peter joined Jesus. He was one of the fishermen.*"

Impressed, Murphy gasped, "*You should talk to Mrs. Hogendobber. She'd have a fit and fall in it!*"

"Oh," Lucy Fur airily replied, "*she wouldn't listen. You know she believes in this charismatic stuff. She ought to submit to the rigor of the Lutheran catechism. I don't believe you sit around waiting until the spirit moves you.*"

"*She hardly sits,*" Pewter noted, herself a sharp critic of human mystical leanings. But in the case of Miranda, the good woman practiced what she preached.

*"Uh-oh. I don't think biblical references are going to help now."* Murphy stared upward.

Herb cast into a tree.

"Christ on a crutch!" he bellowed, then glanced over his shoulder to see if anyone was within earshot.

*"Cats to the rescue."* Murphy leapt off the window ledge, quickly followed by Pewter and Lucy Fur.

Elocution, watching from inside the house, laughed so hard she had to lie down.

The tiger was halfway up the tree before Lucy Fur even reached the trunk. Pewter, not a girl to rush about, sashayed with dignity toward the puce-faced clergyman.

"Now how am I going to get my hook out of the tree? That's one of my best flies." He threw his lad's cap on the grass.

*"Thank you."* Pewter immediately sat on the herringbone cap.

Herb stepped to the right, giving the line a tug. No release. He walked to the left. Pewter watched.

*"What pretty feathers."* Murphy inspected the tied fly.

*"He sits up for hours tying these things. He won't let Elocution or me help. He sputters if we even touch one of these precious feathers. I personally can't understand why fish would grab a feather if a bird isn't attached."*

*"Life's too short to try and understand cold-blooded creatures."* Mrs. Murphy unleashed one white claw, wedging it underneath the hook. *"Stop pulling,"* she ordered Herb.

138

He stopped. "That's my best fly. Don't you eat it!"

"*Get a grip.*" Murphy laughed.

"*Let me help.*" Lucy Fur put her weight on the line so that if Herb did jerk it there'd be a little slack so Murphy could pry up the hook.

"*Here it comes.*" Murphy popped it straight up.

Herb stared up at the cats. He glanced around again. "His wonders never cease." Then he laughed. The cats joined in.

Slowly he reeled in his line, picking up his favorite fly to inspect the damage. None.

He spoke to Pewter, who was all rapt attention. "Best fly in the world for rockfish bass."

"*Good eating,*" Pewter replied; she liked freshwater fish, especially if fried, but more than any other seafood she liked crabmeat.

"You're on my cap."

"*You threw it on the ground, you big baby.*" Nonetheless, Pewter removed herself from the cap, which he promptly slapped back on his head.

"*Why is he wearing that now? Herringbone is for fall.*" Mrs. Murphy paid attention to fashions.

"*He has to get in the mood. You should see him rehearse his sermons. Once when he used* cowboy *as a metaphor he put on cowboy boots and a big hat.*"

"*He's funny.*" Murphy shimmied back down.

"*They all are.*" Lucy Fur backed down.

"*Watch out!*" Pewter warned. "*He's going to cast again.*"

*"Jesus, preserve us,"* Lucy Fur blurted out.

He popped out the line. It sailed over the cats' upturned heads and nicked the bed of the truck, just above the taillight.

*Ding.*

"Pretty good, if I do say so myself." He grinned ear to ear. "Amen." He smiled outright, following his line in to the truck.

The cats scampered along. The shiny sinker tumbled into the truck bed.

Mrs. Murphy leapt into the bed with Pewter and Lucy Fur on her heels.

"Practice makes perfect," he sang out to himself, reaching into the bed and lifting out his sinker and fly as if they were gold-plated.

*"Well done,"* Lucy Fur congratulated him.

He patted her on her magnificent head.

Pewter noticed that the door was slightly ajar to the passenger side of the truck. *"That broke, too?"*

*"Hey."* Mrs. Murphy peered into the cab.

Lucy Fur got on her hind legs and looked inside. Pewter stood next to her.

*"What?"* Pewter said.

*"That bomber jacket."* Lucy Fur's tail flipped left, then right.

*"Herb doesn't own a bomber jacket."* Murphy jumped out of the bed. She tried to pry open the heavy truck door, but, although ajar, it was too much for her.

*"Whoever used the truck last forgot their jacket."* Pewter shrugged.

*"Open the door!"* Murphy hollered at the top of her not-inconsiderable lungs.

"You could wake the dead." Herb leaned his rod against the truck, walking over to the howling cat. "Oh." He noticed the door and opened it wider to shut it firmly. As he did, the cat hopped into the seat. "Now Mrs. Murphy—" He opened the door. "What's this?"

# 23

With no corpse, no motive, and no witnesses, Rick Shaw was in an unenviable position regarding the disappearance of Tommy Van Allen. By contrast he had 30,000 witnesses to the shooting of Sir H. Vane-Tempest—30,003 if he counted Mrs. Murphy, Pewter, and Tee Tucker.

He looked into Mrs. Murphy's green eyes, which stared right back into his own. "Sure of yourself, aren't you?" he whispered to the cat. Then he turned to Herb. "She shows up in the damnedest places. They both do." He stroked Pewter.

Herb was holding Lucy Fur, more to comfort himself than anything.

"Now, Herb, who used this truck last?"

"I did."

"When?"

"A week ago." He sheepishly continued. "I've been meaning to fix the flat but it's always one thing or another."

Cynthia Cooper pulled up to join them. Rick held out the bomber jacket. He wore gloves. "T.V.A." Coop read aloud the initials embroidered on the inside map pocket.

"So the truck has been in the garage for one week," Rick went on. He turned back to Herb. "Have you checked it? You know, come on out to get something from the glove compartment? Anything?"

"No."

"How many people—" Rick stopped himself. Everyone knew where the garage was. In fact, everyone knew everything—almost.

"Do you have any idea why this jacket is in your truck?"

"Sheriff, that's the sixty-four-thousand-dollar question." Herb betrayed his age when he used that phrase.

*"Maybe Tommy put it in there himself."* Lucy Fur posited her idea.

*"No."* Mrs. Murphy concentrated fiercely on the jacket.

"You know, when H. Vane was hauled away in the ambulance, I established the range for muzzle-loaders. About one hundred yards. That meant anyone in either of the two companies could have fired on him. I met the doctor the second she walked out of surgery. I did everything by the book. Three bullet wounds can't be an accident but I have no complaint filed by the victim. Isn't that odd?"

"Yes." Herb crossed his arms over his chest.

"And I have a missing person I am treating as, shall we say, an unfriendly disappearance. We find the airplane. Nothing, except it's covered with pussycat paw prints." He cast

142

an eye at Mrs. Murphy, even though he didn't realize those were her prints. "I've combed through Tommy's house and his office with his housekeeper. Nothing has been taken. The only things missing are what he was wearing—the clothes on his back, a signet ring, and his forty-five-thousand-dollar Schauffenhausen watch."

Herb whistled at the price.

"We've alerted pawnshops across the country. We've sent out photographs to every law-enforcement agency. Not a trace. What I'm driving at is—things are just too damned curious." Rick slapped his thigh in disgust. "I'll check this for prints, fibers, you name it." He sighed audibly. "But I can't put it together."

"Nobody can, boss." Coop brightened. "At least we've got another clue."

"There is that." He smiled.

"Do you think the killer is trying to implicate me?" Herb reached for his rod as though the touch of it would make everything all right.

"No, I don't." Rick smiled. "And I have a suspicious mind. There are so many places to dispose of a jacket.... *Whoever* put it here is in effect giving us the finger—begging your pardon, Reverend."

"Van Allen was probably wearing this jacket when he disappeared," Cynthia said. "Herb, if you don't mind, leave the truck here for a day. We need to check it for prints."

"We've got a portable compressor. I'll fill your tire. Once we're finished tomorrow you can take it down to the garage."

"Thanks, that would be a big help."

Lucy Fur rubbed his leg. *"Don't worry, Poppy. Everything will be all right."*

*"Tommy Van Allen was wearing a trench coat, collar turned up, when I saw him at Tally Urquhart's."*

*"You saw him?"* Lucy Fur stopped midrub.

*"I couldn't see his face but how many six-foot-five men are there? I was far away, it was getting foggy with a hard rain. But he wasn't wearing that bomber jacket."*

*"Maybe he left it in his car and grabbed the trench coat because it was raining?"* Pewter said.

*"It doesn't matter whether he was wearing it, left it in a car, or whether this jacket was in someone else's car or someone else's house. That's really irrelevant at this point."* Murphy's words were clipped.

Pewter disagreed. *"I think it's relevant. The killer or accomplice wanted to get rid of evidence. Maybe he forgot this jacket was in his car or trunk or something?"*

*"No way."* The tiger stood up. *"He's putting down bad scent."*

*"Deliberately misleading us?"* Lucy Fur sat on Herb's sturdy walking shoe.

*"You'd better believe it—and enjoying himself in the bargain."* Mrs. Murphy felt the whole complexion of the events had changed, like a lighting-change during a play. The mood shifts with the light. It can suddenly become treacherous.

# 24

Tubes invaded H. Vane-Tempest's body. Alert but in pain, he lay in the hospital bed counting the minutes until the next shot would bring him relief. What hurt most was his reset shoulder blade.

"Honey, drink a little water. You'll get dehydrated." Sarah held a plastic water cup with a big plastic bent straw in it.

Dutifully he drank. "Where's that goddamn nurse?"

"She'll be here in a minute." Sarah checked her watch.

The heavyset nurse appeared, right on time. "How are you feeling?"

"I've felt better."

She checked his chart and took his pulse.

"He's very uncomfortable. Can't you increase his dosage?"

"No. Only the doctor can do that." The nurse gently removed her fingers from his wrist. "This will help for now. I know it wears off sooner than you'd like, but Dr. Svarski is a firm believer in getting people up and out of here as soon as possible. If you become dependent on painkillers it's that much harder."

H. Vane glared at her as she stuck the needle into his left arm.

"What about his sleep? If you give him a higher dosage at night he'll at least be able to sleep right through. As it is now, he wakes up."

"Mrs. Tempest—"

*"Lady Vane-Tempest."* Sarah was testy.

"Ma'am, you'll have to discuss this with Dr. Svarski. I cannot increase your husband's dosage." She abruptly left the room.

"I hate nurses." Sarah closed the door, then sat next to him. "Would you like me to read to you?"

He smiled at her. "Thank you, but I can't seem to stay focused on anything. My mind wanders. I couldn't even answer Shaw's questions."

"He understands." She lowered her voice. "Henry, it's just us. No repercussions. I understand you don't want to make accusations you can't support. You're exceedingly fair that way. But between us, who would want to shoot you? Is there something I don't know?"

He looked into his wife's imploring eyes. "Sarah, the only person I can think of is Archie."

"Yes, of course." She put her hand on his.

"Lately I'd have gladly shot him." He laughed but it hurt so badly he stopped.

She shook her head. "He's snapped, I suppose. The sheriff can't arrest him until they have more proof....How are you holding up, honey, you look done in."

"Tired."

"Sleep. You need lots of sleep."

"Yes, but it's so boring." He squeezed her hand and promptly fell asleep.

# 25

News of the bomber jacket appeared in the *Daily Progress*. A storm of speculation followed and a plethora of leads—all dead ends.

This Saturday, Harry was determined to wax her Barbour coat. If she didn't do it now she'd regret it in about two days, when more rain was predicted.

She warmed the wax as she brushed the coat, inspected the seams, emptied the pockets. An old movie ticket fell out.

"I can't even remember the last time I went to the movies."

*"You need to get out more often,"* Tucker advised.

Mrs. Murphy, grooming her tail, listened to the blue jay squawking outside the barn door. Birds excited her senses. Blue jays were saucy, fearless, and expert dive-bombers.

*"Shut up,"* Pewter called out.

*"Shut up yourself, fatso!"*

*"I have half a mind to go out there and teach him a lesson,"* Pewter grumbled.

Murphy admired her tail. Having this appendage gave her better balance than Harry but the maintenance could be tiresome. If she forgot to hoist it, she picked up mud or dust. If she was caught in pouring rain, her tail looked like a very long rat tail, which offended her exalted vanity. If she brushed by a lily she would smear her tail with sticky rust-colored pollen. In fall she picked up "hitchhikers."

Biting them out of her tail was a time-consuming process. Still, she'd rather have a tail than not.

She thought Harry would be much improved with a tail. Tucker could certainly use one.

A flurry of squawks, screeches, and whistles drew her from her grooming. She dropped her tail, which she had picked up in her paw.

*"That jay family is pushing it too far."* Pewter shook herself and strolled to the barn door.

*"Death to cats!"* The jay swooped down on Pewter, flew through the barn, and zoomed out the other end.

*"I'll break your neck!"* the humiliated cat hollered.

*"I'll help you."* Mrs. Murphy trotted over to Pewter.

Tucker joined them, too.

Again the jay swirled around the hayloft, then dove at a forty-five-degree angle.

Murphy leapt straight up, the swish of tail feathers by her ear. She clapped both paws together but missed.

*"Ha!"* the jay called out.

*"Let's lure him into the hayloft. We'll cut down his air space,"* Pewter sagely advised.

Mrs. Murphy blinked. *"Forget him, I've got an idea. Follow me."*

The two animals trailed after Murphy as she loped across the field.

*"Where are we going?"* Pewter asked.

*"To Tally Urquhart's."*

*"Why?"* The day was pretty enough that Pewter felt she could endure exercise.

*"The blue jay made me think of it."*

"*What?*" Tucker's soft brown eyes scanned the fields.

"*I should have thought of this before. We need to work in circles around the barn. A human can't see the nose on his face.*"

The animals arrived at the abandoned barn a half hour later. Since the weather was good they had made excellent time.

"*The sheriff has scoured the barn and the out-buildings. My plan is that we each work fifty yards apart in a circle. Pewter, take the closest circle. I'll take the second circle. Tucker, you take the farthest circle. If anyone finds something, yell. If we don't find anything let's work three more circles.*"

"*When you saw the two humans, where did they walk?*" Tucker lifted her head to the wind.

"*Down the dirt road.*"

"*If Tommy was killed out here he could be buried anywhere,*" Pewter said.

"*Yes, but the other human was little. He wouldn't be able to drag that heavy carcass far.*"

"*Let's go to work.*" Tucker trotted out 150 yards from the barn and shouted back, "*We'll use the road as our rendezvous point, but remember, I'm on the farthest circle, so it will take me longer to get back here.*"

"*Okay.*" The two cats fanned out.

Murphy worked quietly. She found old smoothed-over bits of glass from long-ago bottles for poultices, worm remedies, even liquor. Here and there she turned up a rusted horseshoe or a rabbit's nest. She throttled her instincts to hunt.

They worked in silence for an hour. Murphy, on the second circle, came back about ten minutes after Pewter.

*"What'd you get?"*

Pewter shrugged. *"Ratholes and high-topped shoes."*

*"Come on."*

*"A piece of an upper, I think, anyway. Humans sure put their bodies into some pinchy clothes and shoes."*

*"Whee-ooo."*

The sound, to their right, sent them scrambling. Tucker sat on the edge of an old dump. Pieces of tractor stuck out through the brambles, which seemed to grow overnight.

*"What have you got?"* Pewter thought the graveyard of machines eerie.

*"Nothing, but wouldn't this be a great place to dump a body?"* Tucker said.

*"Yes, but we would have smelled it when we led Harry to the barn."* Mrs. Murphy marveled at how quickly brambles grow in the spring. They were already twirling through an old discarded hay elevator.

*"Yeah."* Tucker, disappointed, bulled through the thorns into the pile, her thick coat protecting her. *"I'll just nose around."*

*"No hunting, Tucker. We've resisted."*

*"Pewter, I wouldn't dream of it."*

The cats stuck around just in case. The strong, low-built dog pushed straight into the dump. She would nose through some of the debris, a delightful prospect.

Being next to mountains, the area had

shifted over the years with small tremors. A rusted truck, an ancient Chevy from the 1930s, had been turned on its side by quake tremors. Vines and rusting were slowly pulling it apart.

A faint but tantalizing odor curled in Tucker's nostrils. She sniffed around the truck, then started digging underneath it.

As she ripped into the soft earth, the corner of a sturdy, small suitcase appeared. It might once have sat on the seat of the truck but had probably slid out once the glass broke. Over the decades the truck had settled on top of it, and it was covered with fallen leaves and vines depositing layers of humus.

*"Found an old suitcase."*

*"So what?"* Pewter catcalled.

*"It's heavy leather, got steel corners. It has an alluring odor—faded, very faded."*

*"What's she babbling about?"* Murphy grumbled.

*"Let's go see."*

Tucker gave a hearty tug on the suitcase, then another.

The latch gave just a bit. She tugged some more.

*"Will you get back to work?"* Murphy circled around the worst of the brambles, crawling low to avoid the others. She walked over an old Massey-Ferguson tractor, then dropped onto the side of the Chevy.

*"I'm not going in there!"* Pewter shouted.

*"Who asked you?"* Then Tucker yelled again. *"Golly!"*

The cat stepped up as the dog sniffed the musty odor of old death.

The two friends blinked.

*"It's a tiny skeleton."* A bit of lace still hung over the skull. *"A tiny human skeleton!"* Mrs. Murphy gasped.

*"What will we do?"* Tucker's voice was almost a whisper.

*"Will you come out of there?"* Pewter paced, irritated to the point of putting up her tail.

*"We've found a skeleton,"* Murphy called out.

*"You're just saying that to get me in there."*

*"NO, we're not,"* they answered in unison.

Pewter paced, sat, paced, cursed, then finally crawled in. *"You're lying. I know you're lying."*

*"Look."* Mrs. Murphy leaned back.

*"Liar."* Nonetheless Pewter did look. *"Oh, no."* She sat down.

*"Nobody buries their baby in a suitcase."* Tucker was indignant.

*"You're exactly right."* Murphy licked the dog's ear.

*"Are you thinking what I'm thinking?"* Pewter asked.

*"Someone killed this little thing."* Mrs. Murphy sighed. *"Tucker, do you think we can pull the suitcase out of this rubble?"*

*"No."*

*"The rats will get at it, or raccoons."* Pewter felt quite sad. *"Can you cover it again?"*

*"Yes. It wasn't very deep. If you two help it won't take long."*

Tucker pushed the suitcase back, then turned around, throwing dirt on their discovery with her hind legs.

The cats threw dirt on it as well.

Once it was covered they took a breather, then crawled back out.

*"Let's go home,"* a subdued Pewter requested. *"We won't find Tommy Van Allen."*

# 26

At the eastern end of Crozet, on Route 240, the large food plant, which had been through successive corporate owners, dominated the skyline. On the south side of the white buildings ran the railroad tracks, a convenience should they need carloads of grain shunted off onto sidings. These days huge trailers pulled in and out of the parking lot, a sea of macadam. Each time a driver shifted gears a squelch of diesel smoke would shoot straight upward, a smoke signal from the internal-combustion engine.

The giant refrigerator trucks hauled the frozen foods to refrigerated warehouses from whence the product made it directly to the freezer sections of supermarkets.

Loading the behemoths in the docking area plunged men from cavernous freezers into the baking temperature outside and then into the long, cold trailers. This was not the most desirable job in the United States and many a Crozet High School graduate working on that platform rued the day he had decided not to try for college.

While a lot of the town's residents worked in the food factory, just as many did not. It was odd, really, how little social impact the big corporation had on the town except for creating traffic in the morning and then again at quitting time.

For a manager on the way up, Crozet was a good stop. Most deplored the small town, calling it Podunk or some other put-down. For those who weren't southern, the jolt of Virginia life came like unexpected turbulence at twenty thousand feet. Charlottesville, offering some cultural delights, was disdained because it wasn't Chicago, a fact that Charlottesvillians were keen to perpetuate.

Wilson C. McGaughey, thirty-two, ambitious, organized, and a student of time-management schemes, daily outraged those people working in his unit. Bad enough that he mocked their speech, called them slow and inefficient; now he'd taken to putting up flow charts for the workers' edification. Next to the flow chart and the weekly productivity quota McGaughey had what his underlings dubbed the Weenie List—workers who had excelled. Two were chosen each week. Next to that was the Shit List, the names of those who did the poorest work. If your name made the Shit List three times in one year Wilson fired you. Simple as that.

The huge refrigerated units were part of Wilson McGaughey's responsibility. The

154

freezers housed the raw foods that would be processed into turkey dinners or roast beef or linguini. Occasionally a bottle of shine or store-bought alcohol would be secreted in a back corner far from Wilson's eyes.

Dabney Shiflett, cousin to Market, didn't have a drinking problem as much as he had a specific thirst. A good worker, he nimbly sidestepped Wilson. Chewing Fisherman's Friend lozenges helped.

Dabney slipped away from the loading dock, telling his buddy he was heading to the bathroom. Instead he made straight for the meat locker in the back. He walked in and turned on the lights, revealing sides of beef hanging overhead. The back corner had a joist, slightly separated, providing the perfect place to wedge a slender flask of shine. He needed only a nip to feel wondrous warmth, a general flow of well-being. He hurried to the back, unscrewed the cap, and knocked back a healthy swallow. He opened his eyes, mid-pull. His mouth fell open, grain alcohol spilling onto his shirt. He dropped the flask, running flat out for the door.

# 27

"You won't mention the company? We aren't responsible." Wilson McGaughey pressured Rick Shaw. "Nobody could blame us."

"Facts are facts, Mr. McGaughey. The body was found in a Good Foods refrigerator."

Wilson, revulsion turning to anger, wheeled on Dabney. "Do you have something to do with this? It's bad enough you were drinking on company time—"

Rick interrupted, motioning for Dabney to follow him. "If you don't mind, Mr. McGaughey, I'd like to question Mr. Shiflett alone."

Wilson did mind but he held his tongue.

Rick took Dabney away from the corner where the corpse of Tommy Van Allen hung, by handcuffs dangling from a meathook. He'd been shot once in the temple, a neat job, very little mess. His Schauffenhausen watch remained on his wrist, his signet ring was on his finger, and $523, cash, was in his pants pocket along with his keys.

His glazed eyes were staring; his mouth hung open. But he was perfectly preserved, being frozen stiff.

"Now Dabney, pay that Yankee son of a bitch no mind."

"He's gonna fire me."

"He can try. Man can't be fired for finding a corpse."

At the mention of the word *corpse*, Dabney paled and began shaking. "I feel bad, Sheriff."

"It's a terrible shock."

"I didn't kill him."

"Didn't think you did." He clapped Dabney on the back. "How often is this meat locker checked?"

"Daily." He lowered his voice. "In theory. Maybe someone sticks their head in once a day.

156

But, you know, probably no one has walked all the way back here since Tommy's been missing."

"Unless they're in on it."

"Hadn't thought of that." Dabney was feeling better, as long as he didn't look at the body.

"Do you know anyone who might bear a grudge, who—"

"No. He didn't have anything to do with the company, Sheriff, other than building the new office wing, and that was eleven years back."

"I know you came back for a swig, Dabney. Why hadn't you come in here before?"

Dabney looked away from Rick. "Used up the rest of my stash. This was my last bottle until I refilled the others and started all over again." He lifted his head, his smile weak.

"And Wilson knew nothing?"

Dabney shook his head. "No."

"How long ago did you put your flask back here?"

"Uh...three weeks, I reckon. I dunno."

Rick wrinkled his forehead. "Go on, Dabney. I'm sorry you had to go through this. I might want to talk to you later."

Wilson McGaughey sidled up. "You have influence with the press—"

"McGaughey, you haven't lived here long enough to feel anything for that slab of human beef hanging back there, but let me tell you, as men go, he was a good man, not a perfect man, not always an even-tempered man, but a decent man." He stopped for breath. "I can't keep this out of the news. If you obstruct justice in any way, I'll have your ass. Am I clear?"

"Yes."

"You sounded like a New Yorker for a minute." Cynthia had been standing behind her boss.

He turned around. "Is that a compliment or an insult?"

"Depends."

"Mr. McGaughey, did you know the victim?"

"Only in passing." He clipped his words.

"Did you like him?" Rick felt his nose get colder by the minute.

"What little I knew of him, yes. He was a pleasant fellow."

"All right. You can go." Rick paused. "One last thing. Don't fire Dabney Shiflett."

"Man's got a problem." Wilson was furious that the redneck had put one over on him.

"He performs his duties."

"Drinking during work hours is against company regulations."

"Then get the man into a program. Don't fire him. He has three mouths to feed and he's a hard worker. I've known him all my life. If you want to get along in Crozet, work with people. Do you understand?"

Wilson understood that the sheriff was mad at him. But he didn't understand exactly what was being asked of him.

Cynthia spoke up. "The sheriff is saying that you will lower your productivity and maybe even harm your career if you don't learn that showing a little concern for your workers might boost morale. If Dabney was slacking off on the job, okay, then be a hard-ass. But help him. You might need help yourself someday."

"I'll take it under consideration." He walked off, nearly as stiff as Tommy Van Allen.

"Jesus, what a bonehead. And I'll bet he has his M.B.A.," Shaw said.

"Boss, this was in Van Allen's trench-coat pocket." Cynthia held a condom wrapper in her gloved hand.

"Any sign of the condom?"

"No."

"Coop, how do you think he got on that meathook?"

She shrugged. "He could have been hoisted up the same way they hoist the beef. Come on, I'll show you."

They walked outside and Cynthia pointed out a squarish machine used to move pallets loaded with heavy cartons; modified, the machine could also lift up sides of beef.

"Possible." He walked over. "How much does one of these things cost?"

"About sixteen thousand dollars retail."

"How do you know that?"

"Asked Wilson."

"Ah, yes, he'd know." He heard the gurney rolling down the outside walkway. "Coroner's good. Body may be frozen blue but I bet he can establish the time of death. What he can't establish is, was he killed here or brought here? And why here? Why not just dump him up in the waste unit like dead meat?" His voice rasped. "I have never seen anything like this in my years of law enforcement."

"Me neither."

He shot her a sharp glance. "You, you're still wet behind the ears."

"I've seen enough murders to know most of them are committed in a white-hot rage. This was not."

"The bomber jacket in Herb's truck was a neat trick, too. A little flag to let us all know we aren't on top of this case."

The gurney rolled past them, Tommy tucked into two body bags, since his arms were frozen straight up. Diana Robb, the paramedic, couldn't get him into one bag without breaking his arms, and that would compromise evidence.

She stopped as her coworkers continued to push the body to the ambulance. "Weighed a ton. Like moving a boulder."

"Better than shaking off the maggots that crawl up your leg. Those suckers bite." Rick hated that stench.

"You've got a point there. Never would have thought Tommy would end this way. I could have pictured a jealous husband shooting him maybe, but nothing like this."

"Nasty, isn't it?" Coop said.

"Yep." Diana grimaced, then rejoined her crew.

Rick half closed his eyes to hide his frustration.

# 28

Mrs. Murphy watched a bejeweled hand reach into the post-office box. Playfully she swatted.

Big Mim withdrew her hand. "Murphy, stop it."

*"Hee-hee."*

"Harry, your cat is interfering with federal property again." Mim reached in once more.

"Murphy, behave." Harry walked over to the postboxes. She peered through the brass box as Mim peered in from the other side. "Peek-aboo."

"Back at you!" Mim was in a good mood.

Aunt Tally, however, was not. "A sixty-two-year-old woman acting like a silly school-girl."

"I am not sixty-two."

"And I'm not ninety-three. Or is it ninety-one?" She sighed. "I've lied about my age for so many years, I can't remember how old I really am. But I remember exactly how old you are, Mimsy." A light hint of malice floated through her voice. "My sister said you kicked in the womb so hard you gave her a hernia."

The turned-up collar of Mim's expensive English-tailored shirt seemed to stiffen. "Harry and Miranda aren't interested in that."

"Oh yes we are," came the chorus, the animals included.

Tally leaned across the divider. "Urquharts conceive with no difficulty at all, of course." She called over her shoulder to Mim, sorting her mail, "And Little Mim gave you a couple of whacks." Mim ignored her, so she continued. "I never had children myself but I've spent a lifetime observing them—from birth to death sometimes. I've outlived everyone except my imperious niece and her daughter."

"I'm not imperious, Aunt Tally. That honor belongs to you."

"Oh la!" Tally's eyebrows rose, as did her voice.

Pewter, sound asleep on the table, was missing the exchange but Murphy and Tucker drank in every word.

"I never knew your mother," Miranda Hogendobber told Tally, "but everyone says she was beautiful."

"She was. Jamie got her looks and I got Daddy's brains. We'd have all been better off if that genetic package had been reversed." Jamie Urquhart was Tally's deceased brother. "Maybe not these days, but certainly in mine."

"You're fishing for compliments." Mim joined her at the wooden divider. "You looked good then and you look good now."

"Ha. Every plastic surgeon in America could work on me and I'd still look two years older than God." Her bright eyes darted to Miranda. "Sorry."

"That's quite all right."

"You're still a religious nut, I take it." Tally's smile was crooked and funny.

Miranda opened her mouth but nothing came out.

*"This is getting good."* Tucker giggled. *"Think we should wake up Pewter?"*

*"No, let her suffer. We can tell her every syllable and she'll scream that we made it up."* Mrs. Murphy ducked her head and rubbed it under Tucker's ruff. The cat had jumped off the eight-inch wooden divider behind the mailboxes to sit with the dog.

"Tally!" Mim admonished her.

"She is. She quotes the Scriptures more often and more accurately than those jackleg TV preachers. Ought to get *your* own TV show, Miranda. Make a bloody fortune." She threw back her head and laughed. " 'This moment of Jesus brought to you by General Motors. If the Good Lord were with us today he'd drive a Chevy. Trade in your sandals on a V-8.' "

All eyes fixed upon Tally, her red beret tilted at a rakish angle. Her eyes were merry, her lipstick disappearing into the crevices above her still-full lips.

*"Think Mrs. H. will pitch a hissy?"* Tucker took a step backward.

*"No. She'll chalk it up to advanced age, then go pray for her."* Murphy leapt onto the counter. *"Mim's face is crimson, though. Whoo-ee."*

"We'd better be going now." Mim put her hand under Tally's bony elbow.

"I'm not going anywhere until I hear what Miranda has to say. You were the cutest little girl in Crozet."

Harry looked at Miranda with new eyes. It

163

had never occurred to her that her friend might have once been cute, although she wasn't unattractive now—just plump.

Miranda cleared her throat. "I attend the Church of the Holy Light, from which I draw great comfort, Tally, but I don't think I'm a religious nut."

"You weren't like this while George lived. It's a substitute."

"Aunt Tally, that really is going too far." Mim stamped her Gucci-shod foot.

"I can say what I want, when I want. That's a benefit of advanced age. Not that you'll listen. Like Sir H. Vane getting shot. If you ask me, it's a wonder nobody shot that warthog earlier. All this drivel about being knighted. He hasn't done a damn thing. Probably made his money selling drugs to British rock stars."

"He was knighted. Susan and I got on the Internet to the library of the British Museum in London and searched through peers of the realm. Then we went to the London *Times* and pulled up a bio."

"You didn't tell me." Miranda was more upset by this omission than Tally's assault.

"Slipped my mind. Anyway, we did it over lunch hour."

"Well, what did you find out?" Mim demanded.

"He built airports throughout Africa in the countries formerly part of the British commonwealth. He built other things, too, but he made the millions building these airports. He is the genuine article."

"Oh, hell. I liked believing he was a fake."
Tally pouted.

Susan screeched up in her Audi station wagon and hopped out, forgetting to close the door. She was in her spandex workout clothes. She threw open the door to the post office.

"They found Tommy Van Allen!"

*"Pewter, wake up!"* Murphy jumped on the table to pat Pewter's face.

Grumbling, the fat kitty opened her eyes.

Tucker hopped up and down, trying to get closer to the humans. Harry opened the divider door for her to go out front as she and Miranda walked out to Susan.

"He was hanging in the big freezer room at Good Foods."

"What? Why hasn't Rick Shaw informed me?" Mim believed herself to be the first citizen of Crozet. And her husband was the mayor to boot.

"Mim, even Jim doesn't know," Susan breathlessly said.

"Then how do you come by this unsettling knowledge?" Tally asked.

"I dropped by Ned's office just as the phone rang. Dabney Shiflett was fired by his boss for drinking on the job. It was Dabney who found Tommy. He'd snuck into a meat locker for a quick nip and he found Tommy Van Allen hanging from a meathook by a pair of hand-cuffs. Frozen. Just totally frozen."

"My God." Mim couldn't believe it.

"Did Dabney tell Ned how he was killed?" Harry kept a cool head, as always.

"Yes. Shot straight through the temple.

'Neat as a pin,' Dabney said, 'neat as a pin.' Can you imagine?"

"People've been shot around here since gunpowder. Before that the Indians used bows and arrows, clubs and knives. Killing is one of our favorite pastimes," Tally flatly stated.

*"She's got a point there."* Pewter, riveted by the news, agreed with the old lady.

*"Yeah, but this is—"* Tucker was interrupted by Susan continuing.

"The only good thing is, he wasn't pinned on the meathook. At least he was hanging by handcuffs."

*"It's the handcuffs that worry me."* Murphy paced the counter.

*"Why?"* Tucker's pink tongue contrasted with her white fangs.

*"This was thought out. I wonder how long Tommy was alive wearing those handcuffs before he was killed?"*

Pewter flattened her ears, then swept them forward again. *"Torture?"*

*"Physical or psychological...or even sexual. Those handcuffs bother me."*

# 29

The other news of the day, not quite as shocking as the discovery of Tommy Van Allen, concerned Archie Ingram. When Deputy Cooper met him at the county offices to question him further about the shooting at Oak Ridge he asked her about the Van Allen murder.

He said he had heard about it on his C-band radio.

Cooper, suspicious as to how quickly information like that would get on the C-band, drilled him on this. He lost his temper and slugged her.

The county commissioner was sitting in the county jail for assaulting an officer. Bail wouldn't be set until the next morning.

Cynthia, glad to put Archie in his place, nonetheless called around to check Archie's story. Dabney Shiflett had put the news on C-band along with a most unflattering portrait of the man who had just fired him.

Since Wilson McGaughey drove a car, not a truck, and had no two-way radio, Dabney rightly figured it would be days before McGaughey learned what had been said about him. This small revenge gave Dabney some comfort.

# 30

Harry and Mrs. Hogendobber drove over to Tommy Van Allen's the evening of the body's discovery. His housekeeper, Helen Dodds, now in her late fifties, thanked them for their offer of help but was afraid to make any decisions until Tommy's estranged wife, Jessica, showed up. She was due in from Aiken, South Carolina, in the morning. Aileen Ingram, Archie's wife, joined them in the living room.

Mrs. Dodds said everyone had come by to

help—the Tuckers, Reverend Jones, Sarah Vane-Tempest, Mim and Little Mim, just everyone, no matter what was happening in their lives. She was grateful, she went on, and was only sorry Tommy hadn't known he had so many friends. Then she burst into tears.

Aileen, petite and curly-haired, put her arm around Helen's shoulders. "There, there, Helen. I'm so sorry for all this." She glanced up at Miranda. "Helen feels this is her fault."

Helen sobbed anew. "I always tried to keep track of Tommy's schedule but lately I've fallen behind and"—she dropped her voice—"he's been secretive."

Helen had been a dear friend of Aileen's now-deceased mother, and Aileen had remained close to the older woman. As soon as she heard the news of the body's discovery, she hurried to Helen's side.

"Helen, this isn't your fault. It may not even be Tommy's fault. Terrible things happen."

Before Miranda could guide Helen toward heavenly support, Helen startled everyone by shouting, "Well, I hope they get him. I hope whoever killed Tommy fries in the electric chair!"

Harry cut off any attempt by Miranda to describe the Lord's justice. "Helen, I'm sure Sheriff Shaw will get to the bottom of this. We all need to keep our eyes and ears open. The smallest thing may have significance."

Mrs. Murphy climbed out of the truck. Tucker was stuck in the cab, complaining bitterly. Pewter had stayed back at Market Shiflett's store to be picked up on the way home.

Tommy's fiery red Porsche 911 Targa was parked in the garage. Tommy, Vane-Tempest, and Blair Bainbridge had indulged in competitive consumption. Murphy sniffed the driver's-side door, the tires, the front and back of the machine. Not that she expected to find anything—just force of habit.

On her hind paws, she stretched her full height to look in the driver's window. The keys were in the ignition.

"Mrs. Murphy," Harry called.

The cat scampered back to the truck. Miranda was already in the passenger side, Tucker wedged between her and Harry. The cat soared onto Harry's lap, then snuggled next to Tucker.

Harry backed out, heading toward town. "It was good of Aileen Ingram to come by, considering her troubles."

"Archie needs to turn to the Lord. How much plainer must his message be?"

"Miranda, these days when people are in trouble they think of turning to a therapist if they think of anything at all."

"Won't work."

"I wouldn't know." They passed Boom Boom and waved. "My point proven."

"Mmm." Miranda let pass the opportunity to reprimand Harry for her snideness toward

Boom Boom. "I suppose Aileen was on her way to bail out Archie."

"If she had any sense she'd leave him in there."

" 'Whoever exalts himself will be humbled, and whoever humbles himself will be exalted.' " Mrs. Hogendobber quoted Matthew 23, Verse 12.

"Did that just pop into your head or is there a point toit?"

"Harry, don't be ugly."

"I'm sorry. You're right." She sighed heavily. "I'm upset. Seeing poor Mrs. Dodds break down like that—and what's going to happen to her? Who knows what's in Tommy's will or if he even had one."

"He had one. You don't run a big construction company without something like that. Probably had a fat insurance policy, too. I suppose Jessica will get all of it, even if they have separated."

"He could have changed his will."

"Yes, but they aren't legally divorced yet."

"What made you think of the Bible verse about pride?"

"Oh." Mrs. Hogendobber had forgotten to answer Harry's query. "Tommy, H. Vane, Blair, and even Archie. Ridley was part of it for a little while. It's a rich-boys' club. Expensive sports cars, airplanes..."

"Archie doesn't have that much money," Harry interrupted.

"Enough for a Land whatever-you-call-it."

"Land Rover." Harry paused. "I never

thought about that. I mean, it seemed discreet enough. White."

Cynthia Cooper's squad car was parked in front of the bank although it was after banking hours. Harry turned into the parking lot, pulling in front of the old brick freestanding bank building.

"Hey."

"Hey there." Cooper rolled down her window.

"We just came from Tommy Van Allen's. Poor Mrs. Dodds."

"And Aileen Ingram was there to help out." Miranda spoke over the animals' heads.

"She can't spring Archie until tomorrow."

"What?" both women said.

"The judge won't set bail until then."

"He can do that?" Harry wondered.

"He can do whatever he wants. He's the judge." Coop smiled.

"You've had a hard day," Miranda said sympathetically.

"I've had better ones." Cooper smiled weakly.

All heads turned as Sarah Vane-Tempest drove by with H. Vane-Tempest in the passenger seat.

"He's made a remarkable recovery," Miranda noted.

*"For how long?"* Mrs. Murphy cryptically said.

# 31

Sir H. Vane-Tempest had recovered suffi-
ciently to fight with his wife, who started it.

"Why are you protecting him?" Sarah tossed
her shoulder-length blond hair.

"I'm not protecting him."

"The man tried to kill you. I insist you
press charges."

"Sarah, my love, he was behind me. Hun-
dreds of men were behind me. Anyone could
have fired that shot."

"Archie had it in for you. The other hun-
dreds did not. Why are you protecting him?"

"I am not protecting him."

"Then what are you protecting?" She sat
across from him as he reclined on the sofa, more
tired from this exchange than from his physical trauma.

"Nothing. Why don't you fix me a real cuppa?
That tepid slop at the hospital was torture."

Angry but composing herself, Sarah walked
into the kitchen. It was six-thirty, and the
maid and cook had left for the day. However, she could brew an invigorating cup of tea
without help. She measured out the loose
Irish blend, placing it in the ceramic leaf tray
of the Brown Betty teapot. She shook her
head as if to return to the moment and brought
out two fragile china cups delicately edged in
rose gold. These had belonged to H. Vane's
mother. She hoped the sight of them would
improve his mood.

He beamed indulgently when she returned pushing the tea caddy. Scones, jams, white butter, and small watercress sandwiches swirled around the plate, a pinwheel of edibles. The cook made up scones and tea sandwiches fresh each day. The Vane-Tempests practiced the civilized tradition of high tea at four.

He eagerly accepted the cup filled with the intoxicating brew.

He put raw sugar, one teaspoonful exactly, into the cup.

"Ah." He closed his eyes in pleasure as he drank. "My dear, you are unsurpassed."

"Thank you." She sipped her cup of tea.

"My mother loved this china. It was given to her as a wedding present from her aunt Davida. Aunt Davida, you know, served as a missionary in China before World War I. I always thought she was a little cracked, myself, but her china wasn't." He lifted his eyebrows, waiting for the appreciative titter.

Sarah smiled dutifully. "H., you're awful."

Pleased, he replied, "You wouldn't have me any other way."

Sarah wanted to say that she'd be happy to have him forty pounds lighter, with a full head of hair, and perhaps twenty years younger. Some wishes were best left unsaid. "Darling, you're right. I knew from the first moment I saw you that I couldn't live without you."

He nibbled on a scone. "Americans do some things supremely well. Airplanes, for instance. They build good airplanes. However, they can't make a decent scone and they haven't a clue as to how to produce thick Devonshire cream. Odd."

"That's why you brought over a Scottish cook, yes?"

"Indeed." He reached for another scone. "They want their country back, you know. I read the papers front-to-back in the hospital. Just because I was slightly indisposed didn't mean I should alter my regimen. Why England would even want to *keep* Scotland or Wales is beyond me. And Ireland? Pfft." He made a dismissive motion with his hand.

"That's why we live here."

"Yes. Except here we have to listen to the bleatings of the underclass, interwoven as it is with color. Silly."

"Not to them," Sarah said a mite too tartly.

"Reading the speeches of Martin Luther King, my pet?"

She recovered. "No. What I'm saying is, there is no perfect place, but some are closer than others. And this is very close to heaven."

"Americans are too rude to develop proper tea culture. It takes a great civilization to do that: China, Japan, England. Do you know even the Germans are starting to get it?"

"With ruthless efficiency, I'm sure." She smoothed her dress skirt.

He held out his cup for a refill. "They aren't that efficient. That's a myth, my dear. I've done business with them for years."

"I never appreciated how good a businessman you were until you were nearly taken away from me."

"Oh?" He reveled in the compliment.

"You never discuss business with me."

"Dull, my darling. With you I savor the finer things in life: music, dance, novels. I adore it when we read together and I love it when you read to me. You have such a seductive voice, my sweet."

"Thank you. But I must confess, H., I rather like business. I read *The Wall Street Journal* when you're finished with it and I puzzle my way through *Süddeutsche Zeitung* sometimes. I wish I had gone further in school."

"Beauty is its own school."

"The more I know, the more I admire your acumen."

He placed the cup on the tray. "Sarah, building airports is not a suitable venue for a woman."

"But darling, you don't do that anymore. Now you invest in the stock exchange, here and in London. And you have other irons in the fire. It's fascinating. You're fascinating." She stood up and pressed her hands together, standing quite still. "If you had died, if that fool had killed you, I would have been totally unprepared to administer your empire."

He guffawed. "That's what I pay lawyers for and—"

"But who will watch them? You may trust them. Why should I?"

"Really, my dear, they would serve you as faithfully as they have served me."

"Henry, my experience of life is that each time money changes hands it sticks to somebody's fingers. That army you pay is loyal to you—not to me. And there is the small matter of your ex-wife and your two daughters residing in palatial splendor in England. Well, I forgot, Abigail is in Australia now, in outback splendor."

"My ex and my daughters are provided for. They can't break my will and they'd be fools to try because the astronomical costs would jeopardize their resources. I pay the best minds on two continents. Rest yours."

"No. I want to be included."

"Sarah, you have twenty thousand dollars a month in play money. You can do whatever you like."

"That's not what I'm asking and I am not impugning your generosity to me. What I want is to understand your business holdings."

"I—" Flummoxed, Vane-Tempest began to stutter.

Still standing with her hands pressed together, Sarah half whispered, "Because I did not know whether you would live or die, I sat at your desk and I read your papers. I opened the safe and I read the papers in there. You are an amazing man, Henry, and I don't even know the half of it. I only know what you're doing here in Albemarle County. I haven't a single idea of what you may be doing in Zimbabwe or New Zealand or Germany. I do know you avoid the French like the plague."

His mouth twitched. "I see."

"You formed a corporation with Tommy Van Allen, Archie Ingram, and Blair Bainbridge, I learned. Teotan Incorporated. To date Teotan has purchased over two million dollars' worth of land. I had no idea Archie Ingram had resources at that level. The others, of course, aren't paupers, although no one is in your league."

His eyes narrowed. "Archie put up sweat equity."

"Archie is your conduit to and from Richmond. I'm not in your league either, H., but my brain does function. Archie is a county commissioner. He could point toward those areas that the state will develop or claim for highways and bypasses. Am I correct?"

"Yes."

"And now he has cold feet."

"Yes."

"If the full extent of his participation is discovered, he will certainly lose his seat and may even be raked over the coals, politically and legally, for peddling influence. I believe that's the term for it."

"Precisely."

"Is that what he's been fighting about?"

Sir H. Vane-Tempest sat for a moment. His beautiful wife, that trophy of all trophies, surprised him. He'd been married to the woman for seven years and he'd had no idea her mind was this good. She shocked him. He

177

was also shocked at his own blindness. He had discounted her. Oh, he loved her, he lusted after her, but he had discounted her.

He drew a deep breath. "In part, Sarah, that is what we have been fighting about. Archie is a coward. He wanted the money and he has been handsomely paid by the three of us in terms of his share of the corporate profits. He has a ten-percent share. On top of that we pay him an annual stipend through a complicated trust that I set up, one that leaves no trail to him. I'm too tired to go into the details."

"Some other time, my love?"

His eyes brightened under his ginger brows. "Some other time. Yes."

"But Archie had to have known what he was doing."

"He did. As the county hearings and various other meetings heated up he realized that if his involvement with Teotan ever saw the light of day these grillings would be as little minnows to the whale of discontent, to paraphrase Boswell on Johnson."

"Is there more?"

He shrugged. "He's having problems in his marriage. Tupping some damsel, I should think. That's usually what happens. I don't know who the unfortunate might be. Archie has little to offer, although I suppose he's handsome to women."

"There's no accounting for taste. Some country girl might be thrilled to be sleeping with a county commissioner." She burst out laughing, the silver, tinkling, infectious sound filling the room.

This made Vane-Tempest laugh, too.

Sarah, still smiling, said, "Darling, I want to be part of Teotan."

"Everything comes to you when I die."

"I want to work with you. I want to learn. I don't want to wait until you die. And I want to know why you men have been buying these properties."

"I'm tired." He was, too.

"You can't avoid this. Henry, I want to learn. I've watched you. You can turn a shilling into a pound and a pound into a fortune. I do know that before you built those airports in Africa you bought the land on which they were built."

"Ah." He smiled. "You've been doing your homework."

"Yes."

"Have you studied a map of this county?"

"I have, which is why I want to know why you have bought the particular lands you have bought. There seems to be no rhyme or reason to it."

"Have you spoken to Blair or Archie or Tommy about any of this?"

"Of course not. And I'll never speak to Tommy again. He was found hanging in a refrigerated vault at Good Foods today."

"What!" Vane-Tempest's eyes seemed to bug out of his head.

"Gruesome, isn't it?"

"Why didn't you tell me before?"

"I thought you could hear about it tomorrow. I wanted tonight just for our business. But it occurs to me, darling, that Tommy's death *is* our business."

"In what way?"

"He was a partner in Teotan. He's been murdered and someone tried to kill you. Which is why you must prosecute Archie. You must. He'll strike again. Don't you see? If he kills each of you he's safe. Not only will he cover his tracks, he'll reap the profits of whatever you all have created—you saved him with that trust, that untraceable trust."

"I don't believe it," Vane-Tempest blurted. "Archie Ingram isn't smart enough to do that."

"Weren't you worried when Tommy disappeared?"

"No. Off on a toot, I thought. Slumming." He grimaced. "And then I had other things to think about. I haven't given Tommy much thought. Hanging? Did he hang himself?"

"Sheriff Shaw isn't forthcoming with the details but it's all over town, mostly because the manager of the plant fired the man who found him. Said he was remiss in his duties. And that man, Dabney Shiflett, has been babbling nonstop. I really don't know the details. But Tommy didn't hang himself. Now will you pick up the phone and call the sheriff?"

"No, but I will pick up the phone and call Ingram."

180

She stepped toward him, stooping down to meet his eyes. "Henry, if that man makes one move to harm you, I will kill him."

Secretly excited by her ardor, he replied, "That won't be necessary. Archie Ingram has neither the intelligence nor the guts to pull off a scheme such as you imagine. As for Tommy's death, I wouldn't rush to conclusions. His demise and my—well— accident are unrelated."

"Will you include me in Teotan?"

"Yes. But I must discuss this with Blair Bainbridge—"

She pressed her hands together again. "Unless someone kills him, too!"

"Calm down, Sarah. I must have the approval of the other partners, and that includes Archie. As for Tommy, the corporation is set up so that if one principal dies, his share is parceled out equally among the survivors."

"You can't ask for the vote of a man who tried to kill you!" Her eyes were wild.

"I can and I must. Now if you would bring me the handy, I will arrange a meeting."

She gave him the cell phone. He dialed and got Archie's answering machine. "Hello, H. Vane-Tempest here for Archie Ingram. Call tomorrow after nine. Good-bye." He folded the phone, putting it on the tea trolley. "Now I can't very well call Sheriff Shaw, can I?" He paused, a dark shift clouding his features. "I liked Tommy Van Allen. Did you?"

"Yes."

"Terrible thing."

She settled on the chintz sofa, squeezing in next to him. "Henry, you must be careful. You must. I don't want to lose you."

"Promise." He leaned forward and kissed her.

# 32

Lilacs surrounded the brick patio behind Archie's house in Ivy Farms. Once, open meadows had surrounded the strong-running Ivy Creek, before the property was developed in the early seventies. Now dotted with upper-middle-class homes and manicured grounds, the area had lost all vestiges of its farming heritage.

Aileen Ingram, director of the Jefferson Environmental Council, made a decent salary. She poured what extra money she had into their home and garden. Archie was appreciative of her domestic gifts and he appreciated her. Her fine qualities only exacerbated his guilt.

Sitting on the Brown Jordan lawn chair, smelling the profusion of lilacs, he was startled when she appeared at his side.

"I must have been half-asleep."

"Arch, bail was twenty-five hundred dollars. Blair Bainbridge lent me the money and I don't even know why he offered to help. Your lawyer's bills will be double that. I don't know what's wrong. You won't talk to me. I don't think you talk to anyone. You're unraveling. Resign as county commissioner before it's too late."

"Too late for what?"

"Your political career is over. Get out with as much good grace as you can."

"No."

"You're mad."

"No, I'm not. The worst I've done is lose my temper."

"Smashing Cynthia Cooper in the face was stupid."

He crossed his right foot over his left knee, holding his ankle. "I have one year left of my term. I won't run again. It would cost the county too much money to run an election in an off year."

"The mayor would appoint an interim commissioner."

"You've been scheming behind my back!"

"No. I've been trying to save what I can of your reputation." She twisted her wedding ring, thin gold, around her finger. "But I don't think I can save our marriage. That takes two."

"What's that supposed to mean?"

"I'm not an idiot. I know there's another woman—or women. You don't hang around Tommy Van Allen or Blair Bainbridge without partaking of their castoffs."

"I resent that!" He blushed.

"Because I nailed you or because I insulted you by indicating you're playing with their discards instead of seducing a woman on your own merits?" Steel was in her voice. "Your vanity is touching, under the circumstances."

"I admit I have feet of clay. I don't like myself much but"—he warmed to his subject—"I am trying to salt away money for us. A lot of money. I need one more year. Then I'm off the commission. I won't waste my life in these dull meetings with people picking at everything I say or do. I can apply myself to other pursuits, like making you happy again."

"Better to have money than not but I am not waiting a year for you to get your act together. You've lied to me."

"I have not."

"Omission is a kind of lie."

"What man is going to come home and announce to his wife that he's having an affair? I said I wasn't proud of myself." He dropped his eyes, then raised them. "Did you hire a detective?"

"No. Any detective I could hire around here would know the sheriff. If someone tailed you Rick Shaw would find out in a heartbeat. He's on the county payroll. You're a commissioner. I swallowed my pride and my curiosity."

"I'm sorry, Aileen."

"So am I."

"I can't resign. I can explain it later, but not now. I have to stay on and I have to keep my lines to Richmond open."

"You're a political liability now."

"I'm under a dark cloud, but it's passing.

And at the next open meeting at the end of the month I am unveiling a workfare plan that will employ people and create new housing. It's a good plan and won't cost the county much at all. One-cent surcharge on luxury purchases inside the county."

She wondered if he was a blockhead or purposefully opaque. "Intriguing. Archie, I want you out of the house. If you can resolve this affair, clear up your garbage, then we can talk."

"You can't throw me out of my own house."

"I can and I will. Your clothes are packed. Your computer is in the black-and-white box along with your disks. Everything is neatly stacked in the rented U-Haul in the garage, which is attached to your Land Rover. If you aren't out of here by noon I'm calling the sheriff. I figure it will take you that long to pack whatever else you might want."

"And what's the sheriff going to do?" Archie was belligerent.

"Throw you out, because I'm going to accuse you of wife beating. That will be the end of your career. Totally."

He hurried to the garage. She wasn't kidding. There was a loaded U-Haul. He dashed into the kitchen. Aileen was unloading the dishwasher.

"Where am I going to live?"

"Blair Bainbridge said he'd put you up in his extra bedroom. Failing that, there's an apartment for rent on Second Street off High. Seven hundred and fifty dollars a month.

The number is on a Post-it on your steering wheel." She closed the dishwasher door. "And I informed your mother."

"Why don't *you* run the world?"

"I could."

# 33

The *Daily Progress* spread over the table carried the Tommy Van Allen story on the front page. Pewter sat on the paper. The big news was that cocaine was found in his blood.

The post office buzzed. People were in shock but everyone had a theory. No one was quite prepared for the sight of Tommy's widow, Jessica, cruising down Main Street behind the wheel of Tommy's blazing-red Porsche.

Harry and Mrs. Murphy noticed her first. "She could have waited until he was cold in the ground." Realizing what she'd said, she quickly added, "Sorry."

The group crowding into the post office all talked at once. The Reverend Jones was still upset that Tommy's bomber jacket was discovered on his truck seat. Big Mim declared that no one had manners anymore so they shouldn't be shocked at the behavior of Mrs. Van Allen—formerly of Crozet and now hailing from Aiken. It was rumored she had a polo-player lover who had discreetly stayed back in South Carolina. Tally Urquhart sorted her mail. Sarah Vane-Tempest suggested the whole world had gone nuts. Susan Tucker warned people about jumping to conclusions.

When Blair walked in, Big Mim button-holed him at once.

"What do you think?"

"It's macabre," he replied.

"Not that. What do you think of—" She stopped mid-sentence because she had spotted Archie Ingram driving by, pulling a U-Haul trailer behind his Land Rover. "What in the world?"

Blair swallowed. "Damn. Pardon me, Mrs. Sanburne. I've got to go."

"Blair, your mail," Harry called out.

He shut the door, not hearing her.

"Isn't that the most peculiar thing?" Miranda Hogendobber walked out to the door.

Cynthia Cooper pulled up, as did Ridley Kent, dapper even in an old tweed jacket. He bowed and opened the door for her as Miranda stepped back. Cooper wished Ridley's courtesies presaged genuine interest but she knew they did not.

Everyone said their hellos.

"I knew I'd find the gang here," Cynthia muttered, walking over to her mailbox.

Tucker sat outside the front door. She figured the cats could tell her who said what to whom. She wanted to watch the cars and pick up tidbits of conversation in the parking lot.

"Herb, when's the service?" Mim asked.

"Thursday at ten."

Mrs. Murphy sat next to Pewter on the divider counter, both cats careful to avoid the burgundy stamp pad.

"Why haven't you arrested Archie Ingram?" Sarah pursued Cynthia.

"We did yesterday. He's out on bail today."

The silence was complete.

*"For murder?"* Mrs. Murphy asked.

All eyes swiveled to the cat, who meowed, then back to Cooper, her left cheek covered with a reddish bruise soon to turn other colors. Cynthia walked over and petted Murphy and Pewter.

"I don't mean for hitting you—I mean for shooting my husband." Sarah's pleasant voice turned shrill.

"Mrs. Vane-Tempest, we don't know that," Cynthia said simply.

Ridley Kent spoke up, his rich baritone filling the room. "We're all worried. How could we not be?" He glanced around the group for affirmation. "We're all here now. Why don't we put our heads together?"

Mim, usually the group organizer, coolly appraised the usurper. "Good idea."

Ridley, appreciating his mistake, deferred to the Queen of Crozet. "With your permission, Mim. You're better at this kind of thing than any of us."

She smiled and stepped forward. "The circumstances of Tommy's death are still unknown, are they not?"

Cynthia nodded. "We know he was shot in the head, just as the paper tells you. It will take a while to establish the time of death because he was perfectly preserved, you see. But he did have coke in his blood."

"I don't care about Tommy. He's gone to his reward. I care about Henry. What if the killer comes back for him?" Sarah's eyes filled.

"Is it possible it was an accident?" Herb suggested, not believing that it was.

"Three shots? No." Ridley folded his arms across his chest.

"Is there a connection between Sir H. Vane-Tempest and Van Allen? Something that one of us might have overlooked?" Harry interjected.

"On the surface, no, but we're digging," Cynthia replied. "These things take time, and I understand your frustration. Be patient."

"Wouldn't it make sense to question the people who sold the guns and uniforms?" Harry thought out loud. "Maybe there's something peculiar. You've tested Archie's Enfield rifle, and other people's rifles,"—she nodded to the assembled—"but what about other suppliers? Whoever shot H. Vane had to come up with the stuff. He had to have contact with these people."

"Along with every other re-enactor. But yes, we are chasing them down one by one. I had no idea that Civil War reenactments were this precise."

"Obsessive," Sarah said curtly.

"Do you know of any connection between Tommy Van Allen and your husband, other than social?" Herb asked Sarah.

"No," she lied.

"Doesn't Mrs. Woo make period uniforms?" Harry remembered the seamstress with a small shop behind Rio Road Shopping Center.

"She does everything." Mim nodded. "She can whip up a dress from the 1830s that would fool a museum curator. She made a lot of the uniforms."

"She's on our list. We haven't gotten there yet. Initially we concentrated on the firearms people, hoping we could trace the rifle since we have two bullets, one intact and one flattened, the one that lodged against Sir Vane-Tempest's shoulder blade. The third one is missing."

"Arrest Archie Ingram." Sarah pounded the table, making the cats jump.

"Mrs. Vane-Tempest, you can't imagine the pleasure that would give me, but I can't arrest him without evidence."

"He was behind my husband."

"So was I," Ridley said. "So were Blair, Herb, and half of Crozet."

"You don't care what happens to Henry. You don't like him!" Sarah shouted.

"Ma'am, I abide by the laws of the land and I can't arrest Archie Ingram. Not without compelling evidence."

Herb raised his impressive voice. "What's important is we've got to communicate with one another. If we see anything untoward, call the sheriff or the deputy. Call one another."

"Do you think we're all in danger?" Mim neatened her mail stack. She wasn't frightened as much as she was curious.

"No," Cynthia replied.

"Lucky you." Sarah, furious, stalked out of the post office.

This set everyone off again. Ridley Kent hurried after her.

Tucker listened intently, then came in by the back animal door. *"She's hot."*

The cats jumped down to join her. *"Can't blame her."*

*"What did you make of Blair running out like that when he saw Archie?"* Pewter asked the dog.

*"He folded himself into that car and flew down the road in the direction of home. Makes me wonder."*

*"Let's go over there tonight after work,"* Murphy suggested.

*"Yes, let's,"* Pewter chimed in.

One by one the townspeople left. Cynthia, Tally, and Mim lingered.

Miranda made Tally a bracing cup of tea, as she was flagging a bit.

"Not every question has an answer." The old lady sipped her tea, straight.

"I think they do. But we don't always want to hear it." Mim contradicted her aunt.

"Speak for yourself."

"No one wanted to know the answer when Jamie shot Biddy Minor." Big Mim hated being contradicted, even by Tally—or especially by Tally. "Every place has unsolved crimes because people don't want to know."

"What good would it do to know? Everyone is dead. How they arrived at that state is irrelevant!" Tally snapped.

The cats knew better than to leap on the table with Tally present. They hung out in the canvas mail cart instead, heads peeping over the top. Tucker sat under the table.

"Moonshine," Harry called over her shoulder as she emptied the wastebasket into a plastic garbage bag. "I know that's not the reason but that was the excuse given."

"My brother didn't make any more moonshine than anyone else in Albemarle County in those days," Tally said. "Bad blood."

"Had to be awfully bad if Jamie shot him," Miranda said. "Both such handsome men. I've seen their pictures."

"Never see their like again." Tally stared off in the distance.

"Didn't Jamie have a gambling problem?" Big Mim asked her aunt.

"Mim, my brother had many problems. You name it—gambling, horses, women, wine. Prudence was not his watchword."

"Wasn't Tommy Van Allen's either." Harry, finished with her chore, leaned on the sink behind them.

"Somewhat similar personalities. You'd have thought it would have been Jamie who got shot, not Biddy. Biddy was a sensible man most ways." Tally allowed Miranda to refill her cup.

"Guess we'll never know." Harry walked to the divider and folded up the newspaper. The back section fell on the floor. She picked it up without reading it.

"People do terrible things. They just do," Tally said. "We're animals with a gloss of manners."

*"I resent that."* Murphy's tail twitched.

Harry opened a jar of Haute Feline, giving each cat a fishy.

*"Hey."*

She handed Tucker a Milk-Bone.

"You remind me of your great-grandfather, Mary Minor. You have his eyes and you have his curiosity."

"Did you like my great-grandfather?"

"I adored him. Had a schoolgirl crush. Biddy was the handsomest man. Curly black hair and those snapping black eyes. And the biggest smile! He could light a room with that smile. He bet on horses and cards, chickens...everyone did. He and Jamie bred fighting cocks together. Often wondered if that wasn't it. But it wasn't moonshine, I'm sure of that."

"Where'd they fight chickens?" Miranda said. "Didn't you have a pit out on the farm? Oh, I barely remember. My momma wouldn't allow me anywhere near."

"A beautiful pit out by the back barn." She pointed to Harry. "Out where you found the airplane. Nothing left of it anymore. It's full of rusted trucks and tractors. All illegal now." She shrugged.

After Mim and Tally and Cynthia left, Harry picked up the paper to throw it into the garbage bag. She glanced at the back page. "Miranda, did you read this?"

"What?"

They bent over the story. A big photo of a golden retriever behind the wheel of a Dodge Ram made them giggle.

Harry read aloud. " 'Maxwell, a golden retriever owned by Stuart Robinson of Springfield, Massachusetts, received a ticket today for driving without a license. Robinson said the dog was in the cab of the truck when he got out at the gas station, leaving the motor running. He doesn't know how but Maxwell drove the truck down the street, finally running into a mailbox.' "

Miranda laughed. "Art Bushey will kidnap that dog and put him behind the wheel of a Ford."

They laughed harder.

Pewter said, *"I could drive a truck if I had to."*

*"You could not,"* Tucker said. *"You don't have the strength to hold the steering wheel."*

*"I do so."*

*"She could."* Mrs. Murphy took Pewter's part.

*"I'll believe it when I see it."*

After work the cats crawled into the parked truck and practiced.

*"This is harder than I thought,"* Pewter confessed.

*"Yeah, and we aren't even moving."* Murphy laughed until she rolled over.

*"Come on, let's go over to Blair's."*

# 34

The cats reached the deep creek separating Harry's land from Blair's before Tucker caught up with them.

Running flat out, she skidded to a stop, her hind end whirling around, leaving a semi-circle in the grass. *"Cheaters!"*

194

*"You were asleep."*

*"I was not. I was resting my eyes."*

*"Sure."* Pewter viewed the steep bank with zero enthusiasm, but vaulted over.

Archie Ingram's U-Haul was parked next to the divine Porsche.

The animals inspected it thoroughly, then Murphy bounded onto the Porsche, leaving delicate paw prints on the hood and roof.

*"Babe magnet."* She leaned over from the roof and stared inside at the luscious leather.

*"He hardly needs that."* Tucker sniffed the tires. *"He's been over to Little Mim's. That ridiculous Brittany spaniel of hers has marked it."*

*"You can't stand him because he's perfectly groomed."*

*"Murphy, that's silly."* Tucker turned her back on the cat and walked to the house.

*"You can't go in there without us."* Pewter fell in next to the dog.

*"Don't go in,"* Murphy commanded as she carefully slid off the car.

*"Why not?"*

*"We'll interrupt them."*

*"They won't pay any attention to us. Blair will open the door, feed us something, and then go back to whatever he was doing."* Pewter pulled open his back porch door, which was easy since it was warped.

*"The truth comes out."* Murphy whapped her paw from the door. *"Listen to me. Don't you find it odd that Archie Ingram has pulled into Blair's driveway with a U-Haul? You and I should climb*

*up in the tree. We can see everything—the windows are open. "*

*"You climb in the tree. I'm sitting on the kitchen windowsill. "* Pewter walked to the window and jumped up on the sill.

If there hadn't been a screen in the window she would have vaulted into the kitchen.

*"What about me?"*

*"Tucker, I'll open the door for you a crack. Lie down with your nose in the door. You can see and hear everything that way. If they notice you, act glad to see them and go right in. I'm staying in the tree. "*

Pewter watched as Blair brewed coffee. His top-of-the-line machine cost more than the industrial Bunn at Market's store. A pint of cream sat on the counter next to it. Archie was slumped in a chair at the table, his head resting in one hand.

"Come on, Arch, this will start your motor again."

Archie sighed, toying with his cup. "Yeah."

"Will you snap out of it? She didn't shoot you. She isn't running around town telling tales." He handed him the cream. "You're being given a vacation to sort things out."

"Yeah." He drank some coffee.

"Good?"

"Yeah."

"Dazzle me, Arch. Vary your vocabulary. How about 'Yes'?"

The corner of Archie's mouth curved up. "Yes." He drank more coffee.

"If this doesn't enliven you we'll have to look for cocaine," Blair joked.

"People are saying that's why Tommy was killed. That you and Van Allen bring in cocaine in the hubcaps of your Porsches."

"People will say anything."

Archie shrugged. "You use it?"

"I have in the past. I don't now."

"Get you in trouble?"

"No." Blair sat across from him. "I saw it get a lot of other people in trouble and figured I'd quit while I was ahead."

"Aileen wants me to resign my seat on the county commission."

"Not a good idea." Blair drained his cup, rose to pour another.

"H. would shoot me." Archie laughed a dry laugh. "That damned Sarah is screaming all over the county that I shot H. Christ, I wouldn't shoot him. Strangle him, maybe, but not shoot him."

"What went down between you two? One minute you were—"

Archie slapped the table with his open palm, startling Blair and the watching animals. "I got sick of taking his shit. Who was taking all the risks? Me! Whatever I did wasn't enough. He wanted to know more and he wanted it yesterday. Damn, how many times can I run up and down the road to Richmond?"

"Our peer of the realm likes to give orders." Blair checked the time on the old railroad clock on the wall, a duplicate of the one in the post office. It was six-thirty.

"If my involvement comes out, I'm down the tubes."

"Don't be so dramatic," Blair admonished him. "The law is murky in this area. Someone would have to prove that you abused your office for personal gain. Furthermore, the information you passed on to us concerning road development is public knowledge."

"The timetable is not public knowledge."

"Yes, it is."

"The *real* timetable," Archie shot back, in no mood for Blair's rebuke.

"So? It would have to be proved. Archie, for chrissake, you knew what you were getting into. Information is bought and sold every day in every profession. If you're smart enough to get on the inside track, you win." Blair, leaning against his refrigerator, shoved his hands into his back pockets. "We're almost finished with our buying. All that's left is the Catlett property. But even without it, we're in good shape. After that, Arch, it's all over but the shouting."

"It's the shouting I'm worried about."

"Toughen up. Are you hungry?"

"I've lost my appetite."

"*I haven't,*" Pewter called from the windowsill.

"*You ditz!*" Murphy would have boxed her ears if she could. Pewter had no restraint.

The cat's meow startled the two men.

Blair laughed. "Pewter, you shameless eavesdropper."

Tucker pushed open the door, waltzing in. *"Hi."*

"Wonder if Harry's around?" Archie rose, walking outside to check. He came back in. "No, but I hear her on the tractor."

"That thing is a museum piece." Blair put out cream for Pewter and gave Tucker stale bread he'd been saving for the birds.

Furious, Mrs. Murphy backed down the tree, practically vaulting into the kitchen. *"Idiots!"*

*"Party pooper."* Pewter licked her lips; a drop of cream dribbled from her chin.

The aroma of rich cream overcame Murphy's scruples. She hopped up next to Pewter.

"Full house." Blair scratched the base of Mrs. Murphy's tail.

"Damn cat." Archie, eyes squinting, glared at Murphy.

"She had a big time at the meeting." Blair laughed.

Archie held on to his coffee cup with both hands as though it might fly away. "Do you think Sarah cheats on H.?"

Blair raised an eyebrow. "I wouldn't know."

"Ridley said she was going at it with Tommy." Archie, cunning, did not divulge that Ridley also told him Sarah had slept with Blair.

"Was Ridley drunk or sober?"

"Sober."

"I don't know." He did know, of course, because Tommy had told him about the affair, but Blair had given his word not to repeat it. "Sex gets us all into trouble."

The phone rang. Blair picked it up. "Hello." Then he covered the mouthpiece. "H. Vane."

Archie got up and put his ear to the receiver. Murphy joined them. Archie pushed her away but she was persistent.

"Blair, I'd like to have a meeting with you and Archie tomorrow at three. Can you make it?"

"Yes."

"What about Arch? I know he's with you. He drove past the post office and people saw you run out. You know how small this town is."

"He'll be there."

Archie grabbed the phone. "I'll be there."

"Did you shoot me?"

"No."

"I didn't think so."

"Where's Sarah? I can't believe she'd let you call me after the stuff she's saying."

"She drove down to the market. The way she drives, that will take two minutes. I figured I'd call while I could."

"How will you get away for a meeting? And where do you want to have it?" Blair asked.

"Your place. I can drive."

*"Goody,"* Murphy told the others. *"H. Vane will be here tomorrow at three for a meeting."*

*"We'll be at work."* Tucker was disappointed.

*"Leave that to me."* Murphy strained to hear more.

"If Sarah knows you're going to meet with me she'll bring out the cannon," Archie said.

"She'll do what I tell her. I pay the bills, remember?"

"I remember," Archie replied, a splash of acid in his tone.

# 35

"Where is that cat?" Harry opened closet doors to make certain she hadn't shut the nosy Mrs. Murphy in one.

The phone rang. Harry figured the caller was Miranda or Susan, early risers like herself. Sometimes Fair called after returning home from an all-night emergency.

It was six o'clock. She'd been up for half an hour.

"Good morning, camper, zip, zip, zip. We sing a song to start the day."

Before Harry could launch into the second obnoxious lyric, Mrs. Hogendobber tersely said, "More violence."

"What?"

"Mrs. Woo's shop burned down. They think it's arson."

"I don't believe it."

"On the news. If you'd ever turn on your television, you'd...Just turn it on. It's the lead story on Channel 29. Her shop burned to a crisp."

"Roger. See you at work." Harry hung up, stretched over the counter, and clicked on the small TV, which she hated with all her heart. Since Fair had given it to her for her birthday this year she couldn't toss it out.

"...high today expected to be seventy-two degrees Fahrenheit, a light breeze from the

201

south, clouds moving in tonight, and a fifty-percent chance of rainfall after midnight. Back to you, Trish." Robert Van Winkle, the weatherman, smiled.

Soberly facing the camera, the young woman said, "Our top story this morning, Expert Tailoring Shop behind Rio Road Shopping Center was burned to the ground last night. Nothing is left except the charred remains. Chief Johnson says…"

The fire chief faced the camera in the tape from the night before. "We are fully investigating this incident. If anyone saw or heard anything out of the ordinary in the area around two o'clock in the morning, please call the fire department." He rattled off the number, which was shown on the screen.

"Do you think it was arson?"

Pure frustration on his face, Ted Johnson spoke directly into the camera. "We are investigating all possibilities." He repeated himself. "If you have any information concerning these events, please call our hotline. It's manned twenty-four hours a day." The number ran again several times at the bottom of the screen.

"Then you have no leads?"

"I have nothing further to say at this point." He turned his back on the camera.

"What in holy hell is going on?" Harry exclaimed. "Mrs. Woo is the sweetest person in the whole county."

Murphy popped out from behind the sofa where she was hiding.

"*Mrs. Woo had her shop torched,*" Pewter yelled out.

"*I know. I heard the TV.*"

"Where have you been?" Harry glared at Mrs. Murphy.

"*Hiding. I need to stay on the farm today.*" She was determined to attend the 3:00 P.M. meeting at Blair Bainbridge's.

"Here." Harry opened another can of cat food.

Pewter sidled over next to Murphy. "*Mariner's Pride.*"

"*Butt out,*" Murphy growled.

Harry scooped a big spoonful into Pewter's oatmeal-colored crockery dish.

UPHOLSTERY DESTROYER was painted on Mrs. Murphy's dish, while Tucker's read SUPER DOG.

"*This goes back to the reenactment at Oak Ridge.*" Tucker stated. She sat down while the cats ate and Harry dialed Susan Tucker to discuss the latest news.

"*The new guys had to have uniforms made or altered in a hurry. Everybody went to Mrs. Woo. She knew who was in that reenactment,*" Pewter said.

"*Yes, but so do Herb Jones, H. Vane-Tempest, Rick Shaw—each company commander has a list of men. That's what's sticking in my craw. We know!*" Mrs. Murphy pushed her food bowl away.

"*Mrs. Woo had to know something.*"

"*It could be unrelated, Tucker.*" Pewter pounced on Murphy's rejected food.

"*Don't talk with your mouth full. Humans do that. Vile.*" Murphy sniffed.

"*Miss Manners.*" Pewter swished her tail once.

"*Listen to me. Tucker, you go with Mother. Stick with her no matter what. We've got to stay here today.*"

"*Only one of you needs to go to the meeting.*"

"*Both Pewter and I need to read the map. Really study it.*" Mrs. Murphy sat still like the famous Egyptian statue of the cat with earrings in its ears.

"*Why are you so worried?*" Tucker cocked her head.

"*Because Harry found the airplane—my fault. And because Harry suggested checking out all the suppliers for Civil War re-enactors. Remember? She mentioned gun sales, uniforms. She's eventually going to go one step too far.*"

"*She'd better carry her gun,*" Pewter sagely advised.

"*Let's mention that to her.*" Mrs. Murphy rubbed against Harry's arm while she was speaking to Susan. "*Carry your side arm.*"

"*She's—*" Pewter's attention was diverted by the bold blue jay swooping by the kitchen window.

Seeing Pewter, he sailed straight for the window, then turned, feetfirst, wings flapping while he threatened at the window.

"*I hate that bird!*" Pewter spit.

"*Not my fave either. Come on,*" Murphy said.

He returned for another pass, the bird version of giving the finger. Pewter leapt at the window and smacked it.

*"Come on, Pewter."* Murphy kicked her with her hind leg.

Pewter slid down off the counter. Leaping wasn't her first recourse. If she could put her front paws on cabinets and reach way down, sliding, then she'd hit the floor with less of a thump. Hitting with all that lard made a big *baboom.*

The three hurried into the bedroom. The bedroom door, usually closed, was open, since Harry was still in her robe.

The .357 was in a hard plastic carrying case.

*"Ugh. This thing is heavy."* Murphy tried to push it out.

*"Let's all three try."* Tucker wedged in next to Murphy on the left, pushing over sneakers and old cowboy boots.

Pewter was already on Murphy's right side.

*"On three,"* Murphy called out. *"One, two, three."*

*"Uh."* They all grunted but succeeded in moving the gun case halfway out of the closet. She'd trip over it if she wasn't looking and she had to go to the closet for her boots.

*"Think she'll get it?"* Pewter scratched behind her ear.

*"Fleas?"*

*"No,"* she angrily replied. *"An itch."*

*"Gray animals have more trouble with fleas."* Mrs. Murphy pronounced this as solemnly as a judge.

*"You're so full of it."*

Pewter swatted Murphy, and the two girls mixed it up. Tucker, no fool, stepped away just as Harry stepped into her bedroom.

"Hey!"

Two angry faces greeted hers.

*"She started it."*

*"I did not,"* Mrs. Murphy defended herself.

"Don't you dare fight in my bedroom. The last time, you knocked over Mom's crystal stag's head. Luckily it fell on the carpeted part of the floor. I love that stag's head."

She bent over to fetch her boots.

*"Take your gun,"* Pewter said.

Harry pushed the gray box back in, then stopped. She pulled it out and opened it up. The polished chrome barrel shone. She liked revolvers. They felt better in her hand than other types of handguns. Being a country girl, Harry had grown up with guns and rifles. She knew how to use them safely. Guns made no sense in the city, but they made a great deal of sense in the country, especially during rabies season. In theory rabies occurred all year long, but Harry usually noticed an upswing in the spring. It was a horrible disease, a dreadful way for an animal to die, and dangerous for everyone else.

*"Take the gun."* Tucker panted from nervousness.

Harry plucked out a clear hard plastic packet of bullets. She laid the bullets and gun on the bed, then pulled on her socks, stepped into her jeans, threw on her windowpane shirt, finally yanked on the old boots, and slipped the packet into her shirt pocket. Although the gun was unloaded she checked again just to be sure. Then she carried the gun to the truck and placed it in the glove compartment.

She walked back into the house for her purse and the animals, calling, "Rodeo!"

Tucker bounded through the screen door. The cats followed but then flew into the barn.

"Murphy, come on!" Harry put one hand on the chrome handhold she had installed outside both doors so she could swing up.

"*Forget it.*" Tucker sat on the seat.

Harry dropped back down. She trudged into the barn. The horses walked up to the gate to watch. Harry turned them out first thing each morning.

"*Blown her stack,*" Tomahawk said to Gin Fizz.

"*Uh-huh.*"

Poptart joined them. Human explosions amused them so long as they didn't take place on their backs.

"Let's go!" Harry stomped down the center aisle, not a cat in sight, not even a paw print.

Both cats hid behind a hay bale in the loft. A telltale stalk of hay floated down, whirling in the early sunlight.

"A-ha!" Harry climbed the ladder so fast she could have been a cat.

"*Skedaddle.*" Murphy shot out from her hay bale, streaking toward the back of the loft where the bales were stacked higher.

Pewter flattened as Harry tromped by, not even noticing her. Then the gray cat silently

207

circled, dropping behind an old tack trunk put in the loft with odds and ends of bits, bridles, and old tools.

Harry craned to see around the tall bales. A pair of gleaming eyes stared right back at her.

"*Go to work.*"

"Come on out of there."

"*No.*"

She checked her watch, her father's old Bulova. "Damn."

"*Go on.*"

"I know you're saying ugly things about me."

"*No, I'm not.*" Murphy didn't like Harry's misinterpretation of her meow. "*Just go on.*"

Harry checked her watch again. "You'd better be in that house when I come home."

"*I will be.*"

"*Me, too,*" Pewter called out.

Harry put her hands outside the ladder and her feet, too, to slide down.

As she walked toward the truck a fat raindrop splattered on her cheek.

"The weatherman said it wouldn't rain until after midnight."

Tucker, sitting in the driver's seat, said, "*He lied.*"

# 36

The two cats walked over to Simon's nest. He opened an eye, then closed it.

"*I know you're awake.*" Murphy tickled the possum's nose with her tail.

*"I'm tired. I was out foraging all night,"* he grumbled.

*"In the feed room."* Pewter laughed.

*"Go back to sleep. I'm borrowing this map that I stashed here. I'll bring it back."*

*"Fine."* He closed his eyes again.

They carried the map to the opened hayloft door, unfolded it, and studied it.

*"It's the watershed, like you said."* Pewter sat on the corner.

*"Wish I knew what the separate squares meant. Any ideas?"*

*"No. They're in or adjacent to the watershed."*

*"Well, let's put this back. There may be a good time to show the humans."*

The blue jay streaked past the hayloft, spied the cats, and shrieked, *"Tuna breath!"*

Pewter lunged for the bird but Murphy caught her. *"Don't let him bug you like that. Do you want to fall out of the hayloft?"*

*"I will kill that bird if it's the last thing I do."*

*"Self-control."*

Complaining, Pewter put the map in Simon's nest along with his ever-expanding treasures. The latest find was a broken fan belt.

*"Mrs. Murphy, let's do nothing today. Nothing at all."*

*"Good idea."*

# 37

The massive green Range Rover, outfitted for its owner with a hamper basket from Harrods, rolled down Blair Bainbridge's driveway at precisely 2:55 P.M. Mrs. Murphy and Pewter, halfway across Blair's hay field, observed Sir H. at the wheel. He wore a bush hat, which offset his safari jacket nicely.

Sir H. Vane-Tempest never believed in buying a bargain when he could pay full price. He'd bought his attire at Hunting World in Paris. The French soaked him good.

The brief morning rain had subsided, leaving a sparkling sky with impressive cumulus clouds tipping over the mountains.

Pewter loathed mud. She hated the sensation when it curled up between her toes. She'd have to wait until it dried, then pick it out with her teeth. Mrs. Murphy, while not lax in her personal grooming, wasn't as fastidious as Pewter. But then Pewter was a lustrous gunmetal-gray, which showed any soiling, whereas Mrs. Murphy was a brown tiger with black stripes, her mottled coat hiding any imperfections.

Pewter felt that she was a rare color, a more desirable color than the tabby. After all, tabbies were a dime a dozen.

The cats reached the porch door as Sir H. Vane-Tempest stepped out of his Rover. He'd lost weight since the shooting and actually looked better than he had before he'd been drilled with three holes.

He knocked on the screened-porch door.

"Come in, H." Blair walked out to greet him. "Arch is in the living room."

Mrs. Murphy shot through Blair's tall legs.

Pewter slid through, too. "You stinkers!" He laughed.

As Blair served drinks, Murphy and Pewter edged to the living-room door. Vane-Tempest noticed them when he entered the house, but he paid little attention. To him cats were dumb animals.

"Arch—" Vane-Tempest nodded.

"H.," Arch replied coolly. "How did you leave Sarah?"

"I told you she'd do as I asked." A wrinkle creased his brow. "Actually, Boom Boom came over to give her some soothing herbs. Don't look at me like that—it's what she called them, soothing herbs."

"She still selling that herb stuff? What's she call it, aromatherapy?"

"Yes. The girls are going on a shopping spree. Boom Boom will share her latest catharsis. I'll come home. Sarah will forget to be out of sorts but she'll suggest that we both try Lifeline. That's Boom Boom's latest salvation—she's quite predictable." He laughed.

Archie didn't laugh. "I don't think any woman is predictable. Mine threw me out."

"Won't last. Make amends. Buy her a new car or something."

"I don't have that kind of money." Archie sourly turned and noticed Mrs. Murphy seated under the coffee table.

"You will."

"Blair," Archie called out, impatiently.

"I'm coming." He returned with a silver tray bearing two Irish-crystal decanters and three matching glasses. "Sherry, if you're so inclined, or Glenlivet."

Vane-Tempest longingly stared at the scotch, then sighed. "A cup of coffee or even tea. Early for tea, but I'll brave it. Cutting back." He indicated the booze.

"Tea it is. Arch?"

"I'm fine. What is that cat doing here again? Harry's cat." He didn't see Pewter. She had ducked behind a wing chair.

*"I beg your pardon."* Murphy brazenly strolled into the middle of the room.

"Two days in a row. I guess I rate." Blair loved Harry's cats.

"Get Murphy out of here," Archie grumbled.

"Are you allergic?" Vane-Tempest politely inquired.

"To that damned cat, I am. She made a fool of me at that meeting."

"Hardly needed the cat for that," Vane-Tempest dryly noted.

"I don't trust her. Something uncanny about her." Archie pouted.

Blair scooped up Murphy. "Come on, sweetie. I'll give you a treat, but outside."

Murphy wrinkled her nose. *"You're an asshole, Archie Ingram."* Then she called to Pewter, *"Hide under the sofa. I'll meet you outside later."*

Blair put Mrs. Murphy over his shoulder while Pewter squeezed under the large sofa. He intended to poach salmon for supper, so he sliced off a bit, then diced it while the teakettle boiled. He placed a small bowl of the fresh salmon outside for the tiger.

Murphy prowled around the cars. The windows were open. She might as well investigate the interiors.

Once the tea was served, Vane-Tempest got down to business. Since he had called this meeting no one else could start it.

"I'll get straight to the point: Sarah wants to be a partner in Teotan Incorporated."

"Does she know what we're doing?"

"No, Arch, she does not." Vane-Tempest shot him a baleful glance. "But she knows we're purchasing land."

"Did you tell her?" Archie's right eye twitched nervously.

"No. She went through my papers when I was in hospital. Under the circumstances that was normal. I told her the lawyers would handle everything, but that didn't satisfy her. She was terribly worried. Also, she doesn't trust my lawyers."

"Do you?"

"Of course I do. Some of these men have served me for over twenty-five years. Sarah's feeling is that should the worst befall me, they won't work with her, they won't reveal to her the full extent of my holdings."

"She's worried about them stealing from her?" His tone revealed curiosity as well as irritation.

"No. I don't think that's it. She wants to be in charge. The only way she can make intelligent decisions is to have accurate information. I never thought about it until she raised the issue, but I can see her point of view."

"Why can't you teach her about your invest-ments without bringing her into Teotan?" Blair asked sensibly.

"Oh, I can." Vane-Tempest held up his hands. "But she read some of the real-estate transactions. She understands property, of course, so she wants to be part of this. She doesn't know the full significance of our purchases."

"I see." Blair poured himself a glass of sherry. He enjoyed the nutlike flavor.

"I tried to dissuade her."

"What if we refuse her?" Archie crossed his arms over his chest and leaned back in the chair.

"I don't know." He shrugged. "But I do rather think—what's the expression...it's dis-tasteful but, ah yes—I think she's better inside the tent pissing out than outside the tent pissing in."

Blair and Archie remained silent for a moment.

"I sense this is unwelcome."

Blair cleared his throat. "A surprise. My con-cern is not her response to the purpose of our corporation. Sarah can appreciate profit as well as the next man—woman." He stroked his chin. "My concern is, what would be her function? Whatever resources she puts into the corporation would, in effect, be your resources."

"Quite true. She hasn't a penny that doesn't come from me."

"And she'd have a vote. You'd control Teotan." Archie neatly summed up the situ-ation.

"It does rather appear so, but I would never assume that Sarah would always agree with me. If you two present something sensible she might be swayed. I don't know. I mean, there's little potential for disagreement. Our business plan is clear but I understand your concern. It would throw Teotan out of balance."

Archie rose, put his hands behind his back, and paced. "She's bright. She's beautiful. Once Teotan goes public she'd make a hell of a spokesperson. People tend to trust women more than they trust men."

Blair raised an eyebrow. "Exactly what do you mean by 'going public'?"

"Not public-issue stock, obviously. No, I meant when Teotan presents its plan to the county commission. Who better to present it than Sarah? She's perfect."

"I never thought of that." Vane-Tempest smiled.

Blair poured him another cup of tea. "Do *you* want her in the corporation?"

"Quite frankly, at first, I did not. I was offended when she suggested it and put out that she'd read my papers. She had access only to the papers at home, but still. However, once she explained her fears, I considered what I would do in her circumstances: the same thing."

"Having Sarah in Teotan at this late date..." Blair paused. "You would control the corporation after I've pumped in seven hundred and fifty thousand dollars. That's—"

"I understand." And Vane-Tempest did. He

was a businessman, after all. "You, Tommy, and I put in equal shares and Archie put in sweat equity. We have—I forget the exact term—right of survivorship, in essence, to Tommy's share. We don't need another partner. And she'll be hell to live with." He wiped his brow. "On the other hand, apart from being a spokesperson, she does have a way about her. Sarah could— how did Ridley put it one day? Could talk a dog off a meat wagon." He smiled. "You people have such colorful expressions."

"You could put her in my place," Archie soberly suggested. "She could cover my tracks."

"Your tracks are well covered, Archie." Vane-Tempest spoke forcefully. "An investigator would have to go through two dummy corporations in Bermuda and there are no papers with your name on them. You're paid in cash."

"Aileen told me my career was over."

"Aileen doesn't have the facts," Vane-Tempest flatly stated.

"What I've done is immoral." A flush covered Archie's angular face.

"Balls!" the Englishman exploded. "Spare me Aileen's refined morality. You've made a sound business decision. You supply us with pertinent information, connect us with the proper people in Richmond, and serve your county. Our plan will save Albemarle millions of dollars." He gestured expansively. "And why shouldn't we be amply rewarded for our foresight?"

"Buck up, Archie." Blair agreed with Vane-Tempest, although he recognized Archie's moral predicament. Still, Archie had known what he was getting into.

Archie mulled this over. Their plan *would* save the county money. "It is a good plan, isn't it?"

"We have Tommy to thank for the first glimmer." Blair missed the fun-loving Tommy. "If he hadn't pushed me into flying lessons I'd have never studied the watershed from the air."

"Nor would we have applied ourselves to underground streams and rivers." Vane-Tempest perked up; the tea was giving him a lift. "If one studies the land mass one can pick out those depressions, those possible water sources. The fact that no one had considered this is evidence of precisely how stupid elected officials are. Present company excluded, of course." He nodded to Arch.

"Some are dumb, others are on the gravy train." Archie's eyes glittered with anger. "No one can tell me that fortunes won't be made with a reservoir, and those fortunes won't necessarily be made here. Outsiders will bid on the job and, oh, how interesting that state process can get. I've watched this bullshit mumbo jumbo for years. All they do is waste money, siphon off a nice piece into their own pockets, and let the taxpayer pay through the nose."

"Right. Which is why our plan of wells to service the northwest corner of the county is brilliant." Blair sat up straight. "The wells we have already dug are moving at eighty-eight gallons of water a minute. That's extraordinary. With the underground water we're tapping we can service Free Union, Boonesville, Earlysville, that whole northwestern corner all the way to the county line. The only expense will be for constructing cisterns or water towers, and that's a hell of a lot cheaper than building a reservoir. The county buys the water from us at an attractive rate. If this works, which I know it will, we can do the same thing for the other sections of the county."

"But we'll have more competition. Other people will copy us and start buying up the land." Archie sat down again. "There's talk about these wells being dug but so far as I know no one has figured out the purpose. But people will buy up land. Just wait."

"I'll attend to that. There's no reason we can't absorb some of these entrepreneurs into an umbrella corporation or create limited partnerships for, say, the southeastern corner of the county. We can worry about that later." On a roll, Vane-Tempest continued. "Your job, Arch, apart from keeping us informed of what's cooking at the statehouse, is to introduce the idea of floating a bond to set up those water towers and cisterns."

"I can't do that until you present your idea to the public."

"Which is where Sarah comes in." Vane-Tempest smiled without warmth.

"Let me think about this. I'm not saying no, I just want to think. Give me a week."

"Fair enough." Vane-Tempest opened his palms, a gesture of appeasement. "Now, another matter. Which one of us killed Tommy Van Allen? We all had something to gain."

Stunned, Archie reacted first. "That's a sick joke!"

As the men wrangled, Mrs. Murphy emerged from the Range Rover. She'd already investigated the 911, loath to leave it because it smelled so good. Being small, the Porsche took no time at all. The Range Rover, however, sucked up almost forty-five minutes of precise sniffing and opening compartments.

Next on the list was the U-Haul.

The U-Haul had an open back like a stall with a Dutch door. It hadn't been unpacked. Looked like Archie couldn't make up his mind what to do.

Once inside, Mrs. Murphy picked her way over the suitcases, one small desk, and a chair. Her eyes were adjusting to the light. She noticed a cardboard box with a picture of handcuffs on the outside, haphazardly tossed into a carton. She pushed the box, and something rattled inside. She tried to open it but it was shut tight.

Claws out, Murphy smashed into the cardboard full-force. With her claws embedded all the way through the cardboard, she easily lifted the lid. A pair of shiny handcuffs, key in the lock, gleamed up at her.

The slapping shut of the porch door alerted her to the approach of a human.

The tiger scrambled over the desk and

chair, managing to propel herself out the back. She dropped onto the ground as H. Vane-Tempest reached his car.

Archie cursed on seeing her. "If that damn cat peed on my stuff I'll kill her!"

Pewter scurried out of the house, racing for the old graveyard. *"Vamoose!"*

Mrs. Murphy flew down the farm road to catch her, Archie's curses still ringing in her ears.

# 38

The old gravestones, worn thin by time, stood out bleakly on the meadow's horizon. The buried were members of Herb Jones's family who had once farmed the land now owned by Blair Bainbridge. As is the custom in Virginia, when land passes hands, family members nonetheless continue to care for the graves of their ancestors.

Once a year Herb righted tombstones, planted flowers, and trimmed the magnificent English boxwood hedge bordering the southwest side. Over time Herb's bad back hurt him more and more. Blair had begun to help tend the graveyard and to learn the history of its inhabitants.

Blair mowed the lawn, pruned trees, and trimmed around the edges of the stones. He performed this service out of respect for Herb, who had a large flock and not much help. The good reverend's natural generosity meant he had but little time for himself and even less money.

Pewter caught her breath on a flat gravestone set on graceful piers. *"You won't believe what I heard!"*

*"Well, I found handcuffs."*

*"You did?"*

*"In the U-Haul."*

*"So it is Archie Ingram."* Pewter scanned the fresh green shoots in the field.

*"How many people carry handcuffs?"*

*"Cops and cop wanna-bes. Now listen to what those guys were talking about. The map makes sense. The marked-off squares are lands they've bought through a corporation called Teotan. They've tapped underground rivers and streams. They're sinking wells on these properties and the flow is so strong they can sell water to the county. The county will need to put up water towers or build cisterns—which are a lot better-looking. This plan will save the county a mess of money and provide a good water supply for all of the newcomers. So far no other humans have put two and two together although the well drillers know a mess of wells are being dug."*

*"Hmm, where's the hole?"*

*"There isn't one. I mean, except for Tommy Van Allen winding up as a frozen TV dinner. He was one of the four partners and, the most extraordinary thing, Sir H. Vane-Tempest said, 'Which one of us killed Tommy Van Allen?' Archie screamed so loud I thought my eardrums would burst. He said H. was sick to even say such a thing. Blair wasn't overfond of H.'s crack*

either. *Sir H. Vane said Sarah wanted to come into the deal in place of Tommy. At first Archie was opposed, then he thought it over and said she might be a good spokesperson for when they go public."*

*"Blair?"*

*"He's not sure yet. He's afraid it will give the Vane-Tempests control over Teotan. He's right, too."*

Mrs. Murphy, hearing geese, squinted into the sun. She spied the telltale V formation, flying low. The rustling of the birds' wings was growing louder and just as quickly growing faint as the formation passed.

*"I wouldn't want to be in Teotan right now."*

*"Me neither,"* Pewter agreed. *"One partner hung on a meathook and the other got blasted."*

*"The brilliance of their business plan is the money is steady. Millions will come in over the years. If they sold the land or the water outright to the county they'd lose an enormous chunk of their profit to taxes."* She shook herself, then squeezed through the iron fence around the graveyard. *"Blair's smarter than I gave him credit for."*

*"Smart? He'll be dead soon enough. Archie will control everything."*

They walked across the soft earth, crossing over the creek into Harry's hay field. Tomahawk, Poptart, and Gin Fizz, mouths full of clover and timothy, raised their heads, spotted their feline friends, then returned to grazing.

Mrs. Murphy finally spoke. *"Blair isn't our human. He isn't our responsibility, but I like him."*

*"I'm not risking my neck for anyone but Harry."*

*"No one is asking you to, but we need to be alert. I'm inclined to help him up to a point. He's our next-door neighbor."*

*"That's what worries me: He's next door."*

# 39

When Harry returned from work that evening, Mrs. Murphy was asleep on the sofa and Pewter was dozing by her food bowl.

Tucker burst through the door to share the day's gossip. The cats, at first grumpy, woke up fully and told the corgi of their adventure.

As they were filling Tucker in, Deputy Cooper drove up. She emerged from her squad car, carrying Chinese food.

Harry selected some morsels of chicken for the cats. Cynthia had thoughtfully brought a knuckle bone from Market Shiflett's grocery for Tucker.

"Hear about Little Mim's party?"

Harry shook her head since her mouth was full of chicken-fried rice, so Cynthia continued.

"She's planning an apple-blossom party. Impromptu."

"Ha," Harry replied, knowing that Little Mim's version of *impromptu* meant a small army of workers at the last minute instead of a small army planning months in advance.

*Spontaneity* wasn't a word associated with either Mim senior or Mim junior.

"She's renting small tables, setting them out in the apple orchard. She's hired a band. Her mother is lending her the outdoor dance floor. That takes an entire day to put together. Anyway, she's in a state."

"Where'd you hear this?"

"From the horse's mouth. I met her this morning to ask if she took clothing to Mrs. Woo. Turns out she doesn't since Gretchen, Big Mim's utility infielder, also does the mending. That's when she waxed eloquent about the party."

"Bet she doesn't invite me."

"She has to invite you." Cynthia grabbed pork lo mein with her chopsticks.

"No she doesn't."

"Yes she does, because if she doesn't everyone will notice. She cares about appearances as much as her mother."

"Maybe I'll go and maybe I won't."

"You'll go. Since when have you missed a party?"

"When I first separated from Fair."

"Forget about that. Hey, where's he been?"

"Foaling season. From January through May he's delivering the Thoroughbred foals. When we were married I'd sometimes go days without seeing him."

"There are other vets. He could have passed on some of the work."

"No, he really couldn't. People have a lot of money tied up in a mare. First there's the purchase price of the mare herself. If she's a Thoroughbred with good bloodlines and of a good age that could be, in these parts, anywhere from five thousand to thirty thousand dollars. Then there's the stud fee. Again, the price varies widely. So when that baby hits the ground some of the breeders already have fifty thousand dollars invested in it. For the hunter people it's a little different. But still, it's not just money, it's emotion, too. Fair's the best, so everyone wants him."

"There's a lot I don't know about the horse business."

"Incredible business, because it's not just money and it's not just the study of bloodlines, there's a certain something, a sixth sense. That's the hook. Otherwise, everyone could do it. Harder and harder to make money at it, though."

"Everything's that way. Do you think we'll live to see a revolution?" Cynthia offered the rest of the lo mein to Harry, who refused, so she dumped it all on her plate.

"Yeah, but I don't know what kind of revolution. I do know you can't punish people for productivity and expect a society to last long. Right now an American's answer is to work harder but the harder he or she works the more the government takes. Think of all the money we've already put into Social Security from our wages. By the time the whole system collapses will we be too old to fight?"

"Look at you and me. Single women in our thirties."

"Never too old to fight." Cynthia smiled. "Think you'll stay single?"

"Yes."

"I don't. You'll get married in the next few years."

"Nope." Harry shook her head for emphasis. "I have nothing to gain from another husband. I'm not saying I won't have an affair but, really, what can I get from marriage except double the laundry?"

"Cynic."

"Yep."

"If Little Mim doesn't snag Blair Bainbridge, I think she'll have a nervous breakdown." Cynthia opened a brown paper bag filled with brownies. "Dessert."

Harry inhaled over the bag. "Miranda! She didn't tell me she was making brownies."

"I stopped by after work. She happened to be making some for tomorrow. Hot out of the pan."

"God, these are good." Harry bit into one. "This business about Little Mim and Blair is delicate. Blair and I are buddies. Nothing more to it than that, but it drives her bats."

"Yeah, well, his reticence about the situation doesn't help matters."

*"He likes you."* Mrs. Murphy swallowed the last of her cashew chicken.

"More?" Harry dropped another chicken bit on her plate.

*"Hey!"*

She dropped one for Pewter, too. Tucker, engrossed in her bone, paid no attention to the

Chinese food or the conversation. A joint bone required intense concentration.

"Blair's changed." Harry chose her words carefully since she knew Cynthia, like many women, had a crush on him. "He's distant."

"You know, I thought it was just me—he didn't want to be bothered with me."

"Cynthia, he likes you. It's not you. He's worried about his age. After all, his work is his face. He's getting crow's-feet around his eyes and a few gray hairs around the temples."

"Makes him look even better, I think."

"Me, too, but models have a short shelf life. As he ages he'll wind up in catalogs for tie companies. That's not the same as a spread in *GQ*."

"Never thought of that. It's bad enough when women worry about their looks. It seems somehow"—she groped for the right word— "frivolous when a man does it."

"Yeah. Then again," Harry continued, "I guess the money dries up."

"He's invested wisely, I bet."

"I don't know. He never talks about money. I just see how he spends it." Harry sighed. "I can't imagine buying whatever I want when I want it."

"Me neither," Cynthia agreed. "Course, if he married Little Mim, he'd never have to work another day in his life."

Harry paused. "I don't think he could do that."

"Too moral?"

"Well—he likes beautiful women. Little

Mim is nice-looking but she's not a *Vogue* model. Know what I mean?"

"Yep."

"And when the woman has the bucks, the man dances to her tune unless she's a flat-out fool, and Little Mim is not. Whoever has the gold makes the rules."

"Guess he'll never go out with me." Cynthia smiled wanly.

"Cynthia, Blair's nice enough but you need a good old country boy. A man who isn't afraid to get his hands dirty."

"Oh, I don't know."

"Think you'll ever get married?" Harry asked.

"I hope so."

A horn beeping down the driveway broke the moment.

"Whoo-ee," Susan Tucker called.

"Whoo-ee back at you." Harry didn't get up as Susan stuck her head through the kitchen doorway. "Grab a plate. Cynthia's demolished all the pork lo mein, but there's lots of everything else."

Needing no prompting, Susan did just that. "Since you guys are on dessert I'll assume everything else is mine." She smiled.

"Pig out, Suz."

As she shoveled food into her mouth, Susan's bright eyes danced. "You won't believe what happened to me. Mmm, can't talk with my mouth full."

"We'll talk to you. When you've slowed down you can tell us everything."

Susan held up her hand, indicating that was a good idea, and kept eating.

Mrs. Murphy jumped onto the kitchen counter. The sun was setting; a shaft of scarlet spiraled into the sky. Very unusual, just that one vertical column of color. She dropped down on top of the closed plastic garbage can, then to the floor, and walked out the door. Pewter and Tucker ignored her.

Susan recovered enough to talk. "I was on the fifteenth hole at Keswick. I like to play once a week there and once a week at Farmington. Actually, I'd play every day if I could, but that's neither here nor there. Anyway, there I was moving along at a pretty good clip when who should roll by me in her personalized golf cart but Sarah Vane-Tempest. She was by herself, so I asked if she wanted to join me. She said no, she was on her way home. She'd lost track of the time. She wanted to be there when H. Vane got home. Said she was furious with him because he was driving his car and she didn't think he should be doing that. Then she zoomed on by."

"She's overprotective." Harry reached for another brownie.

"Treats us like dirt." Cynthia shrugged. "But then, a lot of people do."

"What have we here?" Susan noticed Mrs. Murphy carrying what looked like folded paper in her mouth.

Pewter stopped eating. *"Won't help."*

Murphy dropped the map at Cynthia Cooper's feet.

She bent over to pick it up, carefully opening

it. The name in small block print on the right-hand corner read TOMMY VAN ALLEN.

Her expression motivated both Harry and Susan to rise out of their chairs and lean over her shoulder.

"Good Lord!" Susan exclaimed.

Harry picked up her cat and kissed her cheek. "Where'd you find this, pusskin?"

*"In the airplane."*

Cynthia traced the outlined blocks with her forefinger. She quickly folded the map back up and headed for the door. "Not a word of this to anyone. I mean it. Not even Miranda."

Harry followed her out to the car as Susan cleared the table.

Cynthia slid behind the wheel, buckled up, reached over onto the passenger seat, and gave Harry a folder. "I came over so we could read this together, but I don't think it matters too much if you keep it for tonight. I'll pick it up from you at work tomorrow." She started the motor. "Do you have any idea where Mrs. Murphy could have gotten this map?"

"Not one."

Cynthia handed her the file, labeled BARBER C. MINOR, and drove off.

# 40

"*Umph.*" Pewter bit at her hind claws, trying to pull out the mud caked there.

*"Why don't you relax? The stuff will fall out tomorrow,"* Mrs. Murphy advised.

"I'm not going to bed with mud in my claws."

"Least you're not complaining about how you came by it."

"Wish I'd been with you guys." Tucker lay down with her head between her paws, her expressive eyes turned upward to the cats, each of which sat on an arm of the old wing chair. Harry was intently reading the file on her great-grandfather.

"You're good at what you do," Murphy complimented Tucker.

"Anything big happen in the P.O.?" Pewter yanked out another tiny pellet of mud.

"Reverend Jones said Elocution is on special foods to control her weight. Harry wrote down the information." Tucker gleefully directed this at Pewter. "Then Boom Boom and Sarah waltzed in. Major shopping spree but Sarah said that even though she'd spent a lot of H. Vane's money she was still mad at him for driving himself around. She thinks he should go slow and after all, they can afford a chauffeur. Then Big Mim arrived for her mail, told Sarah to shut up and let her husband do whatever he wants, the worst thing she can do is make him feel like an invalid. So Sarah got mad and huffed out to the car. Said she had to play golf. Boom Boom fussed at Mim, said Sarah'd suffered a hideous shock. Mim told Boom to get a life and stop feeding off other people's tragedies. Then Boom huffed out and Harry and Big Mim laughed themselves silly. That was my day."

"We told you ours."

"What's she so absorbed in?" Tucker rolled

over to reveal a sparkling white stomach, a tiny paunch growing ever more noticeable.

Murphy moved to the back of the wing chair and read over Harry's shoulder. " 'File. *Barber Clark Minor, aka Biddy. Born April 2, 1890. Shot dead, May 30, 1927. Born in Albemarle County. Duke University, B.A. 1911. Law school, University of Virginia. Left before receiving degree. Enlisted in the Army. Saw action in France. Achieved rank of captain. Wounded three times. (Awarded Bronze Star.) Returned to Crozet. Finished law school. Entered practice with firm of Roscoe, Commons. Later Roscoe, Commons, and Minor.*

" '*Married Elizabeth Carhart, 1919. Three children. Howard, born 1920. Anne, born 1921. Barber Clark Jr., 1923.*

" '*No criminal record.*

" '*Killed by James Urquhart. Mr. Minor's widow did not press charges.*' "

Tucker broke into the cat's oration, saying, "*You'd think Mrs. Minor would have brought charges. What else does it say?*"

" '*Testimony of witnesses. Sheriff Hogendobber*'—*must be George's father or uncle or something.*" She referred to Mrs. Hogendobber's deceased husband, George. "*Anyway the sheriff questioned three eyewitnesses, the first being Isabelle Urquhart, Mim's mother. She saw Biddy drive up to the Urquhart farm the morning of May 30. She was being driven by her father to market. They had passed the Urquhart driveway and Biddy waved.*"

Harry turned the page, absentmindedly

reaching up to tickle Mrs. Murphy under her chin.

*"Go on,"* Tucker urged as Pewter also moved to the back of the chair to read over Harry's shoulder.

" *'The second witness was James Urquhart himself, aged nineteen. The boy stated, "Mr. Minor called on me at ten in the morning unexpectedly. One thing led to another. I lost my temper and struck him in the face. He hit me back. I usually carry a side arm. Copperheads. All over this spring. I pulled it out and shot him in the chest. He kept coming at me and I shot him again. He fell down on his knees and then fell over backward. When I reached him he was dead."*

" *'The third witness was Thalia Urquhart, aged twenty. "Mr. Minor called on my brother,"* she stated. *"They had words. Jamie went into a rage and shot him. He should have never shot Biddy Minor. He was such a nice man." ' "*

Three brown photographs of the body were neatly pasted on the last page—Biddy's stiff, prone body, blood spreading over his white shirt, his eyes open, gazing to heaven. But even in death Biddy Minor was a fabulously handsome man.

*"That's it?"* Tucker asked.

*"Except for the three old photographs."* Pewter added, *"You've seen a lot worse."*

Harry closed the folder, crossing her legs under her. "Not much of an investigation for a murder. You'd think Sheriff Hogendobber would have shown more curiosity and you'd think Biddy's wife would have thrown the book at him," she thought out loud as the three animals hung on each word. "Course, the Urquharts were rich. The Minors were not."

*"He admitted to the shooting,"* Pewter mentioned. *"She had an open-and-shut case."*

"Know what I think?" Harry leaned against the backrest. "A gentleman's agreement. And gentlewoman's. Bet Tally knows the truth."

*"Maybe."* Mrs. Murphy listened. The owl hooted in the barn. *"What's she blabbing about?"*

*"Who?"*

*"The owl."* Murphy crawled into Harry's lap before Pewter had the chance to think of it.

*"Calling for a boyfriend."* Tucker giggled.

*"That's all we need. More owls,"* Murphy grumbled.

*"I'd rather have owls than blue jays."*

*"Pewter, you're obsessed with that blue jay."* Harry rubbed Murphy's ears so she purred the last part of the sentence.

*"Apart from the insults, blue jays steal. Anything shiny. They're so greedy."*

# 41

Rick Shaw's ashtray overflowed with butts. As he absentmindedly put a live cigarette into the deep tray, the whole mess caught on fire, a miniature volcano of stale nicotine and discarded ideas.

Coop, laughing, trotted to the water cooler, filled a cup, and dumped the contents onto the smoldering ashtray. She had prudently carried a paper towel with her to clean up the mess.

"Goddammit!" He stood up, knocking his chair over backward.

"*You* set the place on fire, not me, grouch."

"I didn't mean you. I meant me."

"Boss, you take these cases too personal."

"I liked Tommy. I like Mary Woo. Hell, I can't even find out who burned her shop down, and she's too upset to remember anything to do with her records. Or maybe too scared. Yes, I take this *personal*." He parodied Cynthia's incorrect English.

"Come on, let's go home." She pointed to the wall clock.

It was two-thirty in the morning.

"No. Not yet."

"Your wife probably forgets what you look like."

"Right now that's good. I look like a vampire reject. One more time." He pointed to the map on the table. "What do these properties have in common?"

"Nothing that I can tell. They aren't connected. They aren't on major roadways or potential road expansions. They aren't in the path of the beltway that the state threatens to build but never does. Just looks like speculation."

"Land speculation ruined Lighthorse Harry Lee."

"And plenty more." Like Rick, Cynthia knew her history—but most Virginians did.

Before schools became "relevant," teachers

led you to the facts. If you didn't study them willingly they simply pounded them into you. One way or the other a Virginian would learn history, multiplication tables, the Queen's English, and manners. Then a child would go home for more drilling by the family about the family, things like: "Aunt Minnie believes that God is a giant orange. Other than that she's harmless, so be respectful."

"God, I'm tired." Rick sighed. His mind was wandering. He sank back in his chair.

"Roger." Cynthia rubbed her eyes.

"Let me review this again. Mrs. Murphy brought you the map. Dropped it right at your feet."

"Yes."

"Harry had never seen the map?"

"No. Boss, I told you exactly how it happened. Mrs. Murphy walked outside and returned with the map. She was quite deliberate about it. She didn't give it to Harry. She gave it to me."

"If we ever go to court, what do we say? A cat gave us evidence?"

"Sure looks that way." Cynthia smiled. She genuinely liked her boss.

"Let's keep this out of the papers. I can't bring myself to drag the pussycat into the glare of publicity. Where did she find it!"

"We've gone over this. Behind the post office? Near the house? In the bomber jacket? The map could have been dropped anywhere. But wherever it was, Mrs. Murphy found it."

"Why would she bother to pick it up?" He threw his hands in the air.

"Because cats love paper."

"Next you'll tell me she reads."

"That one, I wouldn't be surprised." She pulled the coroner's report over to her one more time and thumbed through it. "Guess you have to release this."

"Yes. It confirms he was killed on the night he disappeared. And I guess I'll have to release the fact that he was loaded with cocaine. They'll have a field day with that one."

"You need some sleep before facing reporters again."

"I need a lead. A clear lead." Rick pounded the table.

"We can start visiting these land parcels."

"Yep." He rose, sighed, and clicked off the bright, small desk lamp. "You're right. We both need sleep."

They waved to the graveyard-shift dispatcher.

The cool night air, bearing a hint of moisture, smelled like fresh earth.

"Night, Rick."

"Coop?"

"Yeah?"

"Think H. Vane is in on the drug trade?"

"We don't know if Tommy was dealing. We only know he was full of the stuff."

"That's not what I'm asking."

"H. Vane loves a profit." She turned up her collar.

"H., Tommy, Blair, and Archie took flying lessons. I questioned Ridley, too, but he wasn't in the club for long. Makes sense." He sighed. "Well, let's both get some sleep. Then we can drive over the land marked on the map."

# 42

Earlier that same night Sarah, in a rage, had slapped her husband in the face. He slapped her back.

"You forget your station, madam." He coldly turned his back on her.

"You can't go out alone. You hire a body-guard or I will!"

"Don't tell me what I can do. And don't worry that I'll be killed. Whoever tried was a damned poor shot."

"You can be insufferably smug."

"And you can be a bloody nag."

With some effort, she composed herself. "What happened at the meeting today?"

"Surprisingly, Archie thought your joining us was a good idea, once he had time to adjust to it."

"And?"

"Blair wants to consult his lawyer. It would give you and me overwhelming control of the corporation and there is the small matter that you haven't invested your share of capital."

"Ass."

"He's a better businessman than I assumed he would be. I thought he was just a pretty face and an empty head."

"What does he care what I put in or what

percent of the stock we own? He'll still make a boatload of money."

"Give him time."

"You'll persuade him?"

"Actually, I think you will."

The telephone rang.

Sarah picked it up. "Hello. What are you doing calling here?"

Archie replied on the other end, "I'd like to speak to your husband."

She handed the phone to H. "Archie."

"Hello, Arch. Forgive Sarah. She still believes you shot me." He listened a bit, chewed his lip, nodding in agreement with Archie's ideas. Finally, he turned to Sarah, who had flopped down on the sofa and pointedly picked up a magazine. "He'd like to speak to you."

"No."

He put his hand over the receiver. "Sarah, I insist. You must get over this absurd notion that Arch tried to kill me."

Furiously, she stood; her magazine slithered to the floor. She took the offered phone. "Yes."

"I'm sure H. filled you in on our meeting today."

"Yes."

"I think it would be beneficial to all parties if we sat down and talked."

"I have nothing to say to you." She glared at H., who made appeasing gestures.

"Well, I have a great deal to say to you." He hurried his words before she could cut him off.

"We need to talk, especially if we're going to be in business together."

"That's up to Blair Bainbridge."

"Sarah..."

"Hold on." She covered the mouthpiece. "He wants to talk to me privately. Do I have to do this?"

"I think it would be best for all concerned."

She removed her hand from the mouthpiece. "All right."

"How about my office tomorrow afternoon?"

"Make it Friday. I have a dentist's appointment tomorrow."

"Fine. Friday. My office."

She hung up the phone. "Friday. His office. Are you happy now?"

"Yes, the sooner we get this behind us, the better." His jaw tightened, his eyes narrowed, then just as quickly as the tension showed on his face, he erased it.

"It would be helpful if we knew who killed Tommy Van Allen and why." She flopped back down on the sofa, bending over to retrieve her magazine. "You don't think it was Archie?"

Vane-Tempest lowered his bulk next to her. "Much as I trust my instincts in business, I have learned not to jump to conclusions. We both know Archie Ingram doesn't have the guts to kill anyone in cold blood. You're using these events to express other, repressed emotions such as anger at the fact that I have kept you from my business. I've shut you out of a large part of my life. I've treated you like a child."

"Yes, you have." She lowered her eyes, then looked into his eyes again.

"I'm turning over a new leaf. If Blair obstructs your inclusion in Teotan, I'll start another corporation and you can be president." He put his arm around her. "But, I think he'll see the light of reason just as you will when Archie speaks to you. We were all such good friends once. Let's go back to the way things were."

She put her head on his shoulder. "I'd like that."

# 43

Tommy Van Allen's memorial service on Thursday, intended to be a subdued affair, scandalized Crozet because his widow chose not to attend. It wasn't because she was too shocked to fulfill this last duty to her husband. She just didn't care. She'd already returned to Aiken and she had given Rick Shaw carte blanche to ransack Tommy's records. She also allowed him to impound the Porsche for a week. He promised to send it on to Aiken after it had been searched.

Big Mim hosted a small luncheon after the memorial for Van Allen. Her prize-winning peonies picked that moment to open.

Miranda Hogendobber strolled through Mim's magnificent gardens, which undulated down to the lake. The catamaran, *Mim's Vim*, gently bobbed in the water. The reverend escorted her.

"Young people today have no discipline." Mrs. Hogendobber's hazel eyes were troubled. "Jessica Van Allen should have come to the funeral. God knows she'll inherit all his money."

"Miranda, if people no longer dress as they should it's an outward sign that they've lost all sense of propriety. Dress isn't superficial."

"I quite agree."

"Even Harry, who does have manners, falls down in the dress department."

"Poor dear. She has to be dragged kicking and screaming to shop. Susan and I are considering putting silver duct tape over her mouth on our upcoming foray."

"Not like my dear departed. Her motto was, Shop until you drop." Herb Jones chuckled.

They sat on the wrought-iron bench, two old friends together. "What's become of the world, Herbert?"

"I don't know. Maybe every old person asks that question. But it's a cruder and more vulgar world than the one I knew as a boy. And it's more violent."

"We thought the violence would end with World War II."

"Now we turn it back on ourselves." He drank in the refreshing sight before him. "If nothing else, the gardens are flourishing." He patted Miranda on her gloved hand. "Your tulips this year could have won national awards."

"Do you really think so?"

242

"You outdid yourself."

A sharp voice interrupted their enjoyment. "You two spooning?"

"I haven't heard that word since grade school." Herb burst out laughing.

Tally Urquhart, moving slowly, but moving, descended upon them. "Just what are you doing down here, off by yourselves? You don't appear to be grieving."

"Are you?" Miranda, usually not at all saucy, had been emboldened by Herb's praise.

"No. I've grieved enough in my life. After a while you learn to say good-bye and be done with it. When your number's up it's up. I should have been dead years ago, but here I am."

"You'll outlive us all." Herb stood up, offering her his seat.

Tally balanced on her silver hound-headed cane, lowering herself next to Miranda. "The sheriff is taking Tommy's and Blair's cars apart."

"Yes, we heard that, too." Miranda shifted her position to face the vinegary lady.

"Won't do a bit of good."

"Why is that?" Herb mildly inquired.

"Because science, machines, fingerprints, oh, it's all very impressive. The *how* fills page upon page. But it's the *why* that matters."

"Ah, yes," Mrs. Hogendobber mused while watching two children paddle a dark green canoe at the far side of the lake.

"Such as, why doesn't Blair Bainbridge call on Marilyn? He doesn't appear to be in love with anyone else. She's certainly the most eligible young lady in the entire county."

"I think Harry is the most eligible young lady." Miranda surprised herself by contradicting Tally.

"She hasn't a sou," Tally grumbled, then half smiled. "But she's a far more interesting soul than my great-niece. Don't tell Mimsy, though." She laughed in earnest.

"We ought to get Harry out of that post office. She's too intelligent for that job."

"Thank you, Herbert," Mrs. Hogendobber said with unaccustomed sarcasm.

"Miranda, your husband was the postmaster. It's something else entirely."

"Oh?"

"She graduated from Smith College in art history." Herb hoped this would explain his point of view without further insulting the memory of Miranda's husband.

"I graduated from Mary Baldwin," Tally said, "and I never worked a day in my life. Of course, we weren't expected to then."

"You did work," Miranda said.

"Of course I worked. I worked harder than a stevedore but you know what I mean. For money. I think it's better now."

"You do?" Herb pressed.

"Yes. People ought to be able to pursue their talents."

"My point." Herb beamed. "Harry is not pursuing her talents."

"But perhaps she is," Tally said. "She enjoys life. She appreciates the clouds and the peonies and us. She has before her every day at the post office the peerless entertainment of the human comedy."

"I never thought of that."

"Of course not, Herbie, you're thinking of your next sermon." Tally flicked her cane out at him. "Now, what are we going to do about Little Mim and this Bainbridge fellow? She'll perish if she doesn't land him. I tell her she's better off alone but I don't think a young woman like Marilyn believes that."

"Nor do I." Herb folded his hands behind his back.

"Naturally. Men need women. Women don't need men." Tally sounded triumphant.

"Fiddlesticks." He restrained himself from saying *bullshit*.

Harry headed down to join them. "Why is everyone suddenly shutting up?"

"Because we were talking about you," Tally replied.

"Only good things." Miranda smiled.

"That's a relief."

Mim trooped down to the lake a few moments after Harry's arrival. "What are you all doing down here? I need you in the garden. You all are the social spark plugs of Crozet."

The small gathering looked at one another with resignation, then Miranda piped up. "And what are you doing here, Mim, dear?"

"Came here to get away from all of them."

They laughed together, which lightened the unexpressed tension and worry.

245

# 44

The day started quietly enough. It had dawned crimson, then gold. Harry knocked out her chores quickly, then decided to walk to work, given the exceptional beauty of the morning.

Pewter complained long and loud about Harry's decision. Pewter hated being stranded without wheels.

Harry hadn't gone a half mile down the road before a low rumble captured her attention. Blair Bainbridge snaked around the corner, saw her, and braked. He opened the door from the inside.

"Hop in."

"I've got the critters."

"We'll squeeze in."

*"I've been dying to ride in this car."* Murphy sat in Harry's lap, forcing Tucker and Pewter onto the small backseat.

Blair turned toward the farm.

"I've got to go to work."

"You need the truck. Didn't you listen to the radio this morning?"

"No."

"Big storms are moving up from the south. Fast. You need the truck."

"When they come from the south they're wet. How long before they arrive?"

"The weatherman isn't sure, of course. They always cover their butt. There's a high off the coast that might hold it up for a bit."

*"Oh, goody,"* Murphy sarcastically said.

*"Not fair that you're in the front."* Tucker stuck her nose between the seats.

*"Get over it."*

*"Selfish."* Pewter leaned on Tucker as they turned down the long dirt driveway.

"Are you coming or going?" Harry asked.

"Ever hear the one about the duke who died in the prostitute's arms? The bobby asked what happened and she said, 'He was coming and going.' " Blair scratched his head. "Did I get that right?"

"I don't know, but you're certainly in a good mood."

"I have four hundred horsepower at 5,750 rpm. Of course I'm in a good mood." He pulled up next to Harry's truck. "I'll see you later."

"Come on, gang."

Pewter stubbornly waited to be lifted into the truck. *"I told you to take the truck. Nobody listens to me."*

*"Pewter, stop bellyaching."* Tucker found an old rawhide chew wedged in the seat just under the unused middle seat belt. Harry turned the key; that old familiar cough-then-shake was followed by the motor turning over.

*"See that?"* Pewter put her paws on the windshield.

*"What?"*

*"The blue jay is sitting on the lamppost by the back door. Because he sees us pulling out."*

*"Could be because Mom throws out birdseed there for Simon and the birds."*

Miranda was carrying a big tray into Market Shiflett's just as Harry pulled into her parking space in back of the post office.

"Let me help."

"There's a second one on the kitchen table. You fetch that one."

Harry brought the light, flaky biscuits to Market's.

He wiped down the counter, said hello to his former cat, Pewter, and threw scraps to the animals. "H. Vane-Tempest called to tell me there's a re-enactors' meeting at his house tomorrow to discuss *safety* measures. I like that." He shook his head cynically.

"Are you going?" Harry asked.

"Well, I bought all that stuff for the Oak Ridge affair, I suppose I ought to get my money's worth."

*"You could sell it,"* Pewter, ever the realist, suggested.

He fed her another small beef scrap. "She's a good mouser."

*"Can't catch a bird, though, to save her life."* Murphy stood on her hind paws to catch a tossed morsel.

Tucker, too, grabbed a piece of meat from the air. She was very quick.

"Did he ask Archie to the meeting?" Harry inquired.

"I don't know."

The post-office crew hurried over to the frame building as Rob Collier tossed in the canvas sacks from the main office on Seminole Trail, also called Route 29.

"Time to work." Harry started sorting.

The phone rang and Harry picked it up.

Cynthia Cooper was on the line. "Harry, can you come with me this lunch hour?"

"Sure. What are we doing?"

"Tell you when I see you."

She hung up. "Miranda, will you mind Mrs. Murphy, Pewter, and Tucker for lunch? Cynthia asked me to go with her but she won't say why. Official business, I guess."

At twelve Cynthia picked up Harry in the squad car. Harry asked Miranda to cover for her for two hours.

Within fifteen minutes they were at the airport, at the private hangar.

"Are you afraid of small planes?" Cynthia asked.

"No."

"Glad to hear it." Cynthia bent over to fit through the small door, then reached out to pull Harry in. "This is Bob Green. He's a pilot for FedEx. In his off time he still loves to fly."

"Hi." The square-jawed pilot nodded a greeting.

They taxied down the runway, lifted off, and were airborne in minutes. Harry, on the passenger side, looked down on the patchwork quilts of green, beige, and forest. Creeks and rivers glittered. The tops of the buildings at Fashion Square Mall were flat.

"Boy, hope we never get five feet of snow. Bet those roofs wouldn't take the stress load."

"Bet they can." Bob smiled. "Or there will be lawsuits up the wazoo."

Cynthia, hand on the back of Harry's seat, leaned forward between Bob and Harry to hand her Tommy Van Allen's map. "You grew up here. We're flying you over these parcels. Tell me what you know."

Bob flew over the first parcel, a high meadow adjacent to Sugar Hollow.

"Well, that used to belong to Francie Haynes, an old lady who raised Herefords, the horned kind."

"Haynes. The black Haynes?"

"Yeah."

"Anything special about the land?"

"Not that I know of."

As they flew over each parcel, Harry recounted the history as she knew it.

"Bob, can we go up just a little bit, another thousand feet or so, and make a big circle?" Harry requested.

"No problem."

"Coop, look down. Can you see how the land folds together? Can you see the old reservoir at Sugar Hollow?"

"Yes."

"Okay, we're flying over the watershed. See how everything drains, essentially, in one direction? That's where the state and some in the county want to put the new reservoir, between Free Union and Earlysville."

"I can see it."

"Let's go lower over Sugar Hollow."

Bob pushed in the steering wheel and they gently descended.

"Really obvious here." Cynthia strained

to look over Harry's head, out the passenger window. "And I can see Francie Haynes's land."

"Now, wouldn't it make more sense to use Sugar Hollow?" Harry said.

"From up here, yes."

"Hey, you two, it's just us and the birds up here," said Bob. "The landowners are bigger and richer at the other place. This is poor people. Used to be poor people, I mean. Other folks are moving in now."

"And let's not forget the contractors." Cynthia shielded her eyes as they turned toward the sun. "You know when the state writes the specs for these massive projects they write them so only a few firms can truly compete. What a crock of shit it all is. Sorry, Bob, I don't know you well enough to swear."

"Fine by me."

"So, there's nothing special about these parcels of land?"

"Some are in the watershed and some aren't. But no, there's nothing that I know of that marks these off. Why?" Harry asked.

"Can't tell you that part."

"Since we're up here, can we fly over Tally Urquhart's?"

"Good idea." Cynthia raised her voice because the propeller noise drowned out normal conversation. "The back side of Little Yellow Mountain. I guess Mint Springs is a better coordinate."

"Okay."

Within a few moments they were cruising

over the verdant acres, the miles of crisp white fencing that constituted the Urquhart place. The old hay barn and stone buildings came into view.

"Bob, see that barn down there? How hard would it be to land there? I'm not asking you to land," she hastened to add as he descended, "but how hard would it be?" Cynthia asked.

"Not much of a strip. A little like threading the needle between the two hills. Take a good pilot."

"How about in rain and fog?" Harry asked.

"Take a pilot with brass balls and a sure touch."

# 45

The map lay open on Rick's desk. A pile of financial statements, account books, and manila legal-sized folders were stacked on the floor next to his chair.

"The watershed..." He rubbed his chin.

"It's easy to see from the air," Cynthia said, then added, "I checked the weather the night Tommy Van Allen died, or we think he died."

"You doubt the word of our coroner?"

"When someone's frozen like a fish stick, yes."

He slapped her on the back. "That's what I like—an independent thinker."

"A storm came in quickly and hung on a long time that night. And then today, we just got up in time. As we landed the clouds rolled down like a dirty gray rug."

"Was there any similarity of the properties from the air?"

"Not really."

"Hmm, Harry pepper you with questions?"

"No, she was pretty good."

He sat in his chair. "Close the door." He paused until she returned.

"I've read every comma, semicolon, period, and smudge on Van Allen's account books. He's clean." He swiveled around. "What you're telling me is that Tommy was a damn good pilot."

"Yes. After seeing the small landing strip, he was better than good," Cynthia affirmed.

"H. Vane and Tommy already knew how to fly," Rick said out loud, even though he was really talking to himself. He had found no double set of account books. He wondered if perhaps the other fellows kept accounts. He was pursuing the drug angle. "And they were all part of the Oak Ridge reenactment. At least, Tommy would have been." She nodded and he continued, "Coop, we're in the ballpark, at least, but we still aren't on base."

"Could it be that these land parcels represent just what they appear to: investments against future growth? I guess I should say, for future growth?"

"With the exception of two here bordering Sugar Hollow they're generally in this quadrant." He took out a color copy he'd made of the map and put a ruler on the copy. With a red pencil he drew lines, and a pattern began to form. "See." He slapped his thigh. "I'd like to think this map represents drug customers, but when we checked the farms—before they were purchased—no. There's no way old Ephraim Chiles would buy drugs. I want to make this fit and I can't. And I'm not sure why some of these parcels have new wells on them and others don't."

"I see that there are two roughly parallel lines."

"I see it and I don't know what it means. Think about what you saw in the air. Was there anything to suggest this type of alignment, something obvious like a low hill chain or a creek?"

"No. Besides, if there were a creek it would be on the map. We'd have noticed it before."

He dropped his forehead onto his hand. "When's the next commission meeting?"

"Next Tuesday."

"Okay. We'll tack this on the wall without saying anything. Has to be on the wall before anyone gets to the meeting. We might at least flush out Arch." He smiled. "I think we're getting a little closer to our killer."

"Good idea," she said with little enthusiasm.

He fired his pencil at her end-over-end. "What?"

"Nothing."

"Out with it."

"I've inherited your gut feelings. This doesn't feel right. Maybe half-right. Not complete."

"Yeah, I feel that way, but the look on your face…"

"He's going to strike again. I just know it."

"Something off-the-wall like Mrs. Woo's store. I think that was definitely part of this. The fire destroyed her files—all those re-enactor files."

"Well, she does bring us back to the re-enactors. You're right."

"In a funny way serial sex killers are easier to figure than this one," Rick mused.

"But there may have been sex. Don't forget the empty rubber packet in Tommy Van Allen's trench coat."

"Nah. I don't buy it."

Coop sat on the edge of the desk. "I hope I'm wrong, but this is far from over. H. Vane better hire a bodyguard." As she said that a loud clap of thunder startled them both and the heavens opened.

# 46

When the natural light struck Sarah Vane-Tempest's hair, the blonde highlights glimmered like beaten gold. Her fingernails, perfectly manicured, complemented long, graceful hands. Not only was she a beautiful woman, she had perfected young those wiles so useful in reducing men to putty.

Since most men are taller than most women, the first trick she mastered—by fourth grade—

was the disarming habit of lowering her eyes, then raising them as though only the object of her glance could call forth such a promising response. She modulated her voice so it was never loud, never strident, a bit soft so that he would have to strain to listen.

The more sophisticated snares, such as inflecting each sentence subtly so that it seemed a question only he with his superior wisdom could answer, she acquired by eighteen.

Lowering her shoulder a tad in his direction also sparked fire in the male of the species. The fact that these were calculated postures, as studied as an actress's blocking on the stage, never occurred to men. Even a man as highly intelligent as Sir H. Vane-Tempest devolved into a quivering hormonal puddle in Sarah's presence.

Her demeanor changed completely in the company of women. Her voice, straightforward, was not harsh but certainly not music to female ears. She looked her friends straight in the eye. She said what was on her mind. She never once dropped a shoulder or slightly turned her body to make a woman appear larger.

Her women friends giggled when she'd switch gears the second a man entered the room. Her profound falsity, although a subject of amusement to most and disgust to a few, did not make women mistrust her. Each woman, even Harry, knew why women performed as Sarah performed. It was an unequal world.

Beauty, short-lived, was a weapon to secure food, clothing, shelter, and status. Few women could stand alone and live well. They had to be attached to a breadwinner.

Although bright, Sarah was essentially afraid of the world, afraid she couldn't move in it on her own at the level she desired. She wasn't wrong. Few women have as much power or money as Sir H. Vane-Tempest.

She'd hit the jackpot. It was simple, really. She studied where the rich played. Since it was easier to get to Florida from Connecticut than to some other places like Aspen, she showed up, fresh out of school, then carefully edged closer and closer to the good parties.

She had also been careful not to do something stupid, like sleep with the wrong man or take a job in a clothing shop. That would diminish her mystery. She'd attend polo matches at Royal Palm Polo Club in Boca Raton. She'd watch, alone, hoping to catch a man's eye or that of an older woman needing an extra for a party. Usually men were needed as extras, but occasionally a young woman was needed to pep up an older visiting gentleman.

One Sunday at Wellington, west of Palm Beach, she happened to be standing near a string of ponies. The groom, called away by another groom needing help to catch a runaway, left a pile of polo mallets on the ground. They were organized by length and whippiness of shaft.

Sir H. Vane-Tempest thundered up. "Manuel, 51 green."

Sarah reached into the pile of 51's, having

the presence of mind to grab the one with green tape carefully placed where the shaft meets the head. H. Vane noticed immediately that Manuel had been changed by the good fairy into one of the most beautiful young women he had ever beheld.

The rest, as they say, was history. An expensive divorce from Wife Number One—who was, after all, showing wear and tear—soon followed.

That was seven years ago. Soon, very soon, actually, Sarah would be showing wear and tear herself.

Had someone whispered in her ear, as she walked down the aisle, that the price of marriage would be high, she would never have believed it. Lured by surface glamor, she didn't recognize the price was herself. She had lost herself. Once she realized it, she panicked. Such women seek solace in religion, booze, drugs, charitable work, children, and of course, other men.

When she walked through Archie Ingram's office door on Friday she closed the door behind her. She had made a point of never going to his office or calling him at the office.

"Did you shoot H.?"

"No."

"Why not?"

"I'd never do such a thing. You know that."

"Wish you would," she said in jest, throwing her purse on the desk.

He seized her by the waist, drawing her to him.

She didn't resist. She kissed him, starting

with the cleft in his chin. "I haven't seen you for two long weeks."

Once the frantic mingling of body fluids was over, they had time to review their predicament. A black cloud seemed to follow Archie wherever he moved. As for her, glad though she was that Archie was out of his house, Sarah would never leave her husband. That was what she told Archie. Poor Archie cried.

"It's not that bad." She ran her fingers through his hair.

"It's not that good."

"H. is a vindictive, combative man. He'd stop at nothing to ruin you. Discretion is the better part of valor." She sighed. "He's old. He's not as vigilant as he once was where I'm concerned, probably because his testosterone level has dropped. All will be well."

Blinking back the tears, Archie moaned, "I hate that bastard. I hate him because he's smarter than I am and I hate him because he has you."

"He has me in body only, not in soul," she quietly said.

"Maybe." He frowned, for as much as he loved her, he was learning to distrust her. "But he knew I'd fall for the Teotan plan. The money is good. More money than I could dream of in my job. It wasn't until that meeting in Crozet, the one where Harry's cat jumped on the table, that I realized I had the most to lose. H., Blair, and Tommy risk far less than I do but their profit is higher!"

She smoothed her hair. "Arch, you'll clear

259

a good two million and possibly more. I can't see what you have to lose."

"My reputation. My political career. I'll never be governor."

"Ah." She hadn't realized his ambition reached that high. "Other men have overcome scandal."

"This is Virginia," he snapped.

"Well, yes, there is that. Do you really think you could vault from the county commission to Richmond?"

"Yes. I know I could get elected to the state House of Representatives, for starters. One step at a time. But I blew it." He wiped his brow.

"Maybe you can buy your way in."

"Doesn't work quite that way. Money helps, but—" He smiled sadly. "You haven't lived here long enough, Sarah. Disgrace stains through generations. The reverse of that is all those silly, empty snobs living off the grand deeds of their ancestors. No one forgets anything here."

"That's absurd." She didn't believe it.

"Sarah, you're married to a powerful man. People would like you even if you weren't, but don't let surface acceptance fool you."

"I can ride, garden, and shoot with the best of Virginia's country squires," she boasted.

"So you can." He gave up trying to teach her the real rules of the road. Archie was on the verge of giving up everything, he felt so profoundly miserable.

"Sure you didn't try to kill him? It was a brilliant plan." She changed the subject, a jocular tone to her voice.

"No. I didn't." He pulled himself together, retied his silk rep tie, brushed off his pants. "Sarah, you could have any man you want to play with. Why me?"

"You have imagination. Most men don't."

He nuzzled her neck. "What kind of imagination? Did Tommy Van Allen have imagination?"

She drew back. "About what?"

"About you."

"Arch, don't be absurd."

"I know you had an affair with him."

She waited, sighed, lowered her eyes, then raised them. "I haven't always used the best judgment. He made me—reckless. Of course, I had no idea he was snorting coke. I was as shocked as the next person when the *Daily Progress* reprinted the autopsy results. I never saw any sign of it, but then I'm not sure I know the signs." She sounded convincing.

"Is that why you went up in the airplane with him late at night with a storm coming? To be reckless?" Archie played his wild card, for he didn't really know if she'd been with Tommy or not. He thought maybe he could trip her up.

"No."

"What'd you do, give H. sleeping pills?"

"I never flew with Tommy. Are you suggesting I killed him?"

"Maybe he got in the way."

"Of what?" She pulled back, viewing him with dispassion.

"Your well-ordered life. Maybe he threatened to tell your husband. He might have thought H. would throw you out. He'd have you all to himself."

"Tommy was reckless but he wasn't in love with me. We occupied each other's thoughts for a while—that's all."

"You occupied more than thoughts. Tell me, were you sleeping with him when you were sleeping with me?"

"No," she lied.

"Well—that's something, at least."

"Arch, sometimes if you let things alone they work out better. My husband is an old man."

"And strong as an ox. He'll live to be as old as Tally Urquhart. I wish I did have the guts to kill him, but I need him."

"For what?"

"Teotan. In for a penny, in for a pound. I can't back out now no matter what I'm sacrificing."

"Blair's smart enough to run the corporation. Don't underestimate him. And thank you for speaking up for me at the meeting." She kissed him on each cheek and then the mouth. "I was only kidding about killing H. I could understand if you had shot him. But I'm glad you didn't."

"You certainly ran your mouth about it all over town."

"Arch, what better way to cover *our tracks*?"

"Your tracks." He coolly appraised her but couldn't protect himself from her beauty.

"My tracks?"

262

"Sarah, you could have shot H. You weren't at the reenactment."

"I ran back for H.'s canteen."

"Prove it." He smiled softly.

"You're as bad as Rick Shaw." She laughed it off. "I found witnesses who saw me running back to the tent."

"You could easily have ducked behind the hunter barn or into the woods or even into your Range Rover if you ran fast enough and managed to creep out of the woods. You could have fallen in at the back of the marching line."

"In that gown and hoop? Are you insane?"

"No. You'd change, of course."

He breathed in sharply. "I did not shoot H. Vane. Tommy was already dead. If he had a motive it died with him. You are the only other person with a motive."

"What about Blair? If H. were out of the way, you and he could run Teotan. Two people would control the new water supply."

"It's an interesting theory. But if Blair and I were in cahoots I'd know about it and—" He held up his hands in question.

Unperturbed, she said, "You could have killed Tommy. And tried to kill H. And intend to kill Blair. All threads would be in your hands."

"Thank you for giving me credit for being that intelligent. But I didn't do it. I wouldn't do it and the rock-bottom reality is, I'm not smart enough to pull off a crime like that and not get caught. You, on the other hand, are."

"I didn't kill Tommy Van Allen."

"Not even to cover your tracks, as you say?"

"Well, then you'd be next on my list, wouldn't you?"

"I think I would. Am I?"

"No, darling. I adore you. Can't you tell? Can't you tell when you hold me?"

He sighed. "Sarah, I don't know what I know anymore."

"You're angry at me because I won't leave H. right now. I can't, Archie. We'd have a year of passion if we were lucky, but sooner or later the outside world would tear us apart. My way takes longer but the result is more solid. H. is an *old* man."

"Old and healthy. Old and frighteningly intelligent."

"But still old." She put her forefinger to his lips to silence him, then kissed her forefinger and his lips simultaneously.

"Arch, let me keep saying dreadful things about you. It's the only hope we've got. It's the only cover we've got. You know the truth and you know every chance I get, I'll come to you." She ran her finger across his lips, then along the side of his jaw.

He kissed her hard. "That fool doesn't know what he has in you."

"As long as you know."

"It's funny. I would have thought you'd have the affair with Blair, not me. He's a lot better-looking than I am." He still didn't know whether to believe what Ridley Kent had told him.

"Chemistry." She brushed her hair with a few practiced flips of her wrist. "Besides, Little Mim would die. We've got to leave her something."

"Ridley told me you had a brief fling with Blair." Archie couldn't stand it any longer. He had to hear her response.

Coolly, too coolly, Sarah said, "Ridley's put out that I refused his advances. Why listen to him? I can't believe you listen to him."

"I don't know." His voice wavered.

"Well, I do." She kissed him again and then left for home.

# 47

The underside of a Porsche is sealed. It's as though the bottom is covered by a series of interconnecting skid plates. The mechanic, in white overalls, removed one gray underbody rectangle. Rick peered up as the mechanic shone a light.

"Couldn't hardly hide a tin of snuff up there," the mechanic said.

"Would you like us to remove each panel?" Mike Gage, the owner of Pegasus Motor Cars, politely asked the sheriff.

"No, bring her down. Body panels make more sense."

"Of course."

Blair Bainbridge watched. "You aren't going to cut the upholstery, are you?" He had cooperated with the search, not demanding a warrant, but he wasn't sure what he'd do if it went that far.

"I don't know." Rick ducked his head in the car once it returned to earth. "There's no place to hide anything in those backseats. Hardly big enough for a cat."

"Somebody could remove the padding in the front seats and replace it with cocaine. I think you'd be able to feel it, though." Mike pressed down on the seat.

"Harvey, bring up the new Targa. Let him feel those seats so he has a point of comparison."

Within minutes a lush polar-silver Targa gutturally announced its arrival. Rick opened the door. The smell of a new car made him giddy with possibilities. Dutifully, he pressed on the seats, then pressed again on the seats of Blair's Turbo.

Blair, clasping and unclasping his hands, murmured, "Look, I don't know why you're doing this. You know I'm not involved in drugs."

"Your buddy Tommy Van Allen sure was. Cocaine packed behind his hubcaps—come on, it must have given you a charge to fake out everybody."

"No," Blair flatly replied.

"Fast money. Fast cars."

"I don't sell drugs."

Mike Gage interrupted the increasingly tense exchange. "Let me show you something, Rick. See these air inlets on the front end?"

"Yes." Rick pressed at the small sloops in the metal.

"Could stash small amounts of coke in them but it would lead to undesirable consequences later." Mike had briefed Rick earlier on the basics of an air-cooled engine.

Blair spoke up. "If I was going to deal drugs I'd find a better place than that."

Rick ignored him as Mike continued to point out small areas where drugs could be secreted.

Blair shifted his weight from foot to foot. "You know I'm innocent."

"You knew about Tommy." Rick pushed him.

"Tommy didn't run drugs. It's crazy. A Porsche attracts attention. It'd be crazy to carry drugs in a Porsche."

"If you don't calm down I'll haul you out of here," Rick threatened.

"Listen, I'm allowing you to search my car out of courtesy. You don't have a warrant. I have nothing to hide, so give me some credit."

Mike looked away as Rick scowled.

Rick hesitated a moment, then spoke to Mike. "Don't rip up the leather. Keep searching, though. Mr. Bainbridge and I will be right over there in the squad car if you need me."

"Okay." Mike nodded.

Blair slid into the squad car passenger seat, slamming the door.

Rick wedged himself behind the wheel. "Would you like to tell me the purpose of Teotan? I have Tommy's maps. I know you've sunk wells. Let's have it."

Blair waited a moment, then cleared his throat. "Teotan's purpose is to supply potable water to the northwest quadrant of the county while saving the taxpayers considerable expense. We were intending to present our plan at the next water commission meeting—next week, in fact."

"No new reservoir?"

Blair shrugged. "My hope would be no. Teotan could save this county a fortune in construction costs. There's enough water running underground to fill the need. Millions of gallons."

Rick dropped his head a moment, then raised it. "Sir H. Vane-Tempest said the same thing."

"It *is* a good plan."

"Have you approached Archie Ingram? He opposes any idea of Vane-Tempest's." Rick didn't know of Archie's involvement, for Vane-Tempest, true to his word, had said nothing.

"Archie's a weathervane." Blair sounded noncommittal. "He's not the same man since his wife kicked him out."

"Wasn't impressed with the original." Rick sighed a long sigh. "I'm a paid public servant. I'm not supposed to harbor political opinions."

Blair shrugged. "Won't go past me."

"Changing the subject, what are you going to do if the county rejects your concept? I suppose you have supporting figures?" Rick asked.

"We do. Much of the seven hundred and fifty thousand dollars apiece we each put up to create

Teotan went for a feasibility study. We used a firm out of Atlanta. Washington, New York, and Richmond were too close in the respect that too many people from Albemarle work in those cities or have strong ties there. What we are about to offer this county is economical and sound."

"What if they reject it?"

"If we can get it on the ballot as a referendum, I think we'll prevail despite the vested interests in a reservoir and dam. But, should we fail, we'll sell the water as bottled water."

"You'll have to tap-dance again on that one. Environmental studies and water purity." He shook his head. "We're so over-regulated. It's lunacy. Generations of Virginians drank water right out of the ground. They had more common sense. They didn't build on drained marshland or put their homes where runoff would leak into the well. People sit in front of computers and know nothing of the real world."

"We're prepared for the bottled-water battle. We've retained Fernley, Stubbs, and Marshall in Richmond."

"Then you are prepared." He tapped on the steering wheel. "One member of your company is dead. No suspects. One member was shot. Many suspects, including Mr. Ingram. Is there something about Teotan I ought to know?"

"No."

Rick warned Blair, "If I were you, I'd look over my shoulder. I don't think it's coincidence but I still couldn't say why, exactly."

"Unfortunately, I don't know why either. If our plan works it means a steady flow of profits for as long as we live. If one partner dies, his share is equally divided among the survivors. On the surface of it that would be motivation for murder."

"Blair, have you seen this ticket before?" Rick reached into his breast pocket and pulled out a white locker ticket, Number 349.

Blair examined the Greyhound locker ticket. "No."

"We found this in Tommy's car."

"I assume you went to the locker?"

"Yes. We found accounting books for cocaine deals."

"That's too easy. I know Tommy Van Allen wouldn't sell drugs. No way!"

Rick paused. "Actually, Blair, I think you're right but I have nothing else to go on."

"I don't sell drugs. Tommy didn't sell drugs. I don't know what this is all about or why, but it's not true."

"Is there something about Teotan I don't know? That might have a bearing on this case? Blair, for God's sake, a man has been killed and another wounded. *Tell* me."

Blair inhaled sharply. "Archie is a hidden partner."

"Arch doesn't have that kind of money. You other boys put up big bucks."

"He put in work." Blair left it at that.

Rick whistled. "He's using public office for private gain. And H. Vane-Tempest risks nothing. Archie risks everything."

"H. Vane risks the start-up money."

"That's nothing to him and you know it." Rick turned to face Blair. "This changes everything."

"I don't know. I mean, yes, it compromises Archie politically but people's attention span is two minutes. Look at all the crap politicians get away with, Rick."

"I'd say Archie Ingram has more motivation to kill than any of you. He'd be sitting atop a fountain of profits."

"It doesn't seem possible."

"A lot of things don't seem possible but they happen anyway. Blair, I'd be careful if I were you."

# 48

Mrs. Murphy slept on the divider counter, her tail hanging down. Pewter, on her back on the small table, meowed in her sleep. Tucker snored under the big canvas mail cart.

Harry felt like sleeping herself. A low-pressure system was moving in.

The front door swung open as her head nodded. She blinked. Dr. Larry Johnson waved.

"I'm ready for a nap, too, Harry. Where's Miranda?"

"Next door. She's planning a menu for Market. He wants to sell complete meals. It's a good idea."

"And Miranda will cook them?"

"Part of them. She works hard enough as it is, and the garden comes first."

Larry eyed Murphy's tail. "Tempting."

Harry stood on her tiptoes, leaning over the counter. "She's proud of that tail."

Mrs. Hogendobber entered through the back door. "Hello," she sang out.

Mrs. Murphy opened one eye. *"Keep your voices down."*

Sarah and Sir H. Vane-Tempest came in with Herb right behind them.

"Glad I ran into you," Larry said. He walked back outside and returned, handing Vane-Tempest his Confederate tunic top. "Is this genuine homespun?"

Vane-Tempest examined the material in his hands.

Miranda flipped up the countertop and walked out to the front. "I can tell you."

*"I wish everyone would shut up."* Mrs. Murphy opened both eyes.

Tucker lifted her head. *"They complain when I bark."*

Miranda held the material in her hands, rubbing it between forefinger and thumb. "Machine."

"How can you tell?" Vane-Tempest held the other sleeve.

"If this were spun on a home loom there'd be more slubs and the color dye wouldn't be as even. Also, the boys in gray were often called butternut. Dyes weren't colorfast, you see, and dyeing could be an expensive process. A foot soldier would wear homespun for so long

272

that the color would go from a sort of light brown to a gray-white over time."

Harry joined them. "Bet that stuff itches to high heaven."

"Your shirt would be spun from cotton. Probably better cotton than what you buy today," Miranda noted. "So you wouldn't feel your tunic so much."

Harry took the jacket from Vane-Tempest, slipping it on.

Herb laughed. "You'll drown in that."

Mrs. Murphy sat bolt upright. She soared from the counter into the mail bin. *"Wake up."*

*"Dammit!"* Pewter, surprised and therefore scared, spit at Murphy.

Tally and Big Mim dropped by to pick up their mail.

"You know what I don't understand?" Tally put one hand on her hip. "If a man dresses as a woman, everybody laughs. They'll pay money to see him. If a woman dresses as a man, stone silence."

By now Pewter had hopped onto the divider counter and Murphy roused Tucker, who padded out front to the people.

"Want to try?" Harry handed the tunic to Big Mim.

"I'll leave that to the boys."

*"That's it!"* Murphy crowed.

Pewter blinked, thought, then she got it. So did Tucker.

That same afternoon, as Sarah fed the domestic ducks on her pond, private investigator Tareq Said discreetly delivered county-commission tapes to her husband, as he did once a week. He'd bugged Archie's office along with the others. Vane-Tempest did not fully trust Arch and wanted to make certain he was getting his money's worth. Also, this way he could keep tabs on the other commissioners. Surprisingly, Arch had not disappointed him. He really was working for Teotan's acceptance. He was all business.

However, this week's tape proved substantially different. Tareq handed over the legal-sized folder, then swiftly left.

# 49

The brass buttons rolled around in the palm of her hand with a dull *clank*. Harry pushed them with her forefinger.

"First Virginia." Blair leaned against his 110 HP John Deere tractor—new, of course, like everything on his farm. "They're genuine. Cost five hundred and fifty dollars."

"Wonder who wore them and if he survived the war?"

Blair shrugged. "I don't know."

The warm sun skidded over Mrs. Murphy's coat; she glistened as she lounged on the hood of the 911 Turbo. Neither human had yet noticed her chosen place to display her glories.

Pewter prowled around Blair's equipment shed with Tucker. She was on a blue-jay kick. Determined to find and bait the raucous bird wherever she could, she had sharpened her claws on the side of the shed. Pewter could perform surgery with those claws.

"Looks like you're throwing yourself whole hog into reenacting," Harry said.

"I kind of thought it was silly at first. But I felt something at Oak Ridge, and, Harry, that wasn't even a true reenactment. We weren't on sacred ground, if you will. I want to go to the Seven Days, Sharpsburg." He looked sober at the word; Sharpsburg was the scene of the worst carnage in that bloodiest of wars. "I can't explain what I felt, just—just that I have to do this."

"Have you ever noticed that all the reenactors are white?"

"The combatants were mostly white."

"I'll feel a little better about this when someone resurrects the 54th Massachusetts." Harry cited the all-black regiment renowned for its courage.

"Harry, I'm sure someone is already doing that. Really, I don't think this is a racist program." His warm hazel eyes flickered.

"Maybe you're right." She sighed. "Maybe it's me. Maybe I don't like being reminded of a war of supreme foolishness, a foolishness that soaked this state in blood. So many battles have been fought here in Virginia since the Revolutionary War. All that blood has soaked into our soil. Makes me sick, kinda. I think I fail to see the romance of it."

"Maybe it's a guy thing." He smiled.

"Guess so." She paused, then swung up

into the cab of the elegant, expensive, coveted John Deere. "Blair, I've been thinking. A guy thing?" she said, louder than she intended. "What if Sarah was in uniform? What if she shot H. Vane?"

*"What?"*

The animals stopped in the shed. Mrs. Murphy, on the Porsche, pricked her ears.

"I know it sounds crazy but today in the post office when I tried on the jacket, it occurred to me—she could have worn the trousers under her hoop skirt, stepped out of it....Of course, she'd have to run back like mad, get out of the uniform, stash it, and get back into her dress— but it's not impossible. Heavy smoke covered everything. You couldn't see the hand in front of your face sometimes. And it was pandemonium. Who would notice one person sneaking off? And besides, nobody noticed H. had been shot for quite a while. She'd have had time."

He blinked. "I don't know. Never thought of it."

"Mrs. Woo made lots of the uniforms— too many to remember. But she probably kept receipts, if not records. So what happens? Her store gets burned down."

Blair wondered if Sarah was capable of murder. "Harry, that's pretty extreme."

"But why? Everyone just jumped to the conclusion that it was Archie Ingram."

Slowly, his deep baritone low, Blair said, "Well, I don't know. It's possible. But why kill him? She'll eventually inherit his estate anyway, most of it."

"He's a tough bird and a demanding one. She's in the prime of life. Servicing H. Vane, you'll forgive the expression, may be losing some of its luster."

His face reddened. Mrs. Murphy carefully slid off the Porsche hood. She walked over to the tractor as Pewter and Tucker joined her. Harry stepped down from the cockpit.

"Nice, huh?"

"Beautiful. If I had to pick between your Porsche and your John Deere it would be one of the hardest decisions of my life." She laughed, leaning against the giant rear wheel. "I think I'd better talk to Coop."

"Don't do that," he said too rapidly.

"Why not?"

"Because you can't ruin someone's name like that."

*"She's not ruining her name,"* Mrs. Murphy said. *"She's only conveying an idea. Coop has tact."*

"Hadn't thought of that."

*"Mother, you're not ruining her name. And you're right!"* Pewter meowed.

Harry picked up the cat, putting her on her shoulder. "Hush."

*"Put me down."* She wiggled.

*"Pewter, stay put. You'll get her mind distracted. Humans can't focus for very long. That's why they can't catch mice."*

Pewter glared at Mrs. Murphy but settled down on Harry's shoulder.

Tucker lifted her nose in the air. *"Blair's body temperature is rising. He's upset."*

"The other flaw in your theory is that if Sarah shot at H. Vane, then who killed Tommy Van Allen?" Blair said.

"There's no proof that the two murders are connected. We've all been assuming. They could be unrelated."

*"They're related. We just don't know how."* Tucker was resolute on this point.

Blair blushed. "Yeah."

"What's the matter?"

*"Took her a while,"* Pewter dryly commented.

"Oh." He clasped his hands behind his back. "Nothing. Say, would you like to borrow my tractor? You could disc your fields in one-third the time." He pointed to a disc, its round metal spheres tilted slightly inward toward a center line.

Murphy noted, *"That's a quick change of subject."*

Harry eyed the huge implement, which would make short work of her chores. Good farmer that she was, she disced first before plowing. She disced the fields for hay, too. They didn't need plowing but she was a great believer in working the soil thoroughly before planting. If the hay was already established she'd merely thatch and aerate every few years. She loved farming, desperately wishing she could make a good living from it. But she just squeaked by.

"This is brand-new."

"Hell, you know how to use this equipment better than I do."

"Tell you what." Harry would feel better if she could make a trade. "I'll show you how to prepare that cornfield you want to put in down on your bottomland. Then I'll borrow this baby." She patted the field-green side of the square, powerful tractor.

"Deal." He stuck out his hand then withdrew it. "Sorry. Forgot my manners."

"Oh, Blair, I don't care. I think that stuff's outmoded." She referred to the fact that a man wasn't supposed to extend his hand to a lady, but wait for her to extend hers first.

"Big Mim would kill me." He grinned.

Harry noticed Archie's U-Haul. "Is he ever leaving?"

"Today, in fact."

"Bet you're relieved."

"Archie is curiously stubborn."

"What a nice way to put it." Harry smiled as she headed for her truck. "Where's he going?"

"Tally Urquhart's."

"What?"

"She'll let him live in one of her outbuildings if he'll restore it. He said he needs a positive project."

"*I'm nervous.*" The tiger walked over to Harry's truck. "*We've got to get her to call Coop.*"

It was too late for that.

# 50

Sir H. Vane-Tempest noticed the peculiar waxiness of the magnolias—grandifloras—he'd planted along his southern drive. The long shadows of late afternoon heightened the colors and the sense of melancholy at the day's passing.

A troop of gardeners worked behind the house.

Usually the garden delighted him. Vane-Tempest was not a man to delight in people, since he viewed all relationships as a power struggle, a struggle he must win in order to feel important. He saw people in terms of a vertical scale. Perhaps the Windsor family ranked above him, certain Rothschilds and Von Thyssens, but he believed he sat very near the pinnacle. Usually that fact thrilled him.

Since reading Tareq's transcription he'd been unthrilled, indeed, deeply miserable.

"The days are drained into time's cup and I've drunk it dry," he whispered to himself, turning on his heel to go inside.

He stopped, turned around, and looked again at the gardens. He noticed Sarah walking among the workers. Her beauty soared beyond explanation, like the beauty of creamy peonies. It just was.

He turned once more and walked into the house. He strolled down the long parquet-floor hallway, barely noticing the Monet. He strode into Sarah's room, opened her closet, clicked on the lights, and closed the door behind him.

Row upon row of cashmere sweaters in plastic see-through boxes attested to her acquisitiveness as well as to her insight into the fact that she was valuable only as long as she was beautiful.

He headed for the long rows of canvas garment bags. He unzipped them one by one. Sumptuous evening gowns of emerald, sapphire, ruby, silver, white, and gold spilled over the sides of the opened bags. He could picture his wife in each of these extravagantly expensive confections.

He reached into the bottom of each garment bag, swished around with his hand, then moved to the next one. The last bag tucked in the cedar-lined closet swayed slightly.

He opened it. The zipper clicked as the tab moved down. Her shimmering peach gown fluttered. He reached down. Nothing.

The door opened. "H., what are you doing?"

"Where is it?"

"What?" She noticed the shine on his brow, the gleam in his eye.

"Your uniform."

"What uniform?"

"Don't play games with me. You dressed up and shot me. Archie doesn't have the guts."

"I did no such thing."

"Liar!" He lunged toward her but the closet was huge.

She slammed the door, locked it, and cut off the lights. She took her unregistered snub-nosed

281

.38 out of the nightstand by her bed and threw it into her purse. Then she ran like hell for her car.

# 51

Harry was just turning into her driveway when Sarah flew past her without waving, her car a blur.

She stopped at her mailbox, watching as Sarah turned into Blair's driveway a quarter of a mile down the road.

"I wonder—" she said out loud, then shook her head. "Nah."

Sarah roared up to the house, parked her car next to the Porsche, and ran to the door.

"Archie! Archie!"

Archie, who'd just come back from dragging the U-Haul to Tally's, was surprised to see Sarah burst through the doorway, even more surprised when she flung herself into his arms.

"I think I'll go to my office." Blair, who'd been helping Archie, put his papers in a box, then walked upstairs.

Sarah waited until she heard the door close. "He's going to kill me."

"H.?"

"Archie, I've got to get out of here. Help me!"

"Why does he want to kill you?"

"Because I tried to kill him."

"What!"

"It *was* me at Oak Ridge. You were right.

I dressed as a soldier, just as you said. Those damned old rifles—it's a wonder anybody hit the broad side of a barn during that war."

Archie held her at arm's length. "Sarah, you really shot H. Vane?"

"I'm only sorry I missed killing him."

"He knows?" Archie was amazed.

"He thinks he knows. I caught him in my closet going through my garment bags— looking for the uniform, damn his eyes. Well, he won't find it. I'm not stupid. I burned the thing."

"So he has no proof?"

"No, but what does that matter? He's in a rage. He'll kill me if he finds me and he's so rich he'll get off. People like him always do."

"Why did you want to kill him?" Archie coolly asked.

"Because I couldn't stand his fat body one more minute. Because I hate him. I hate the sight of him. You've never been a servant, Archie, you wouldn't understand."

"You were a very well-paid one."

Sensing his withdrawal, she said, "I couldn't tell you. You would have tried to stop me. As long as he's alive I can't be with you. And why should I go to the poorhouse? I've worked for that money. If he caught us together my divorce would be an open-and-shut case. Shut the door. Bang."

"I see."

"Archie, help me!" She threw her arms around him.

"Where is he now?"

283

"Locked in my closet. He'll eventually break the door down. His shoulder still hurts but he's strong. You've got to hide me until I can figure something out."

"Jesus, Sarah, didn't your mother tell you, Look before you leap?"

"If I'd done that I'd never have fallen in love with you."

"I wish I believed that." He sighed. Beautiful women acquired men like dogs acquire fleas. All they had to do was walk through a room.

"Did you shoot Tommy? Tell me the truth this time."

"No. I loved Tommy once." She looked him square in the eye. "He had magic. It didn't last long but I was so miserable with H. Archie, can't you understand?"

"I—"

"He'll kill me!"

"All right. All right." He stroked her hair.

Try as he might, he couldn't stop loving her. He kissed her. "Everything will be all right." He walked to the foot of the stairs. "Blair."

The door opened. "Yes."

"I'm taking Sarah to the airport."

Blair clomped halfway down the stairs. "Everything okay?"

"No," Sarah tearfully confessed. "Blair, I can explain everything later. I just have to get out of here."

Archie hustled her into his Land Rover. Blair watched them start down the driveway. If he'd watched longer he would have seen that

Archie turned right out of his driveway, not left toward the airport.

# 52

Pewter wedged herself underneath the camellia bush. She felt certain the blue jay would perch there and since she'd squeezed herself in and was still, he wouldn't notice.

Hunting was best in the morning or late afternoon. No animal likes to go to bed on an empty stomach. She knew she could grab the blue jay. She'd even gone to the trouble of scattering about bread crusts, which she fished out of the garbage when Harry's back was turned.

Pewter dreamed of ways to dispatch the bird, her favorite being a straight vertical leap, grasping the offender between her mighty paws, pulling him to the ground, and staring him in the eye before breaking his neck.

*"She who laughs last laughs best!"* she told herself, revving her motor.

She was ready!

*Pop.*

Mrs. Murphy, sitting on the haywagon next to the barn, out of Pewter's way, heard it, too. She looked out toward Harry, who'd been inspired by the vision of that new John Deere to get up on Johnny Pop and overseed the front acres. Harry rolled along, the small seeder attached to the back of the tractor.

*"Pewter."*

Pewter wouldn't answer.

Tucker, half-asleep under the haywagon, did. *"What?"*

*"Hear that?"*

*"Yes."*

*"That wasn't Johnny Pop."* Mrs. Murphy was worried.

The old tractor would *pop, pop, pop* along but this *pop* was crisp.

*Pop!*

*"Pewter, get out from under there. We've got to get to Blair's."*

Pewter backed farther underneath the camellia bush. *She'll do anything to spoil this. She* doesn't *think I can kill the blue jay. She thinks she's the Great Striped Hunter. I'll show her,* she thought to herself.

Mrs. Murphy peeled off the haywagon, covering eight feet in the launch without even pushing hard. Tucker scrambled out.

Pewter noticed the two racing across the fields toward Blair's house. Torn, she grumbled, then slowly extricated herself from her perfect hiding place.

*"Fatso!"* The blue jay, who'd been perched on the weathervane on top of the barn, screamed as he swooped over Pewter's head.

She leapt up, twisting in the air, but missed. *"You're toast,"* she threatened but hurried after Mrs. Murphy and Tucker. The jay dive-bombed her part of the way, shrieking with delight.

Mrs. Murphy didn't turn to look for Pewter or wait.

Pewter switched on the afterburners, her ears

swept back, her whiskers flat against her face, her tail level to the ground. She veered right toward the creek, then dropped down onto the bank, ran alongside, found a shallow place, and ran through the water. No time to fool around and find another path. She reached Mrs. Murphy and Tucker as they crossed over by the old graveyard on the hill. The three animals flew down to Blair's house.

*"Too late,"* Mrs. Murphy said.

Blair sat in his car, the door open. Blood ran down his forehead, marring the leather seat. He was slumped over to the right, his long torso behind the gearshift, his head on the passenger seat. The motor was running. He appeared to have been shot.

Tucker licked his hand but Blair didn't move.

Sarah Vane-Tempest's car was parked in front of the barn. Archie Ingram's car was gone.

Mrs. Murphy jumped into his lap. Pewter followed by gingerly stepping onto the floor on the driver's side. The car was in neutral. Blair's left foot was on the clutch, his right had turned up sideways.

*"Where's he hit?"* Tucker stood on her hind legs.

*"I don't know."*

*"His legs are okay."* Pewter sniffed for blood. *"What about his head?"*

Mrs. Murphy put her nose to Blair's nose. She sniffed his lips, put a paw on his lower lip, and pulled it down. *"Gums are white."*

*"But is he hit in the head?"*

*"There's a lot of blood, but I can only see the left side of his face."*

*"Put your nose to the seat. See if you smell blood or powder,"* Tucker advised.

Murphy carefully laid the side of her face on the seat, her eye level with Blair's closed one. *"Blood's oozing on the seat. Must be the right side of his head,"* she said, cool in a crisis. *"Pewter, sit in his lap and lean on the horn. I'll keep licking him."*

Pewter, both paws on the horn, put her weight into it. The horn sounded.

*"Who's going to hear it?"* Tucker sat down. *"Archie's not here. Mom's on her tractor."*

*"He's in a bad way."* Murphy kept licking Blair's face. *"We've got to do something fast."*

*"Let's think."* Pewter, over with Murphy now, put her paw on Blair's wrist. His pulse was erratic.

*"We could run back to Harry,"* Pewter said.

*"She's on the tractor. Can't hear us. She might not notice us. We've got to convince her to come over here."* Murphy checked the gearshift on the floor. *"Tucker, are you thinking what I'm thinking?"*

*"It's his only chance,"* the dog solemnly said.

*"I wish somebody would tell me!"* an upset gray kitty exploded.

*"We're going to drive this sucker,"* Murphy resolutely stated.

*"You're out of your mind!"*

*"Pewter, go home then,"* Murphy sharply told her. *"Tucker, give him a shove."*

Tucker nudged Blair with her front paws and her head. He slowly slumped over just a bit more.

"*Pewter, are you in or out of this car?*"

"*I'm in. What do you want me to do?*"

"*We've got to get the car in first gear.*"

"*His foot is on the clutch,*" Pewter said.

"*Okay, Tucker, can you fit in down there?*"

"*Yes.*"

"*Sit on his foot while Pewter and I push the gearshift into first. Then slowly move his foot off the clutch and we'll steer.*"

"*Won't work. We'll stall out,*" Tucker panted. "*The trick is, I have to get his foot off the clutch and mine on the gas pedal. Luckily his foot isn't on the gas pedal.*"

"*We have to get this right on the first try.*" Murphy crawled over into Blair's lap while Pewter sat in the passenger seat, patting his face with her paw.

The idea was for Murphy to push the shift stick from the top while Pewter pulled from the bottom.

"*Ready?*" Murphy tersely asked.

"*Yes,*" the other two replied.

The cats moved the gearshift into first. That part was easy. The next part was hard because if they stalled out they'd have to turn the key and feed gas at the same time. They didn't think they could do that.

"*Tucker, it's better if we shoot ahead than stall out,*" Murphy advised.

Pewter had joined her in the driver's seat. She stood on her hind legs, staring out the window. Murphy sat in Blair's lap, her paws on the bottom of the steering wheel.

*"God, I hope this car is as responsive as all those ads say it is."* Murphy sent up a little prayer to the Great Cat in the sky for Blair. *"Let's go."*

Tucker pushed off Blair's foot as she pushed down on the gas pedal with her right paw. The car lurched forward and sputtered.

*"More gas."*

Tucker, both feet free now, pressed on the accelerator.

The car smoothly accelerated at amazing speed.

*"Keep on the road! Not so much gas!"*

*"Help me,"* Murphy called out.

Pewter, claws unleashed, sank them into the leather steering wheel. She struggled to keep the car on the gravel driveway. Even a small motion turned the wheels. *"Tucker, let up a little,"* Pewter screamed.

*"I'm trying."* Tucker took her full weight off the flat pedal. *"We've got it now. We got it."*

*"What are we going to do when we get to the paved road?"* Pewter shivered with fear.

*"Pray that no car is coming our way because if we stop we won't get started again."*

Pewter, eyes huge, chin quivering, steered for all she was worth. By God, she might be afraid but she wasn't a coward.

They reached the end of Blair's long driveway. A truck was past them on the right. With all their might the two cats turned the wheel to the left. The car door still hung wide open.

*"Not too much! Not too much!"* Pewter directed.

*"More?"* Tucker couldn't see a thing. This was truly an act of blind faith.

*"No, keep it right like it is, Tucker. You're doing great. Okay, okay, here's our driveway. Another left. Not too much, it's curvy."* Murphy kept her voice calm.

*"Slow, slow. Oh no—there's another car!"* Pewter's fur stood on end.

*"He sees us. He's not going to hit us without messing himself up."*

The car swerved around them, horn honking.

*"Asshole!"* Murphy spat. *"Yeah, okay, now keep your eyes on the road, Pewts. We'll make it."* The car dropped down a bit on the dirt road; the stones had moved to the sides, as they always do. It's a waste of money putting stone on a driveway, but who can afford macadam?

*"I see Mom!"* Pewter almost wept with relief.

*"Tucker, keep it steady. We have to roll past her line of vision. Okay, okay, she sees us. Pewter, hit the horn."*

Pewter laid on that horn for all she was worth.

*"Off?"*

*"Yeah."*

Tucker lifted her weight off the gas pedal. The car shuddered to a stop. Harry stopped the tractor and hit the ground running. She tore over her newly seeded field.

"Oh my God," was all she could say when she reached the stalled-out Turbo. She put it in neutral, started it, then picked up the activated car phone and dialed 911.

"Crozet Emergency—" Diana Robb didn't get to finish her sentence.

"Diana. Harry. Blair's in my driveway. He's been shot. There's blood everywhere. For God's sake, hurry!"

She dropped the phone. She was shaking so hard that Tucker, now on the ground, licked her hands. Then she remembered to turn off the motor. She no longer needed the power for the telephone. Harry felt Blair's pulse, which was surprisingly strong. Fearful of moving him, she ran around to the passenger side of the car and opened the door. The two cats got out of the car and looked up at her blankly.

Within minutes they heard the siren. The rescue squad halted behind the Porsche. Diana reached Blair first.

"Call the E.R. Let's get him out of here."

"Is he going to make it?"

"I don't know." Diana held his head. "Help me lift him upright from the passenger side. We'll slide him out on the driver's side." She turned to Harry. "How did he ever make it over here?"

"If I told you, you wouldn't believe me."

The animals watched, tears in their eyes, their ears drooping.

As Harry and Diana lifted out the injured man, Joe Farham, Diana's assistant, rolled out the gurney from the back of the ambulance.

The three humans gently placed Blair in the gurney.

Joe took Blair's pulse as Diana, still stabilizing his head, examined the wound.

"I can't find an entry point." She stared at the bloody right side of Blair's head.

Blair moaned.

"Dear God, what can I do to help him!" Harry, in tears, cried.

"Take a couple of deep breaths. We'll get him to the E.R. as fast as we can. You wait for Rick to get here. I'll call for him on my way to the hospital. Oh, Harry, don't touch the car. Okay?"

"Okay." Harry wiped her eyes.

Joe had shut the ambulance doors and hopped into the driver's seat as Diana jumped in next to Blair, closing the doors behind her. They hit the siren and flew down the gravel road as Harry tried to collect herself.

*"Please let Blair live,"* Tucker whimpered.

"I don't believe what I saw." Harry cried anew, reaching down to stroke her animals. "You guys are heroes."

*"We couldn't let him die. He has a fighting chance,"* Murphy solemnly said.

Harry sat down on the grass to wait for Sheriff Shaw.

# 53

A crowd of people kept vigil in the hospital hallway: Harry, Miranda, Big Mim, Little Mim, Herb Jones, Boom Boom, Susan and Ned, Market Shiflett, Jim Sanburne, and Dr. Larry

Johnson. Finally, Larry's young partner, Hayden McIntire, emerged from the operating room.

Everyone stood up.

"He'll live."

A collective sigh of relief passed through the group and tears withheld from fear suddenly flowed in gratitude.

"Dr. Chan's closing him up now, but he'll definitely make it."

Larry rushed down immediately once he heard the news. Hayden took him to look at the X rays.

"There's swelling in the area of damage. The brain is fine. Luckily the bullet didn't shatter his skull. It made a deep crease." Hayden pointed to the X ray. "Right here is where the bullet grazed. Like a crease in a piece of paper that tears just a bit."

"Thank God." Larry closed his eyes for a second.

"It's very hard to say what his prognosis is until the swelling goes down. He should be fine. He's young, strong, healthy, but this is the last place you want swelling. Time and rehab will tell."

Later Larry walked with Hayden to see Blair in post-op.

"Any ideas about what happened?" he asked.

"Yes. Given the position of the wound, I think he'd turned away from his attacker."

"He didn't anticipate being shot?" Larry rubbed his forehead with the palm of his hand.

"No. He turned his back."

"Any other signs of struggle on the body?" Larry gazed at the tall man, seemingly asleep except for all the tubes running into him.

"No. Not a mark."

# 54

When Blair regained consciousness Rick and Cynthia were there waiting for him.

Hayden gave them five minutes only, because Blair's condition was still critical.

"Did you see who shot you?" Rick quietly leaned over Blair's bed.

Blair didn't answer because he could barely focus. He had the world's worst headache.

"Archie?" Rick whispered to the wounded man.

"No." Blair whispered, then lost consciousness again.

# 55

The high sun shone over central Virginia. Each leaf, a bride in spring green, smiled at the radiant afternoon light. The trumpet vines opened their orange flowers. Bumblebees appeared in squadrons. Honeybees, decimated by a fatal mite, buzzed but in reduced numbers.

Harry, dazed that her friend had been shot, worked hard but her mind kept returning to yesterday's sight of the cats driving the car with Tucker down in the well. She knew that any animal recognizes injury and pain in any other animal. What was remarkable was that they brought the bleeding man to her. They drove him right in front of her.

Each time she envisioned Murphy and Pewter, both with their paws on the steering wheel, she'd get the shakes.

Living close to nature, Harry was better connected to reality than many people. Now she had to face the depth of her ignorance. She had credited her animal friends with human traits. She'd insulted them. By masking their true natures with human characteristics, she missed what was unique about each species. It was entirely possible that Mrs. Murphy and Pewter, along with Tucker, operated at another level of intelligence than she did. It was also possible that theirs was higher but not measurable by human standards.

Harry was being humbled by life in its myriad forms.

# 56

In the west an inferno illuminated the sky, the spring sun setting in a scarlet blaze. The sky, as though put to the torch, exploded in scarlet and gold.

Cynthia noticed the drama of it as she checked her service revolver. Rick, his mouth a straight line, carefully coasted down the road toward Tally Urquhart's haybarn, where Tommy Van Allen's plane was stowed.

He'd stopped at Miss Tally's to inquire if she'd seen Archie. She said he was renting a room in her house while he fixed up an old farm-worker's stone house down the farm road.

When Cynthia inquired as to how they'd get along, Tally curtly replied, "I need some-body to fight with."

Rick ordered her to stay in her house. She said she had seen Archie's white Land Rover go back there a while ago. She'd heard another car not ten minutes ago but she didn't get to the window in time to see it. However, she was sure it was another car going in, not one coming out.

Rick was no sooner out her front door than Tally phoned Mim.

"Boss, should we wait for backup?"

"No time. God, I hate these kinds of things." Like all police officers, Rick knew domestic violence to be the most irrational of situations. Armed robbery was easy compared to this.

After speeding down the old farm road toward the haybarn, Rick cut the motor at a curve out of sight from the barn door. Both cops got out, drew their guns, and slowly walked toward the old barn, which they could not yet see. Before they rounded the curve they heard a curse, two shots, and a scream. They ran but with practiced caution.

As the two officers approached the barn doors they saw Sir. H. Vane-Tempest bent over Archie Ingram. Sarah was clinging to her husband.

"Freeze!" Rick commanded.

Vane-Tempest spun around, a .357 in his right hand.

"Drop your weapon," Rick ordered, and Vane-Tempest threw the gun on the ground.

Rick kept his gun on the Englishman while Cynthia ran over to Archie. She pressed her index finger into his neck.

"Gone."

"He tried to kill me after abducting my wife," Vane-Tempest said calmly.

Sarah, sobbing, stood between her husband and her lover.

"Have you anything to say?" Cynthia stood up, facing Sarah.

"Sarah, you have the legal right to remain silent," Vane-Tempest forcefully said. "This has been a dreadful situation. You take a deep breath. You're safe now."

"Am I?" She put her face in her hands.

"Put your hands behind your back, sir."

"Rick, I killed him in self-defense. You're making a mistake."

"That may be true, but for right now, the handcuffs go on." Rick snapped the steel bracelets on quickly.

"Don't handcuff him. He had no choice." Sarah wiped her eyes. "Archie abducted me from our home after locking H. in my closet."

"Why would he do that?" Rick put his gun in its holster.

"Because I was having an affair with him. He wanted us to ride off into the sunset together." She didn't realize the irony of her words as the gorgeous sunset deepened.

"You knew about this?" Cynthia directed this to the handcuffed Sir H. Vane-Tempest.

"I did. Yes."

"Oh, H., I'm sorry. I'm so sorry. I never thought he'd try to kill you." She walked over to her husband and threw her arms around his neck.

"I'm an old man. You're a young and beautiful woman. Maybe one of the most beautiful women on the face of the earth," he whispered.

Another squad car pulled up along with the Crozet Rescue Squad. Diana Robb had had a busy day.

Rick motioned to his officers to go slow, then he put his hand under Vane-Tempest's elbow. "Let's go down to HQ."

"May I phone my lawyer?"

"When we get there."

"Do I have to wear these?"

"Until we get to the station, you do. Come on, before the goddamned television crews get out here." That made the old man pick up his feet.

Sarah slid into the backseat next to her husband. She never looked backward at Archie, sprawled on the ground, her snub-nosed .38 in his right hand.

# 57

Mim watched with her aunt as the last of the police cars drove out.

"Shall we go down there?" Mim asked.

"Not in the dark. Let's go in the morning." Tally watched the flickering red-and-blue lights. "Mimsy, stay here tonight, please."

"Of course."

# 58

News of Archie's death spread like a prairie fire.

Susan Tucker burst through the kitchen door to tell Harry, who'd already heard it via telephone from Mrs. Hogendobber, who'd heard it from Mim, who'd heard it from Rick Shaw.

"I can't believe Archie would kidnap Sarah." Harry lay at one end of the sofa while Susan stretched out on the other end. The cats joined them, stretched across the back. Tucker curled up on the wing chair nearby.

"Well, he did," Susan matter-of-factly stated.

"*Bull,*" Pewter said.

"*Sex does short-circuit people's brains,*" Tucker agreed with Susan. "*But why would Archie shoot Blair?*"

"*Her car was parked at Blair's when we found him,*" Mrs. Murphy said.

300

*"Well, why would she go to Blair's?"* Pewter stretched her hind leg straight out for grooming.

"Pewter, do that later. I hate that licking sound when I'm having a conversation," Harry ordered.

*"Priss,"* Pewter complained, but nonetheless tucked her hind leg under her.

*"All the girls go to Blair's,"* Tucker said.

*"Archie was at Blair's, too. He didn't kidnap Sarah,"* Murphy said.

*"Blair must know that. When his mind is clear and he feels better."* Pewter tried to think who else might know.

*"Archie was moving out,"* Mrs. Murphy continued. *"She went there for him. Archie didn't kidnap her."*

*"He's not here to defend himself,"* Tucker sagely noted.

Murphy lay down. *"A wasted life, Archie's."*

"H. is out on bail." Susan put her hands behind her head. "Big surprise."

"Was Sarah harmed?"

"No. She says Archie kidnapped her. He wanted to live with her. He wanted her to run away. He didn't mean to harm her."

"What do you think?" Harry asked.

"I don't know what to think. I'm glad it's over."

"Is it? We still don't know who killed Tommy Van Allen."

"Sarah confessed to Rick Shaw that Archie confessed to her that he killed Tommy over a drug deal gone sour."

"I don't believe it," Harry said.

*"He did not,"* Murphy protested.

"Hush. You've had enough to eat."

*"Sarah shot H. Vane. I don't know who killed Tommy Van Allen but she shot H."* Murphy stuck to her guns.

"She gets a notion..." Harry commented on Murphy's conversation.

*"And they're usually on the money,"* Tucker said.

*"Thank you."* Murphy rested her head on her paws. *"We'd better get over to Tally's place tomorrow. First light."*

*"Why so early?"* Pewter moaned.

*"Before people start crawling over it. The ghouls will show up whether Tally wants them or not."*

*"Weird. Humans fear death but they can't stay away from it."* Pewter remarked.

# 59

A line of gray illuminated the eastern horizon. Mrs. Murphy, Pewter, and Tucker were already on the ridge above Rose Hill.

As they dropped down into the fertile plain the golden rim of the sun pushed over the horizon and shafts of gold, like spokes on a wheel, radiated into the lightened sky.

By the time they reached the barn and stone buildings they were surprised to find Big Mim and Tally already there.

A pool of blood, dark brown, stained the dirt road where Archie had fallen. Big Mim and

Tally stood in silence in the circle of buildings. When Mim finally spoke, she said nothing of the evidence of murder. The women knew each other too well for Tally to be surprised.

"Why don't you let me restore these?"

"I've got no use for them," Tally replied.

"You could rent them out. Make a little money. After all, you were going to rent one to Archie." Mim smiled suddenly as Mrs. Murphy and Pewter came up to her. "Why, look who's here." Tucker lingered at the blood until Murphy sharply reprimanded her.

"You characters certainly cover the miles." Mim petted the cats' heads.

"I say let the whole damn place fall down." Tally thumped the ground with her cane.

"That's foolish."

"Who are you to tell me what's foolish? I knew you in diapers."

"The day may come when you want to sell Rose Hill. You need to keep up the place. I can repair all this. I have a good crew."

"I don't know." She paused, looking skyward as the colors changed from gold to pink to red to gold again and the sun flooded the world with light. "Crazy."

"Hmm?"

She pointed with her cane to the pool of blood.

"Yes. It's all over now."

"It certainly is for Archie. Damn fool. This is the South. You don't steal another man's wife without expecting retribution."

"That's why the rest of the country thinks

we're uncivilized. We erupt. Underneath the veneer of manners we're animals."

"Are you an animal, my dear?" Tally raised a silver eyebrow.

"Yes. If pushed hard enough I am. Why kid myself?"

"The question is, what pushes people? Love? Money? Prestige? Property? I don't know. What people kill and die for seems thin gruel to me."

"You're old. You forget."

Tally whirled on Mim, her cane over her head. "Damn you."

"Passion, Aunt Tally. You see, you still have it."

Tally brought her cane down, then laughed. "You are clever. Sometimes I forget how clever you are."

"Back to business." Mim deflected the compliment.

"Oh, what!" came the irritated response.

"First order of business, let me get my men in here and clean this barn. I'll bring this place back to the way it was when I was a child. How I loved to play back here. And the barn dances! Mother would wear gingham dresses and Daddy would laugh and laugh. What days those were before—well, before everything changed so."

"Change is part of life. Sometimes it's good and sometimes it's not. Most times it's both. A change can be bad for me but good for the man down the road."

"*Maybe I can get them to look at the suit-*

*case.*" Tucker wagged her tailless bottom as Mim winked at her.

"*You can try.*" Pewter shrugged.

Tucker bounded into the thicket, barking like a maniac.

"What's she got in there?" Mim wondered.

"Tractor graveyard. Rats or mice."

The two women returned to arguing about the stone houses but Tucker continued to bark.

"I'll go see. Maybe she's hurt." Mim pushed through the budding bushes, which included nasty thorns. She heard the little dog under the Chevy.

Raised in the country, Mim was hesitant to squat down and find herself face-to-face with a snarling fox or other burrowing creature. But Tucker's entreaties overcame her natural caution. She knelt down, noticing dirt fly up as Tucker dug furiously in the loam.

"*Look!*" Tucker tugged at a corner of the suit-case.

Mim reached in and grabbed the corner sticking out. She edged it toward her, grasping the handle. As soon as Mim had the suitcase Tucker shut up.

"This is what you want?" Mim stared into the beautiful round eyes.

"*Open it.*"

Mim clicked open the top. "Oh, God," she gasped, stepping back.

"What are you doing in there?!"

"Tucker dug out an old suitcase with a tiny skeleton in it and what's left of a lace headcap and dress." She closed the suitcase, fighting her way back through the foliage, Tucker at her heels.

"I don't want to see it." A ghastly pallor covered Tally's face. "Put it back, Marilyn."

"I can't do that. I have to turn this skeleton over to Rick Shaw. The child was murdered. Why else would she or he be stuffed in a suitcase?" Mim noticed Tally clutch at her chest and falter. "Aunt Tally." She dropped the suitcase, the skeleton tumbling out, and grabbed her aunt.

"Oh, no." Tally saw the child's bones.

Mrs. Murphy and Pewter silently watched. Tucker sat by the skeleton.

"Put it back," Tally sobbed.

Mim sank to her knees with the old lady. No fool, she said, "What do you know about this child?"

"It's mine!" Tally sobbed so hard Mrs. Murphy thought her old heart would break.

"Is this why Uncle Jamie shot Biddy Minor?"

"Yes. I wanted to die. I loved Biddy Minor. I loved him like no other man on earth and he loved me."

Mim put her arms around her aunt and softly asked, "Did you kill your baby?"

"No, no, I could never do that."

"Did Biddy?"

"No."

"Who, then?"

"Daddy. He took the baby from my arms and he smothered her."

Mim shivered. "I'm so sorry."

"I didn't show much. I got away with being pregnant. Momma suspected but I lied through my teeth."

"What did Biddy do?"

"Daddy said if Biddy set foot on his property he'd kill him—a married man trifling with a young thing, that's what he called me, a young thing. But, oh, I loved Biddy Minor and I found a way to get a message to him. Veenie—do you remember our maid? She was born in slavery she was so old—Veenie told him I delivered the baby and Daddy killed her. I wanted that baby. She was all I would ever have of Biddy. He couldn't divorce, you see. Nobody could then."

"Yes, I remember."

"And Daddy wanted me to marry well. If anyone knew I'd had an illegitimate child he couldn't have married me off to the milkman."

"I see." Mim stood up and brushed off her knees. She helped Tally up.

Tally, once on her feet, walked over to the skeleton with hesitant steps. She knelt down. Tucker whimpered.

Tally looked at Tucker. "She was the most beautiful little girl, with red curls, red curls just like mine when I was little." She touched the hand. "And I'll never forget when she wrapped her tiny fingers around my finger. She was my living memory of Biddy." Tally put her head in her hands and sobbed, racking sobs.

Mim, eyes wet, too, knelt down and gathered up the bones, putting them back into the suitcase.

"I thought Daddy buried her but one night he got drunk and said he put her in a suitcase and threw her in with the junk. I thought about looking for her but I couldn't, you know, Mimsy, I couldn't."

"You were a girl and had no control over your life. How is it that Jamie shot Biddy?"

"When Biddy heard what Daddy did to the baby, he came up here to kill him. I told Jamie I trusted him, and he loved me, I thought. Wild as he was, you could trust Jamie. But as soon as Biddy put one foot on our land Jamie killed him because he knew Biddy would kill Daddy for what he'd done. And I think in Jamie's heart he thought he was protecting me. He knew I'd run after Biddy again and ruin all our lives. I never hated Jamie for what he did but I hated Daddy. I hated Daddy for the rest of his life and I hate him still." She touched a piece of pink ribbon on the bonnet and pleaded, "Don't give her to the sheriff."

"I won't. We'll bury her on the hill with the rest of the family. She's one of us. You can tell or not tell." Mim closed the suitcase as though it carried the most precious items in the world, then she helped up Tally and they both walked slowly back to Mim's Bentley.

Tucker walked over to the girls. *"Poor Tally."*

*"It's like a tom killing kittens,"* Pewter said.

*"Bet old man Urquhart went to his grave believing he did the right thing."* Tucker watched as Mim opened the door for her aunt, setting the suitcase on her lap.

*"Humans can justify anything. Kill one. Kill millions. They'll come up with a reason why it's all right."* Pewter had the last word.

# 60

On a glorious afternoon the following week, Sarah Vane-Tempest was directing her gardeners. H. Vane-Tempest, in a cashmere-and-linen turtleneck, worked in his secondary office, used only in good weather, a twenty-by-twenty glassed-in porch with French doors across the entire breadth. He could open all the doors on an especially good day.

He had little sense of the ordinary work week. He did whatever he wanted whenever he wanted and expected his help to be there. For this demanding schedule he paid quite well.

Seated across from him, Howard Fenton organized blue-covered legal packets, twelve of them. His assistant, a young man fresh out of Yale Law, carefully double-checked each document.

Vane-Tempest, using a fountain pen, the only appropriate writing utensil, signed the last one. Behind him stood his two secretaries, whose function today was to witness the documents and affix their signatures to the bottoms.

Howard viewed the two men—Vane-Tempest would employ only male secretaries, multilingual at that. "Does the subject appear to be in full possession of his mental faculties?"

"Yes," they answered in chorus.

"Does he appear to sign this document freely and without coercion?"

"Yes."

Vane-Tempest raised an eyebrow. "Would you like my blood type?"

Howard, humorless, replied, "Not necessary, sir."

"Next." Vane-Tempest held out his hand, his ultrathin watch half hidden by his cuff.

The Yale Law graduate handed him another legal-sized document. This one had beige covers to distinguish it from the others.

"Mmm." Vane-Tempest read quickly. He understood the law quite well for a civilian. Then, too, those many decades of business, real estate, and one jarring divorce had taught him the basics: Screw them before they screw you.

In this instance he wasn't interested in besting someone. He was acting with largesse.

"I think you'll find it is just as you dictated, sir...."

"I know, Howard, but it's a damn fool who signs a contract without reading it, even if he did dictate it. If you're bored,"—his voice dripped acid and well it should, since he kept this law firm on a million-dollar retainer—"walk with my beautiful wife in her beautiful garden."

"I'm not bored."

"I'm so glad to hear it." He read on and ten minutes later signed the beige-covered documents, again twelve copies.

The black ink, specially purchased from

Italy for its richness of hue, glistened on the last page of the last document. Vane-Tempest blew on the page.

The young assistant surreptitiously sneaked a glance at Sarah, the lush light outlining her breathtaking features. *This is what money buys,* he thought to himself.

"Shall I hand deliver the Teotan papers to Mr. Bainbridge?"

"Yes. Mr. Bainbridge, as you know, is in hospital. Don't tire him."

"Despite his injuries I do believe this will revive his spirits."

"Hope so, Howard. Nasty business. The police will never find the criminal. They never do, you know. You Americans display a curious disregard for punishment and deterrence."

"Sir?" Howard stood as his client got to his feet.

"If you catch them you let them off on parole. If they're in jail they work out with weights or watch TV. Devil's Island, by God, send them to Devil's Island. You'll see your crime statistics plunge."

"I agree." And he did.

"Off with you, then." Vane-Tempest smiled genially as Secretary Number One showed the two lawyers the front door.

He clasped his hands behind his back. Butterflies covered his Italian lilacs, late bloomers, but everything was late this year.

He strode outside feeling better than he

had in a while. Putting his arm around Sarah's shoulders, he guided her to the expanse of manicured lawn, the croquet pitch, facing the north. The direct western view, the best mountain views, he wisely left unmolested, the lawn merging with the edge of a hayfield.

"Spring. Finally. Unequivocally."

"Yes."

"I have resigned my interest and by extension your interest in Teotan," Vane-Tempest informed his wife.

"What?" Dismay read over her face.

He held up his hand. "Patience. Hear me out. I have turned over the corporation to Blair, to which he has agreed. He has only to sign the documents I have prepared and Teotan is his with my investment. I apologized for taking out my jealousy on him and speaking harshly to him. He apologized for an 'immoral escapade.' Exact words."

"What about me?"

"I thought we could go into business together. The two of us. What would you like?"

Turning to view her garden she replied, with a hint of determination and excitement, "A nursery. A wholesale business to supply the landscape architects."

"How interesting. I thought you might pick a dress shop or a theater."

"A nursery. It's healthier." She beamed at him.

"So it is."

"H., why are you relinquishing Teotan? There are other ways to buy off Blair Bainbridge."

"The fellow doesn't have to be bought off. He doesn't remember much about that afternoon. Not uncommon with head injuries, I'm told. So let's just call it insurance...in case he does remember on some distant day. Besides, I think it imprudent for us to be in business with your former lover. I thought I was very clever in keeping Blair and Tommy close to me. They never suspected, I know, and I had ample time to study them. Archie, however, was a complete and dismal surprise." He didn't admit that he figured out about Blair from hearing her answer Archie's accusation during their tryst in Archie's office. He knew from the tone of her voice.

Not missing a beat, she said, "I hated you, H. You dismissed me."

"How did you keep all those balls in the air, forgive the pun." He heard what she said but changed the subject.

"I've always been good at scheduling." She stifled a laugh.

"Did you love any of them?"

"No. Blair is a sweet fellow but too languid, ultimately. And that *was* the briefest of affairs, H. Two weeks."

"Tommy Van Allen?"

"A flameout. It was fading before he died." She bit her lower lip, turning to face her husband. "I hated you and I wanted to hurt you. Don't change the subject. I wanted to hurt you, Henry. You hurt me."

H. Vane-Tempest could withstand news, no matter how bad, as long as he was the center of it. "You succeeded."

"I'm desperately sorry."

"No, you're not. But you will behave and we will create a successful nursery. And I suggest you give Mrs. Woo a great deal of business, for all the trouble you've caused her." As Sarah remained silent he continued. "The reason you'll behave, Sarah, is that I changed my will just now. If my death is in any way suspicious you inherit nothing. Nothing. You do understand?"

"I understand that you will live a long and healthy life." She kissed him on the cheek.

"You had pluck trying to kill me. I underestimated you, undervalued you. That won't happen again."

"You killed Tommy Van Allen, didn't you?"

He shrugged. "I doubt Rick Shaw will solve that crime."

"Henry, I know you..."

"Tommy Van Allen was an impulsive fool. He had enough cocaine in his bloodstream to kill three people. The rest was window dressing." He neglected to mention that he had shot the cocaine into Tommy's veins. Cocaine was ridiculously easy to get in this wealthy county. She stuck her thumb in the waistband of her wraparound skirt. "Teotan is, I should think, generous recompense to Blair." She paused. "Do you think the county will buy the well water?"

"I do. I think Blair will become a wealthy man, not serious money, but some money."

Sarah laughed, because in her husband's

world, less than ten million dollars qualified as some money.

He kissed her lightly on the mouth. "I'm going to lose forty pounds. I've let myself go." He kept to himself the daily shots of testosterone he would be taking. Some things were best left unsaid.

As for putting Tommy's bomber jacket in Herb Jones's truck, and the handcuffs in Archie's van—no one had even found those, more's the pity—he did that for the sheer devilment of it. It was exciting to watch everyone come unglued.

The presence of Sarah's black Jaguar at Blair Bainbridge's still bothered the police. But Vane-Tempest had crawled to the top of the heap by understanding people in a cynical fashion. If the police had a solution that the public accepted, then what was one odd piece that didn't fit into the puzzle? They could prove nothing against Sarah or him.

He knew Sarah had been in the plane with Tommy. He had gotten up in the middle of the night, called Tommy to meet him at the food plant under the pretext of a Teotan emergency, shot him, and loaded him with cocaine. It took all of fifteen minutes. He was home in bed by three o'clock, with no one the wiser. Planting cocaine and a locker storage ticket in Tommy's car was child's play. Faking a set of accounting books was easy, too. He'd run numbers off his computer, then put them into a leather binder.

As for himself, he didn't fear Sarah. This episode, as he chose to consider it, only whetted his appetite for her. He saw her now for what she was, a tiger. And so was he.

# 61

Harry and Miranda sat on two chairs next to Blair's bed. Each woman had visited him two and three times a day since his shooting.

"Is any memory coming back at all?" Miranda politely inquired.

"No," he truthfully replied. "But the doctor said bits and pieces may come back to me. Then again, I may never remember. The last thing I remember—and it's so stupid—is I heard a car come up the driveway. I opened the back screened door and I tripped. Just took a mis-step. That's all I can remember."

"You must be tired of everyone asking you." Harry smiled. "You look good."

"I feel pretty good. The swelling is down. Doc wants me to wait a few more days to be certain. I'll tell you what's driving me crazy." He pointed to the bandages on his head. "My scalp itches like poison ivy. I can't scratch it."

"Means it's healing." Miranda patted his hand. "You'll be back to good health in no time. Thank you, Jesus." She closed her eyes in fervent prayer.

"Yes. I have been very lucky." Blair's eyes misted. "Thank God for you, Harry."

"You've thanked me enough already." Harry warmly smiled.

"And Mrs. Murphy, Pewter, and Tucker." Blair smiled broadly.

"Yes." Harry hadn't told him or anyone the full extent of their efforts. She knew no one would believe her.

"Maybe it's better not to remember. You and Archie had been friends." Miranda assumed Blair's attacker had been Archie.

"I just don't know, Miranda. I don't know if it's better to know or not to know and there's not much I can do about it. I'm just so grateful to be alive." He stopped as his eyes filled with tears, and Harry's and Miranda's eyes filled also.

# 62

Miranda's hand flew to her face. "I hate to hear about drug deals. I so liked Tommy."

Cynthia, in regulation sunglasses, continued her story. "He must have brought the stuff in by private plane after picking it up in Florida or from local airports closer by. You know those training runs that Tommy used to do? They weren't training runs."

"Good job," Miranda congratulated her.

"We've got the records. That's the real break. We found cocaine and a locker ticket from the bus station in Tommy's Porsche. So we went over to the bus station, of course, opened the locker, and that's where the accounting books were."

*"How about that?"* Tucker watched people drive by the post office. Spring worked its magic on everyone. People were smiling.

It galled Cynthia that Blair could not remember whoever shot him. The bullet had never been found—the sign of a careful killer. She knew the other shoe hadn't dropped and she suspected H. Vane-Tempest. Whatever her suspicions might be, suspicions weren't facts, and Blair's doctors confirmed he could have "lost" the hours leading up to his being shot. She sighed. "How is Blair today?"

"His color is better." Mrs. Hogendobber offered a biscuit to Cynthia after shooing Pewter off the table.

Too late, though, for Pewter had yet another fresh biscuit firmly clamped in her jaws. She chewed some of it, then tore the remainder with her claws. *"That's what I'm going to do to that blue jay."*

*"Dream on."* Murphy listened, unmoved, to the details.

*"Doubting Thomas,"* cooed Pewter, who at that moment felt glorious, since she had successfully stolen a biscuit.

*"We're lucky."* Murphy hopped off the counter and rubbed against the corgi's snow-white chest. She dearly loved that dog, although she wouldn't say it out loud.

*"We saved Blair."* Tucker licked Murphy's ear.

*"Yes."* She rubbed her cheek against Tucker's cheek.

Big Mim, Little Mim, Herb, and Tally came in. Cynthia didn't tell them the news about finding the drug records because Big Mim already knew. If Rick Shaw didn't call her the second he knew something, she'd make his life miserable. It helped that she made major contributions to various law-enforcement events and charities.

"We're all feeling better, thanks to you." Mim shook Cynthia's hand.

"I don't deserve any credit, really."

"You're too modest. All those hours of questioning people, investigating sites, poring over evidence—no one sees how much work there is." Mim smiled.

Tally spoke up abruptly. "This Saturday at three at my place, the old cemetery, you are invited to a funeral."

"Oh, no! Who has—" Miranda rushed to console Tally, who held up her hand for silence.

"I'll explain at the funeral. Reverend Herb will conduct the service and afterward I will serve refreshments with the help of my niece and tell you who died and why. I won't live much longer myself. I need to tell you—" She paused, reaching for the counter to steady herself. "I need to tell you how things stay with you. The past, I mean. The past lives right through us. Even if no one ever reads another history book, even if whole nations resign themselves to ignorance, the past pulls like the moon on tides. Please come."

"Of course we'll come." Miranda's voice, filled with warm sympathy, almost made Tally cry.

"I'll be there. Thank you for inviting me," Harry said.

*"How about that?"* Pewter was amazed.

After the group left, including Cynthia, Harry and Miranda sorted, then swept the floors.

"I wonder why Tally invited me to this funeral?" Harry asked.

"I believe it has something to do with you."

"Me?"

"Your blood. There was talk about Tally and your great-grandfather. I was too young to pay attention. But there was talk. This was before my time. Mother remembered, though."

"I guess we'll find out on Saturday."

"You know that you were ransomed from the futile ways inherited from your fathers, not with perishable things such as silver or gold, but with the precious blood of Christ, like that of a lamb without blemish or spot." She put the broom back into the broom closet. "Redemption. I should think that whatever she tells us, Saturday is about redemption."

"What chapter and verse?"

"First Peter, Chapter 1, Verses 18 and 19."

"You amaze me."

"In my day we learned by rote. Stays with you."

Harry scooped up Murphy and kissed her head. She was thinking about the animals driving the Porsche and knowing she couldn't tell anyone.

"Miranda, do you really believe that people can be redeemed? A murderer can be redeemed?"

"Certainly I do, if he but accepts Christ as his savior."

"What about Murphy and Tucker, and Pewter, even though she's a little thief?" She smiled.

"A thief is the only person guaranteed a place in paradise. Remember, it was a thief crucified with Christ who accepted him as the Son of God, and Jesus promised him everlasting life."

"Hope for Pewter."

Miranda, years ago, would have been offended at this discussion, at the idea that animals have immortal souls and spiritual lives...but working with them and watching them, she had changed her mind. Not loudly. Not even so much that others might notice by observation. "There's redemption for Pewter. God loves all his creatures and I believe we will be reunited in heaven." She stopped, and this, for her, was a revelation. "Harry, sometimes I think that animals are closer to God than we are."

*"Not blue jays,"* Pewter announced, being uninterested in theological discussions.

"I do, too." Harry looked around. "It's a wrap, partner."

Miranda put her hand on Harry's shoulder. "I've known you since you were born, Mary Minor. And I know you have doubts. Your faith gets shaken. But it's there. Your mother and father gave you rock-solid beliefs. When you need it, it's there."

"I hope so."

"In time of trouble—" Then Miranda stopped herself. "Let's hope few troubles come your way. I think of them as tests, God's tests. Blair is being tested. He needs us. He's hurt physically and harmed morally."

"Little Mim will be at his side."

"We must all be there." She glanced at the old railroad wall clock. "Oh, dear, I'd better hustle my bustle."

Harry laughed as Miranda scooted out of the post office. Her old-fashioned phrases delighted Harry. She dropped the paper shades and double-checked the lock on the sliding door that closed off the office part of the post office, then walked to the back, dropped the hard plastic sheet in metal slots through the animal door, and secured it with a steel pin. Lastly she opened the back door. "Come on, gang."

Three furry behinds scampered into the late afternoon as Harry locked the back door to the post office.

She opened the door to the blue Ford truck, lifting Tucker in. Pewter and Mrs. Murphy had already jumped up onto the bench seat.

Harry turned the key. The starter clicked, then the motor turned over. She let it idle for a few minutes. No point in pushing the old girl.

Once the motor hummed, she pushed down on the clutch, reaching for the long black stick shift on the floor.

Mrs. Murphy moved over to sit in her lap.

"Want to drive?" Harry asked her as Pewter laughed.

*"I only drive Porsches."* Mrs. Murphy giggled.

Dear Reader,

Cats will conquer the world! Well, if not the world, then the Internet. I now have my own domain on Mom's website. Our address is:

www.ritamaebrown.com

It's not necessary to address me as Your Most Exalted Striped Presence. A simple "Miss Pie" will do.

So many of you ask whether Harry and Fair will get back together again. In my mystery following this one, *The Yearbook Murders,* Harry prepares for her twentieth high-school reunion. This gets her all wispy and misty about Fair, but then, humans are prone to nostalgia.

Cats don't have twentieth high-school reunions. We're too vain.

Others of you have visited Crozet, Virginia. You have discovered that the post office does not exactly parallel what I describe in my books. That's because I've blended the look of the Crozet Post Office with that of the Whitehall Post Office. Artistic license. Other than that, Crozet physically is pretty much Crozet. The characters are my own creations.

I dispatched seven field mice yesterday. Top that!

Affectionately yours,
Sneaky Pie